Smith's
MONTHLY

Every Month Original Novels, Stories, and Articles

USA Today Bestselling Writer
Dean Wesley Smith

TABLE OF CONTENTS

SHORT STORIES

FULL NOVEL

SERIAL NOVEL

NONFICTION

Smith's Monthly Issue #18

Introduction
IT'S A NEW WORLD

I suppose the statement that "It's a New World" is sort of obvious, since you are reading a magazine with only one writer's stories and novels in it. The old world of publishing (or at least the last fifty years of publishing) would not have allowed this sort of thing to happen.

Or if someone tried it, the economics of it would have crushed it quickly in the old world. But now this is issue #18, and the economics of this magazine in this new world of publishing are great.

And I'm still having fun, so onward we go with a crazy idea that to my knowledge has never been done in publishing before.

Back in the pulp era, one writer often filled issue after issue of different magazines. But they did it under varied pen names. That happened regularly, but not so much in an advertised fashion.

And not month after month. Sure, there were magazines such as *Zane Gray's Western Magazine*, or *Ellery Queen's Mystery Magazine*. But they only licensed their names to the product and other writers filled the pages.

Now, in this issue, I hark back a little to the old days. I have a story in this issue I have published under one of my many pen names. "Mated from the Morgue" under the name Dee W. Schofield. I have five or six Dee W. Schofield stories out there, one of which was in the last issue.

The Dee W. Schofield tales were only published originally as stand-alone short stories, and I think before appearing here, maybe ten people read them. Dee. W. Schofield was a writer with only five short stories available. There was just not much chance of anyone finding one of them.

Even with the history of publishing stories under pen names in one magazine, I'm not pretending anything in here was written by someone else. For good or bad, everything in this issue was written by me.

Thanks for the Support

Dean Wesley Smith

And the ranges of the stories this issue are pretty amazing, in my opinion.

"The Balance of a Heart" that starts off the issue is a long Poker Boy novella. It's an adventure, as most Poker Boy stories are.

"Mated from the Morgue" is a meet-cute romance with a slight horrific twist.

And "After the Dance" plays off the idea from an old teenage death song. If you don't like dark, might want to skip that one.

Then, after the start of a golf mystery novel that will be serialized here, I jump to a short story social commentary story in my Bryant Street series, and then end the short stories with a funny meet-cute start of a romance in a grocery store called "Me and Beans and Great Big Melons."

With a title like that, it had better be funny. And weird. And readers tell me it is both.

The novel *Calling Dead: A Cold Poker Gang Novel* is as twisted as a soft-boiled mystery gets. That's the third book in that series and I'm proud of all three.

So a fun romance, a dark romance, a twisted horror story, a Poker Boy urban fantasy adventure, a straight urban fantasy story, a golf mystery serial, and a full mystery novel. That's covering a lot of genres. I hope you enjoy the diverse offerings in this issue. I really have been trying to keep every issue interesting and surprising.

And once again I want to thank the subscribers and the Patreon supporters for the backing on this project. This is a crazy idea, not done before in the history of publishing.

I am thankful you all are along for the ride.

—Dean Wesley Smith
March 15th, 2015
Lincoln City, Oregon

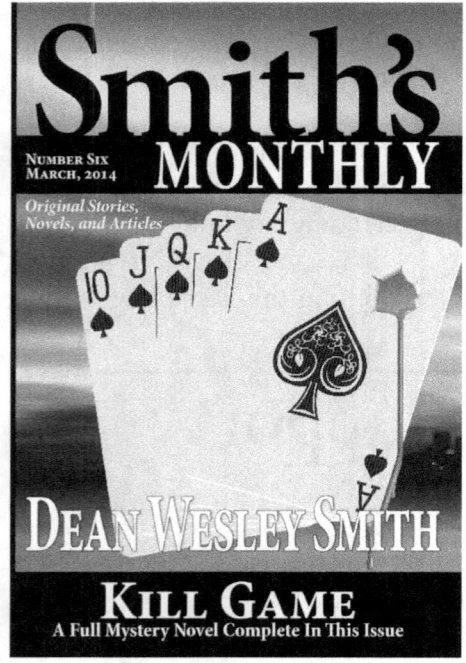

Coming Next Issue in Smith's Monthly
A return to the Ghost of a Chance Series
in a brand new novel.
HEAVEN PAINTED AS A FREE MEAL

Dean Wesley Smith

USA Today **Bestselling Writer**

For the Balance of a Heart

A POKER BOY STORY

As a superhero in the gambling universe, Poker Boy works directly for Stan, the God of Poker.

Poker Boy's job? To save those who need saving and take money at the poker tables from those who need it taken.

But when Lady Luck herself comes calling and asks for a personal favor, Poker Boy and his team must travel far beyond the edges of Las Vegas to find the Queen of Hearts.

FOR THE BALANCE OF A HEART
A Poker Boy Novella

ONE

I ALWAYS FIGURED that when Lady Luck needed a favor from me, things had to be really, really bad.

Laverne, aka Lady Luck, appeared a little after noon on a Friday. My entire team was in my new office eating take-out Chinese and talking about our plans for the weekend. I had a poker tournament I hoped to play in later in the evening at the Bellagio and Patty Ledegerwood, aka Front Desk Girl, my sidekick and girlfriend, had to work swing at the MGM Grand Hotel front desk.

In other words, a pretty standard weekend night for us.

Then Lady Luck appeared.

When that happens, normal becomes a laughing matter.

Laverne had on her standard business casual gray pantsuit. Her dark hair was pulled so tight into a bun on the top of her head that it had to hurt. Her eyes looked neutral as they always did. Lady Luck seldom showed anyone any emotion and it was always impossible to get a read on what she was thinking.

She looked around my new office and smiled and then nodded. "Original."

I thought that meant she liked my new office layout. At least I hoped that was what she meant.

She glanced at Stan, the God of Poker, who was trying to choke down the remains of a spring roll. "Good job."

Stan, who had on his standard gray cardigan sweater and gray slacks, only nodded. Compliments from Lady Luck herself were rare and Stan knew that. The expression on his face and in his dark eyes never changed.

At times I couldn't believe my new office, or the fact that a superhero poker player like me even had an office. But I did, and it was invisible and floated above the city of Las Vegas, about a thousand feet above the MGM Grand Casino and Hotel.

I doubted I would ever get used to how amazing that was.

Since Patty worked at the MGM Grand, I figured directly above the MGM Grand just seemed like a great place to anchor the office. Besides, since I got a lot of my superhero power from casinos funneled through my black leather coat and Fedora-like hat, being parked over a major casino never hurt.

And I seldom took off my coat and hat. Even now over a Chinese lunch that was about to get very cold.

The office in this spot also allowed for a great view of all of Las Vegas and the surrounding mountains and desert since all four walls were glass and perfectly clear. At first that had scared me so much I stayed to the center of the room. Finally, after a day of almost crawling around the room on my hands and knees for fear of falling off the edge of my office tile floor, I had decided to put in a wooden rail about a foot wide and waist-high across the glass. On all four walls. That helped. I now could actually go to the edges of my own office and look down.

Compared to normal offices, mine really wasn't much of an office. No desk, no couches, no pictures or awards hanging on the glass walls. The entire center of the square office was filled with a large, oblong wooden booth. It was an exact replica of the booth in the Diner Restaurant from downtown Las Vegas where we had all met for the last couple of years.

Plastic-covered booth seats and a scarred tabletop made it feel real. Bottles of ketchup and mustard sat next to the salt and pepper and a pile of white paper napkins in the center.

Every detail was the same as in the Diner.

In other words, my nifty new office was nothing more than a hunk of tile floor and a diner booth floating in the air over a major casino. I liked it.

So did the rest of the team, or so they had said.

The booth was large enough to handle the six members of my team. There were two or three extra chairs in the room that visitors could pull up to the end of the booth and a couple of lawn chairs in one corner where Patty and I could just sit and stare out at the city and the mountains.

I'd only had this office for a week and I was starting to love sitting in those lawn chairs in the evenings before sunset.

Lady Luck turned around, grabbed a chair and pulled it toward the end of the booth where we were all sitting. It had been Lady Luck herself who had suggested that Stan, my boss and the God of Poker, teach me how to build and secure a floating office for me and my team.

Over the last few years my team had saved the world more times than I wanted to count, so it seemed like a great idea to me and it was turning out to be just that. But while I was building it, I hadn't been so sure.

It had taken two very long days and just about every ounce of energy I had, even with Stan helping, to put it all together and get it secured somehow in its floating and invisible location. But now it took no energy at all for me to keep it there.

Stan tried to explain to me how that worked, but I flat didn't understand a word he said. I figured there had to be some things only the gods could or should know. Since I was only a lowly superhero in the gambling universe, I wasn't meant to know what we had just done or how it even worked. Honestly, I was fine with that, as long as the office stayed in the air and we could go and come from it.

Lady Luck pulled the chair to the table and sat down. Then she sampled a bite of an extra spring roll and nodded. The food was from a restaurant called Larry's Chinese Place just off The Strip. The locals knew it was the best in town.

My entire team was there, plus Stan. I could tell they were all as shocked by Lady Luck's action as I felt. One of the most powerful gods in the universe just didn't join a bunch of superheroes and a poker god for lunch.

The Smoke and Screamer both eased away from her on the left side of the booth. The Smoke was basically a werewolf who could walk through walls. He stood about my height at six foot, but had shoulders so large it made him seem shorter. His most striking feature was his deep blue eyes.

Screamer was shorter than me and usually just wore Las Vegas tourist clothes like bright shirts and ugly shorts.

He worked for the law enforcement side of the gods and seemed far, far harder than he actually was.

Madge, the food-service-superhero waitress who always wore a too-tight pink diner uniform and owned and ran the Diner, had been sitting on the end on the right side. She now stood and moved to a position behind the booth facing Lady Luck and behind Stan, who sat in the middle.

Patty and I moved closer to Lady Luck on the right side, taking up some of the room left by Madge.

No one said a word and the smell from the Chinese food filling the middle of the table wasn't helping my stomach any. Since my team covered five different branches of the gods, we were unusual, but I just never expected Lady Luck to join us for anything.

"Poker Boy," Laverne said, looking at me. Then she looked at Stan. "Everyone, I need a personal favor."

Now I really, really, really wished I hadn't just eaten that last piece of sweet-and-sour chicken. Lady Luck never asked for personal favors. She had been alive for longer than any written history. Civilizations over the centuries had come and gone, but Lady Luck had lived through them all. So her asking us for a personal favor had to mean things were really, really bad.

"Anything," I managed to say. Stan only nodded and even though he was the God of Poker with the best poker face I had ever seen, I could tell he was too surprised to even speak.

Everyone else nodded slightly, clearly too stunned to dare move much.

"Thank you," she said. Then she took a deep breath. "I need you to find Helen, my daughter."

I was fairly certain at that moment I had stopped breathing.

Lady Luck had just told me she had a daughter. I had thought I was starting to get a grip on all the different gods and superheroes and who worked for whom and who hated whom. But now it was clear there was still a great deal I didn't know about all the whos and whoms of the world of gods.

"Do you know where she was last seen?" Stan asked.

Thank heavens Stan knew about Lady Luck having a daughter and was managing to keep his wits about him. That was the difference between a god and a bunch of superheroes. He'd been alive a lot longer and could roll better with very, very strange requests.

And even better, he could explain it all to us after she left.

"Helen is somewhere here in Las Vegas," Lady Luck said. "And I have no idea what she is doing or why she has vanished. I can't even sense her."

"How long has she been gone?" I managed to ask, at least trying to sound logical and in control and leader-like. Thankfully, my voice didn't squeak.

"About twelve minutes now," Laverne said, clearly serious. "I am very worried."

She started to take another bite from the spring roll, then changed her mind and pushed it away.

"We'll do our best," Stan said.

"Thank you," Lady Luck said, nodding. "I know you will."

With that she vanished, leaving the chair empty at the end of the booth.

I stared at the empty chair for what seemed like hours, but it must have only been a few seconds. Then I turned back to the stunned faces of my team.

"Wow," Madge said from behind Stan. "The Queen of Hearts has gone missing. Imagine that."

Now all I could do was stare at Madge.

She just shrugged. "I'll get some milkshakes for everyone if someone gets rid of all that dead food. Looks like we got some planning to do."

With that she turned and vanished. I had put in an invisible door right behind the booth—with Stan's help—that allowed Madge and most of the team to move back and forth between the real diner in downtown Las Vegas and my office.

I also put a door from my office to Patty's apartment so Patty could be in the office as much as she liked as well, even when I wasn't here. I was the only member of the team besides Stan who knew how to teleport.

Across from me in the booth, The Smoke, a part-human, part-wolf superhero in the world of animals, looked completely shocked, his blue eyes wider than normal by a ways. That was going some.

Beside him, Screamer just looked down at the pile of uneaten Chinese food and shook his head. Screamer worked under the gods of law enforcement and his superpower was the ability to take thoughts from one person and put them in another person's head. He had seen more than I ever wanted to imagine and yet he seemed bothered by this.

I honestly couldn't believe what had just happened either.

Lady Luck had a daughter, who was missing, and Lady Luck had come to us to find her.

That did not bode well for anyone involved.

I looked out over the city of Las Vegas. Helen, the Queen of Hearts, was out there somewhere. And up until a moment ago, I didn't even know she existed beyond the faces of the cards I played poker with.

Had she been the one to pose for those early cards? Or was that just her nickname? So many questions.

In the distance, a Southwest airliner turned for final approach to McCarran Airport. Sometimes a plane landing at the airport got a little too close to this invisible office for comfort, but Stan assured me that a plane could hit the office and it would go right through and no one would notice. Something about the office and everyone in it being a half-turn out of normal time and space.

Again I didn't understand what he meant, but I was fairly certain I didn't want to be in the office the day a plane passed through it.

I was drifting. I had to get focused.

I turned to Stan who was just sitting staring out over the countryside as well, his eyes blank.

Beside me, Patty took my hand and squeezed it, sending waves of comfort and calm through me. She worked under the Gods of Hospitality. Calming people was one of her many superpowers. I loved it.

"Stan, can you tell us about Helen? And why Madge called her the Queen of Hearts?"

"Because for centuries, even before I was born, which was before Atlantis, she has been called that," Stan said. "Her beauty is legendary. Red hair, very tall, and a temper when unleashed that could level a city."

"And she's been gone now for thirteen or so minutes?" I asked. "How does Laverne know that?"

Stan shrugged. "Some sort of connection, a family bond, at a level I am not familiar with."

"And that clearly was broken," I said.

Stan nodded. "I can't sense her either."

I sat back and looked out at the view. I had no idea where to even start on this problem. And that scared me a lot.

"We're missing a lot of information here," Screamer said. "First off, who would have the power to cut the link between Lady Luck and her daughter?"

"Good question," I said. "Can't be many people I would imagine."

"Unless Helen did it herself," The Smoke said in his level, deep voice.

I glanced at Stan who sat calmly, not saying anything.

"Stan?" I asked. "You know who could do this, don't you?"

Stan nodded, but said nothing. Instead he made all the food on the table just vanish with a simple wave of his hand, leaving the scarred wood top as clean as if Madge had spent an hour wiping it down. I had no idea where he sent it all.

"Stan?" I pushed.

He looked up and seemed almost afraid to say what he was about to say. And when a god was afraid to say something, it couldn't be good.

Finally he put both hands on the table and looked first at Patty, then at me. "There is only one person who could break the link between Laverne and Helen purposefully."

"That's going to make the search a lot easier," Screamer said. "Who is it?"

"Laverne's husband," Stan said softly, again looking down at the table.

At that moment you could have heard a pin drop in my new floating office over Las Vegas. Nothing is ever supposed to be that quiet in or above Las Vegas.

TWO

I FINALLY MANAGED to choke out the most logical question we all had to be thinking, since we were all staring at Stan in shock. "Lady Luck is married?"

"Separated, actually," Stan said. "Centuries before I was born."

"His name?"

Stan shrugged. "He's gone by a lot of names over the centuries, just as Laverne has. Last I heard he liked Benny. Before that I think he went by Jonah. In Atlantis it was Belial."

"Evil one?" The Smoke asked, his voice almost a growl.

"Not really," Stan said. "Are you all familiar with the concept of Yin-Yang?"

I was slightly, only because that circle with the two black-and-white shapes inside it was sold as trinkets all over Vegas in just about every form.

Everyone else nodded and Stan went on.

Stan looked at me. "Ever wonder why you have as much bad luck as you have good over time?"

I honestly hadn't wondered that, or at least given it any meaning. I just knew it always balanced out in poker and skill always won out in the long run.

"Benny is the God of Bad Luck?" Screamer asked.

"Not really," Stan said, shaking his head. "Any more than Laverne is only good luck. But Benny and Laverne must both exist for the other to exist. Yin-Yang. Dark and Light. Masculine and Feminine. Only down through time the two sides of that have been confused when it comes to sex."

I was confused as well, but managed to ask "How?"

"Today the sunny, light side is called Yang," Stan said, "and is also associated with masculine. That got flipped. Actually, when all this started, Yin was masculine and in the shadow while Yang was sunny and feminine. The key is that everything stays on the Golden Mean."

"The middle between two extremes," Patty said.

"That's right," Stan said.

I looked at my girlfriend in awe, then back at Stan. I had no doubt I could keep asking him questions and he could keep me confused for hours, And Patty could keep impressing me with her knowledge, but it seemed we had a task to do, so I needed to get that task in motion somehow.

"So, why would Benny cut off connections between Laverne and Helen?"

Stan shook his head. "I can't think of one reason. They both love Helen."

"So if she went to visit her father," Screamer asked, "where would she go?"

"He lives right here," Stan said. "You don't see him out much. He has a walled compound over near the university. He mostly stays to the dark side."

"And we live on the sunny side?" I asked.

Stan pointed at the clear blue sky around the booth.

"Yin-Yang," The Smoke said, his voice very soft as if he understood.

I honestly didn't, and I had no doubt Patty was going to have to help me understand later. But right at this moment, with Helen the Queen of Hearts missing, my understanding of ancient philosophy and aspects of how the gods work didn't much matter. I hoped there would be time to learn it all. For some reason, this problem felt world-ending serious and I had no idea why.

"Would crossing into the shadow side cause the connection to break?" I asked Stan.

"And if we crossed over there, what would happen?" Patty asked.

"And how could we cross over?" Screamer added.

Before Stan could answer, Madge appeared carrying milkshakes, the drink of choice for all of us when working on a case.

"You guys talking about going over into the shadow world?" Madge asked as she put the milkshakes in front of us.

Mine was vanilla with whipped cream stacked high. I really wasn't in the mood for a milkshake, but I forced myself to take a taste anyway. It was as wonderful as usual. I had no doubt that if this meeting kept going for another ten minutes, I would down the entire thing.

Patty nodded thanks to Madge for the milkshake, then answered her question. "We're just discussing if Helen crossing over would cause the connection between her and her mother to be broken."

"In some extreme areas of the shadow world, I suppose it might," Madge said. "But I honestly doubt it."

"I agree," Stan said.

Madge went on as she moved around the table delivering our shakes. "I've worked both sides of the line over the years. Not much purposely crosses the line because that line is always moving for everyone."

"She's right," Stan said. "Every action, every reaction by everyone moves the line for that person."

I was so confused I just wanted to slump down into the booth and cover my head. So I focused on the first question that came to mind.

"Madge, what's it like living on the other side of the line?"

"Exactly the same as here," she said, finishing putting out the milkshakes, napkins, straws and spoons for everyone. "You can't tell the difference, actually. It's the same world."

Banging my head on the table would probably do no good, but I sure felt like doing that. And clearly Stan read me like a book.

"You ever sat at a poker table with a cheater?" Stan asked me.

"Sure," I said.

"How about a guy who couldn't buy a good card if his life depended on it, or played just a little too long and lost all his money."

"Sure," I said. "A normal table."

"They are living on the other side of the line," Stan said. "At least for their time at the table."

"So the shadow side isn't an actual place?" Screamer asked just slightly before I could.

"Yin-Yang," Madge said. "They both exist together and one could not exist without the other. Although I have to admit there is very little Yin in this room. All Yang."

"We all have our dark sides," The Smoke said.

Screamer nodded.

"Of course you do," Madge said. "There are no exceptions. But this group tends to not use the dark side without reason. And that's why I like to hang around with you all. I've spent far too much time solidly over on the other side of that line."

I looked at Madge with a brand new level of respect. Some day I was going to have to ask her a ton of questions about her past.

Patty just shook her head. "So if crossing the line would not normally block any connection between Helen and Laverne, and visiting her father here in Las Vegas would not do that either, what would?"

I had the same question, but decided to ask it from another angle. I looked directly at Stan. "What exactly do you think Laverne is actually asking us to do?"

"Go into the tunnels," Stan said without looking at me.

"Not me," Madge said, turning and vanishing through the invisible door back to the Diner.

"I cannot go down there," The Smoke said, his eyes almost flashing anger.

"I understand," Stan said.

"Well, I don't understand much of anything we've been talking about," I said. "Laverne having a daughter, Laverne being married, Yin-Yang, and now tunnels. My head is starting to hurt. So would someone who understands these tunnels please explain them to me? Slowly."

Before anyone could say a word, Laverne appeared back in the chair at the end of the booth. She looked at Stan, her eyes intense. "You believe Helen might have actually gone down into the tunnels?"

"It would seem to be the only logical conclusion I'm afraid," Stan said.

"I came to the same conclusion," Lady Luck said and sat back, clearly shaken.

These tunnels, whatever they are, must be something very nasty to have Lady Luck act like that.

"I was so hoping it wasn't going to be that," she said. Then she took a deep breath and looked at Stan. "Explain to Poker Boy and his team everything you can about the tunnels and I'll go talk with Helen's father. I'll see if he has any suggestions or has heard from Helen. I would imagine he's getting as worried as I am."

With that she vanished again.

The Smoke pushed to the end of the booth and stood. "I am sorry, I cannot help with the tunnels."

"I understand," Stan said.

I stared at The Smoke as he moved around the booth and vanished into the doorway to the Diner. I considered The Smoke one of the bravest I had ever met. And now he didn't seem to be afraid either. There was something else.

"You want to explain what just happened?" Screamer asked Stan before I could. There were only four of us left now to try to save Lady Luck's daughter.

"In a very ancient agreement between gods to end a war, The Smoke's people were banned from certain ancient cities back when the cities were inhabited. The agreement still holds even after hundreds of thousands of years."

"The tunnels are a part of an old city?" I asked.

"An ancient one," Stan said, nodding. "From the time of the Titans."

"I didn't know they were real," Patty said, saving me from asking yet another

> *These tunnels, whatever they are, must be something very nasty to have Lady Luck act like that.*

stupid question such as who were the Titans?

"Very real," Stan said. "Far before my time. They ruled this planet for almost two hundred thousand years, then one day they all suddenly vanished."

"Anyone know why?" I asked. "And I thought there were only a few of them. Why did they need cities?"

Stan shook his head. "The myths of their leaders is all that has survived. There were millions of Titans at one point in time. They are said to have ascended to a higher plain, or gone into space, or got locked up by a powerful curse in a hidden prison."

"And the tunnels under Las Vegas is the remains of one of their cities?" Screamer asked.

"Actually," Stan said, "It is their main ancient city, their capital city. It is supposed to be completely preserved. It was buried by the gods who followed them into the position of ruling the planet. No one knows why. This area holds a great deal of unseen power, which is why so many of the gods live here, and why the city of Las Vegas even exists in this dry desert."

"And The Smoke can't go down there because his people got in a fight with the Titans?" Screamer asked.

Stan shook his head. "His area of the gods and a few others fought the Giants. In one battle they destroyed part of a Titan city and were forever banned from any Titan area ever since."

I took a deep breath and forced myself to focus through the thousand questions to stay squarely on the task Lady Luck had given us. "So Helen might have gone down there into an ancient protected city? Would that break the connection with her and her mother?"

"I'm assuming it would," Stan said. "The field surrounding that huge city is very powerful."

"How did she find her way in there?" Patty asked.

"Everyone knows how to get in," Stan said. "But no one has ever figured out how to get out."

"Wonderful," was all I could say.

THREE

AFTER A FEW more minutes of confusing me with more mythic history than I could begin to learn in a very long semester of college, I finally held up my hand.

"There is only one question we don't have an answer to," I said. "We don't know why Helen would go down there without a way back. What was she after?"

At that moment Lady Luck appeared. "She went after this."

In front of her and floating over the booth was an image of a golden key, turning slightly in the air. "Her father said she had been spending the last hundred years researching it and he says Helen thinks it is hidden in the old city."

As the key turned in the air over the table, it slowly transformed into a sneering, ugly man's face and then back into a golden key.

"That was one of the faces of Janus," Lady Luck said. "The key is one of his four faces. Some believe when combined with the other three keys, it will release the Titans to return to this time and space."

I had scooted away from the image of the floating key and finally Lady Luck snapped it out of existence.

"Why would she want to release the Titans?" Stan asked, his voice hushed.

I glanced at him. Clearly there was still a lot of very real history I had to learn.

Lady Luck sighed and dropped into the chair in front of the booth. "From what I understand, Helen has researched the Titans for centuries. Her father tells me she believes them to be an honorable race that has been unfairly imprisoned over time."

"And what do you believe?" I asked.

Lady Luck shook her head. "My beliefs are of little value now. We need to go into the old city and find Helen."

"No!" a deep voice said from just behind Lady Luck. "You cannot go into that city and you know it."

A small man, not more than five feet tall and as round as a basketball stepped up and looked into Lady Luck's eyes. If she hadn't been sitting down, she would have towered over him.

Now it was Stan's turn to push back as far as he could into the back of the booth.

Lady Luck said nothing.

After I stopped holding my breath for anyone talking to one of the most powerful gods in the world like a child, it dawned on me who the man was.

"Benny, I presume?" I asked.

He glanced at me. "Got it in one, Poker Boy."

Then he looked back at Laverne. "She's my daughter as well. But you and I both know you can't go in there after her. If you did not return, the world as we know it would collapse. We have both worked far too hard for that to happen. We must stay balanced. And to do that, you must stay here."

The silence in my little office felt like a heavy weight. Finally Benny looked away from his wife again and back at me, and then Stan.

"Find our daughter," he said softly. "We'll give you all the help we can from out here."

With that he and Laverne vanished.

I looked at the white faces of Screamer and Stan, then took Patty's hand in my own and squeezed it.

But all I could think about was that we were so screwed.

FOUR

FOR THE NEXT HOUR Stan explained to me and Patty and Screamer what "the tunnels" were. And how big they were supposed to be.

"But no one really knows what they can see from the doorways, since no one has ever returned after going in there."

Finally, I had to ask.

"So where is this entrance?"

Stan shook his head. "There is an old metal door right on the edge of Binion's Horseshoe Casino, about a hundred paces from Freemont Street down a side street."

"You're kidding," Screamer said.

"I'm not," Stan said. "No one notices it and you have to have some powers to open it. But all of you could do it."

"And no exit?" I asked.

"No one that I have heard of has gone in and come out again."

"Ever?" Patty asked.

Stan just shrugged, about as clear an answer as there was.

My stomach was so twisted into a knot around what was left of my Chinese food lunch, I couldn't even think of a response or another question.

"Well," Screamer said, finally, breaking into the silence, "let's hope we can find a way out once we are in there."

My mind was twisting again, struggling on what Screamer had just said. But I couldn't get it.

I turned to Screamer. "What you just said bothers me, but I can't put my finger on why."

"Bothers me as well," Screamer said, shaking his head. "For obvious reasons."

"Link us, would you?" I said, taking Patty's hand and then reaching my other hand across the booth between the empty milkshake glasses. "There's something I'm not seeing and I feel it might be the answer."

Screamer shrugged and glanced at Stan.

"I think I would only confuse the issue," Stan said. "Sometimes too much history and knowledge can hurt more than it can help."

I knew Stan was right, so Screamer reached over and touched my arm and suddenly he and Patty were both in my mind. We had done this sort of thing so many times over the years, it didn't even feel strange anymore.

It just felt familiar.

After only a few seconds, Screamer pulled his hand away from my arm and I was back alone in my own head.

Patty gave my hand a squeeze, but didn't let go, for which I was glad. Her touch kept me calm and thinking clearly, at least most of the time.

"See anything?" I asked Screamer, then Patty.

"Something about the exit," Patty said.

"You were thinking we should find it first, before we go in."

Suddenly I knew the answer.

"That's exactly right," I said. "And I have an idea. I'll be right back."

I instantly teleported to the Diner.

Madge was scrubbing a counter far harder than it needed to be scrubbed. Clearly she was upset at herself for not wanting or being able to help.

"I need a thermos of hot chocolate," I said.

She looked at me and frowned. "Official or otherwise?"

"Official," I said. "How long?"

"Two minutes," she said, turning for the kitchen. "I'll bring it to you."

"Thanks." A moment later I was sitting next to Patty in the booth in my office.

And I was smiling. I knew how to find the exit, at least from this side.

"What was that all about?" Stan asked, looking as puzzled as the rest of my team.

"Call Laverne and Benny and I'll explain," I said.

"No need," Laverne said as she appeared again in the chair facing the booth. Benny was standing beside her and she still seemed taller than he was. "You think the exit is controlled by the Silicon Suckers?"

"I do," I said. "In fact, I'm convinced of it."

The Silicon Suckers were an ancient race of beings that lived in huge tunnels and caverns under desert regions of the planet. The gods, a long time ago, had negotiated a truce with them to keep humans and Silicon Suckers from fighting.

"How can you be so sure?" Benny asked, his voice deep and low and almost rumbling with power.

"There was a point when I was trying to save a superhero from the Keno side from her time with the Suckers. I had to watch her negotiate with the leader of the Silicon Suckers for an exchange of land

Now Available
from all your favorite booksellers in trade paper and electronic editions.

for a number of thermoses every month of hot chocolate."

"Strangest thing I had ever heard about," Benny said, shaking his head.

"During the negotiation, the leader of the Silicon Suckers floated a map in the air of the land around Las Vegas, showing what humans controlled and what they controlled. There was a giant round area under the city of Las Vegas that had neither human nor Silicon Sucker color on it. At the time, I assumed it was that way because it was under the city and no one cared."

"The ancient city," Laverne said, nodding. "From what I understand, the original protective screen over it was a dome, so it would be round."

"I'm willing to bet," I said, "that the Silicon Suckers know of the exit and have just kept it locked or blocked."

"Worth finding out before going in there," Laverne said, nodding her head. "We'll be watching if you need help."

With that she and Benny both vanished again before I had a chance to ask them why they didn't just go and talk to the Silicon Suckers instead of me. More than likely there was some reason I didn't know about. Just another question I would have to ask later.

Before anyone could say anything, Madge appeared out of the invisible door carrying the thermos of hot chocolate, the most sacred and valuable of drugs to the Silicon Suckers.

I was going to need to negotiate for Laverne's daughter's life with hot chocolate. I just hoped I could offer them enough.

FIVE

FIVE MINUTES LATER, after making sure my plan was solid with Stan and Screamer and Patty, I found myself standing alone on the edge of Highway 95 leading north out of Las Vegas.

The Silicon Suckers' main entrance was under a billboard, hidden from view for anyone not welcome in their castles, as they called their caverns and tunnels.

The hot wind was whipping my coat around me and I had to hold my hat on my head with one hand to keep from having to chase it up the highway.

I waited until there were no cars coming in either direction, then slipped off my shoes and left them in the sand next to a sagebrush. I stepped into the wide tunnel and took ten steps into the sand tunnel, as showed respect, then stopped.

Silicon Suckers were big into respect. And rules. They had a million rules.

A few seconds later two Silicon Suckers appeared. They were, as normal, completely naked, but I had no idea what sex they were, or if Silicon Suckers even had a sex. Their bodies were very, very skinny and a pasty gray, but their heads were huge, with wide, unblinking eyes.

Over the centuries, humans who had seen them called them aliens and lately they had become known as the Grays. But as far as I knew, they had lived on Earth longer than humans, and that was going some I was starting to discover.

Both of the Silicon Suckers bowed slightly to me and I returned the bow, then followed them down through what seemed like miles of sandstone tunnels, illuminated by something I had never been able to figure out. The light just seemed to come from everywhere in the tunnel.

When we broke out into the open into the huge cavern that was the main area of this city, I was stunned. Never had I seen so many Silicon Suckers in this area, and they all seemed to be moving at a normal pace, clearly all busy.

From what I understood, hot chocolate not only was a wonderful drug to the Silicon Suckers, but it was a critical element in their health and ability to reproduce. And clearly they had been doing a great deal of reproducing in the year we had been giving them a number of thermoses of hot chocolate every month in payment.

After almost thirty minutes of walking behind my guides, I was shown into a large room I knew to be the Great One's throne room. Only it was as empty as every other room and tunnel I had seen in this place.

I was told to wait and my guides left me standing alone.

Then from one side of the room, a tall and clearly elderly Silicon Sucker appeared and walked slowly toward me. I knew, without a doubt, even though most of the Silicon Suckers looked identical to me, that I was facing their great leader.

I bowed very deeply.

"It is a great honor that you have blessed us once again with your presence, my friend," the Great One said.

"The honor is mine," I said, carefully respecting their tradition. "May I offer the people of this fantastic castle a gift?"

The Great One nodded slightly and I pulled the thermos of hot chocolate from my coat and sat it on the ground in front of me.

Two others came from a side tunnel and carefully picked up the thermos and carried it away.

After they had left, the great one indicated that I should sit and he did the same, facing me.

Then he nodded, a sign I had permission to speak.

"Great One," I said, bowing slightly as was the custom when someone spoke in front of the Great One, "I am honored by your gracious gift of time to listen to me. I have a very serious problem that only you and your wisdom can help me solve."

The Great One just nodded, signaling I could continue.

"Helen, the daughter of Laverne and Benny, two of our greatest leaders, has vanished."

The Great One leaned forward, clearly reacting in some way to my news.

"Helen is such a wonderful child," the Great One said. "Full of spirit, yet very respectful, as are her parents."

I actually was so stunned he knew Helen, I got off my planned script and for a moment sat there not moving.

"Has she gone into the ancient city?" the Great One asked.

"We think she has, oh Great One," I said, bowing again. "And I am afraid we do not know where the exit is."

The Great One said nothing, so I continued on.

"We would be willing to offer four more containers of the sacred liquid per moon cycle for ten sun cycles if you knew where the exit is from the ancient city and would allow my team to enter the city from our entrance, find her, and bring her back to her parents."

"As I would expect of you, your willingness to risk yourself is admirable."

I bowed slightly in acknowledgement of the compliment. However, a sentence like that usually was followed by the word, "But…"

"We will create a special and separate tunnel from the exit of the ancient city to the surface and allow you to use it for ten sun cycles. But for such work and use, we will require six containers per moon cycle."

I sat dead still for a few seconds. I was expected to negotiate. It was a custom.

"Great One," I finally said, "your kind offer is very generous. If I am allowed to make a counter proposal?"

He nodded, so I went on.

"We can only bring five more than we are doing now per moon cycle for the first year. But then, after that, we can add one more per sun cycle for the ten years of the use of the tunnel you are so graciously willing to build."

I was making sure that he understood that we valued our thermoses of hot chocolate as much as he did, even though we did not. And yet I was giving him a chance to continue to let his people grow and multiply.

He nodded slightly. "Your proposal is very fair. We have an agreement. You can enter the ancient city from above at any time. It will take us only a very short amount of time to open the new tunnel from the ancient city exit to the surface."

"The first payment will be at your entrance tomorrow at sunrise and then with the other regular payment every moon cycle."

"It is always an honor," the Great One said to me, bowing slightly.

"The honor is always mine," I said, bowing as deeply as I could while sitting down.

He stood and without another word left the room.

I waited until he was gone before standing. My legs screamed at me for sitting cross-legged on the dirt floor, but I had had no option.

Two guides appeared a moment later and after thirty minutes of sweating in my black leather coat, we had climbed back to the surface.

I grabbed my shoes and an instant later was in the cool air of my new office floating over Las Vegas.

"Well done," Laverne said, looking like she wanted to hug me.

Benny just smiled and nodded.

"We're not done yet," I said as Patty handed me a large glass of water and I took off my black coat. "We still have to find Helen and get her out of that city."

"At least there's a way out now," Laverne said. "Thanks to you and your fantastic thinking. Not sure why someone hadn't thought of that before now."

With that she and Benny vanished and I slumped into the booth to tell the rest of my team what had just happened.

After I was done, Patty gave me a little kiss on the cheek and then squeezed my hand.

"So we're going in," Screamer said, nodding.

I nodded and turned to Stan. "Is there a map of the ancient city?"

"I'll find out," he said, and vanished.

"I thought you had the exit cleared with the Silicon Suckers," Screamer said.

"I do," I said, "But that ancient city is as large as the entire city of Las Vegas. We first have to find Helen. After that, I honestly have no idea where exactly that one door out is."

"Oh," Screamer said, looking shocked again.

I felt the same way.

SIX

LAVERNE FOUND a very old map of a city that seemed to be not only the size of Las Vegas, but a hundred times larger. In fact, from what I could tell from the old map, at one time the ancient city filled the entire valley.

Stan held that map and the rest of us carried supplies. In packs we had enough food and water to last us a month if we rationed.

We were standing on a side street off of Freemont looking like we were heading into the wilderness for two weeks instead of through a simple door I had never noticed before.

We waited until there was no one on the sidewalk around us, then Stan pulled the door open and held it for us to step through.

I glanced around once more at the city I loved, hoping I would see it again, then holding Patty's hand, I stepped through and into what looked like a long, simple hallway.

Screamer followed, then Stan who pulled the door closed, plunging us into complete blackness.

Patty was the only one who was thinking and had a flashlight in her hand. She snapped it on and pointed it ahead down the hallway that now looked a great deal like a tunnel.

Now I knew where the ancient city got its nickname of "tunnels."

My stomach was in a tight knot and I could barely breathe the stale, dust-smelling air. Only Patty's superpower ability to keep me calm allowed me to move forward. Otherwise I was sure I would have turned and fled for the door and the street beyond.

"Feel that?" Screamer asked.

"Sense of dread spell," Stan said, nodding.

A moment later it was gone as was my need to panic and run. Now all I felt was just plain old fear.

"Thank you," I said.

"Yes," Patty said. "I was barely holding on against it."

"You were doing fine," I said, squeezing her hand as I led us down the hallway and around a corner.

There the beam of her flashlight found another door made of old wood. It had a metal pull handle with strange inscriptions on the metal and the plate under the handle.

"Here we go," Stan said.

I nodded and pulled the door open, sending waves of dust swirling around us in the hallway.

It was now or never.

I stepped through the doorway and into the ancient city.

And stopped cold at what I saw spread out in front of me.

"How can that be?" Patty asked breathlessly beside me.

"Oh, oh," Stan said.

"You have got to be kidding?" Screamer said.

And then, behind us, I heard the door close with a loud thump that sent a chill down my spine.

We were standing on a high balcony with an iron railing protecting us from a very, very long fall. From the looks of it more than thirty or forty stories.

The ancient city was spread out below us. But it wasn't ancient and it certainly wasn't underground and it certainly wasn't empty.

In fact, snow was falling gently on the massive city and I could feel the faint wind and the not-so-faint sounds of a busy city very much alive below us.

We were no longer under Las Vegas.

Or if we were, this was the strangest illusion I had ever seen or felt.

Because we had stepped from a warm afternoon in Las Vegas to a cold, snowy night in a very strange city.

SEVEN

AS I STARED OUT over the fantastic city, suddenly I wished I had listened a little more carefully when Stan explained to me how my new office was out of time and space a half turn. Because I had a hunch this city was the same.

And if we went down into those streets, I was pretty certain we would meet some real Titans. Or at least the descendants of the real Titans from legend.

I really wished I had studied history and legends more back when I was in school. I just never expected to need it like this.

The city stretching into the light snow looked like a fantastic alien science fiction city you might see in the movies with towering beautiful buildings and walkways crisscrossing from building to building mixed up with an ancient Eastern city with arches and columns and narrow, stone roads.

A huge boulevard wider than The Strip in Vegas wound its way through the city and as far as I could see, lined by sleek glowing buildings that seemed to vanish up into the snow. Futuristic cars that looked like they were polished met-al without windows seamlessly flowed up and down the boulevard only on the wrong side of the road as far as I was concerned, like they did in England.

There were a few pedestrians out along the roads, but we were so high in the air I couldn't get any idea of what they looked like.

The snow was thin and the lights from the bustling city made it all seem sort of like I was staring over a fairy tale city inside a snow globe.

For all I knew, I was. I was starting to learn that anything was possible when it came to my world. So maybe we were in a huge snow globe that was the prison to the Titans.

I tried to clear that thought out of my head without much success.

I turned and looked at the door we had come in.

It had vanished. Just a blank, gray cement wall filled the area behind us. No going back that way.

I knew that would be the case, but now being faced with it scared me more than I wanted to admit.

And I had a hunch that finding the exit from this huge city wasn't going to be easy.

We had all stood there on that high balcony in silence for a good minute before I squeezed Patty's hand and turned to Stan. "Got any idea how we might find Helen in this place?"

"I know exactly where she's at," he said, shaking his head and coming back to our situation.

"That's good," Screamer said. "But anyone besides Poker Boy here think to bring a coat?"

For the first time I noticed just how cold it was. Even my black leather coat didn't cut the chill.

An instant later all of us were wearing heavy parkas of varying colors. Patty's was a stylish pink, mine was plain and black like my leather jacket under it, so it matched my fedora-like black hat. Screamer's coat was green with deep pockets that he instantly stuck his hands into. Stan had put himself in a blue parka with a hood and gloves.

I was glad he hadn't given me and Patty gloves. I got a lot of strength from her touch.

"That help?" Stan asked, smiling.

"Thanks," Patty said.

"So how do you know where Helen is at here?" I asked Stan.

"We have a connection when we are close in distance," Stan said. "I've kind of ignored it for years, but it's still there."

"A connection?" Patty asked.

Stan nodded, turning to stare out over the beautiful and very alien city around us. "We were married once."

I just stared at my boss like he had become an alien.

Stan had been married to Lady Luck's daughter. That must have been some divorce.

"Can you jump us to her?" Patty asked, since I hadn't said anything.

He nodded and a moment later we were standing in the snow in what looked like a garden surrounded by stone walls. A brown stone patio filled the center of the garden and in the background was a single-story home with warm orange lights coming from the windows.

The most stunning, redheaded woman I had ever seen was smiling at us.

She wore a white dress that looked more like a thin nightgown. It sort of drifted around her frame and blew in the wind. She had to be cold since I was pretty certain I was seeing through most of that dress or nightgown or whatever it was.

She moved barefooted in the snow across the stone of the patio toward us, her bright red hair blowing in the wind.

All of us stood frozen as she approached and kissed Stan in such a way that most of the snow in the garden area must have melted.

Then she broke the kiss and said, "Wonderful to see you again, my husband."

"Ex-husband," Stan said.

She ignored him and extended her hand to me. "I'm Helen. You must be Poker Boy."

I'm not sure if it was the thin blowing white dress around the naked body in the snow, or her radiant smile, but something caused me to pause before extending my hand as well. "Nice to meet you."

Then Helen turned to Patty. "The famous Patty Ledgerwood, I presume."

"An honor," Patty said, shaking Helen's hand.

Then Helen turned to Screamer and nodded and said nothing.

"Nice seeing you again as well, Sheila," Screamer said, smiling.

I managed to take my eyes off of Helen long enough to look at Screamer with a puzzled look. Clearly he had met her before, only she had called herself Sheila to him.

Wow, did I have a lot of questions when we got out of here.

The woman in the thin, white blowing dress seemed like no Sheila I had ever met.

Screamer just kept his eyes on Helen, and she shrugged and smiled at him.

The next moment we all were inside in a warm living room with a crackling fire in a huge stone fireplace. Helen now had on regular jeans and a flannel shirt and her hair was pulled back. It didn't decrease her beauty in any respect. But it sure made her seem far more human.

Outside in the snow, she had been a goddess. Now she seemed almost normal, if that was possible.

I pretty much doubted it.

The room around us reminded me of a mountain lodge, with warm-brown logs as walls and high ceilings with log rafters. Tan overstuffed couches and chairs surrounded the fireplace and a couple of scarred coffee tables filled the center area.

The air had a faint smoke smell from the burning logs and every so often the fire would pop or crackle.

Thick, dark-brown carpet covered all of the floor except a stone area in front of the fireplace. The carpet added to the feeling of warmth in the room.

I could spend a lot of time in a place like this, especially if it was snowing outside.

"Nice entrance," Stan said to her as he pulled off his parka and dropped down onto a couch.

"You know I always play the part, dear husband," Helen said, laughing. "Thought I was going to freeze off a part or two for a moment there."

"Ex-husband," Stan said more to himself.

"It was a show all right," Screamer said, taking off his parka as well.

"I thought it impressive," Patty said as we both took off our coats and sat on a couch facing Stan.

"Thank you," Helen said, nodding to Patty.

Screamer moved to a chair near the fireplace and Helen sat alone in a large, overstuffed chair facing all of us.

"So did you find what you came for?" Stan asked Helen, his voice clearly telling me he wasn't into any idle chatting, even though I had about a thousand questions I would have loved to have answered at that moment.

Helen smiled and her eyes lit up like a child's eyes with a new toy. "And what do you think I came for?"

"One of the keys of Janus," Stan said.

She laughed, a perfect laugh that might draw someone from across a room. "I did. I had researched it well and knew exactly where it was hidden. I found it within twenty minutes of arriving here."

"And how did you plan on getting back with it?" Screamer asked, also clearly not interested in just having a social visit.

She turned to me, then glanced at Stan. "I knew Mother and Dad would send a rescue party. And I knew it would be you and Poker Boy and his team. And I knew Poker Boy knew the Silicon Suckers and would bargain with them to open the exit, since I am pretty sure the exit has to go into their territory."

She turned to me. "You did that, didn't you?"

"I did," I said, stunned that she had played us like I played a sucker at a poker table.

"Great," she said, clapping her hands together. "Then let's get out of here before the Titans discover some of the gods are among them. I have a hunch they won't like that much."

"Do you know where the exit is at?" I asked.

Helen looked at me like I now had two heads. "No. Don't you?"

I shook my head. "The Silicon Suckers just promised me it would be open with a tunnel to the surface. They never showed me where it was."

She turned to Stan.

"Sorry," he said.

She looked at Screamer.

"We didn't even know this city was here," he said. "We thought we were going into ancient ruins to look for you."

"Oh, no," Helen said, slumping in her chair and covering her face with her hands.

I glanced at Patty, then back at Helen, the Queen of Hearts.

Looks like there was one little detail the Queen of Hearts hadn't figured out in her little scheme.

A very important one.

EIGHT

ACTUALLY, what she hadn't been thinking about, I had, from the very first moment I learned that Laverne wanted us to go down into the "tunnels" as this city was called by those who had never been here.

I wondered what people who lived in this beautiful place actually called it. And exactly where it was in reality. It certainly wasn't under Las Vegas.

"Okay, a couple of questions," I said to the group sitting silently around the fire. "Where exactly is this city in time and space? And what the heck is it called?"

Stan shrugged and looked at Helen.

"The city's name is Elysium," she said without looking up. "It exists in a time in the distant future from what I understand."

Patty coughed, glanced at me, then asked, "Elysium, like in Elysium Fields, like in a form of heaven?"

Helen shrugged. "All myth and rumors of this place. But it is actually a pretty nice city from what I have seen of it."

"Great, just great," Screamer said. "We haven't died and we're stuck in heaven."

I didn't know what to think about her answer. Something was nagging at me, but darned if I could figure it out. Something about this city being in the far future, yet we had come into it in our time, and it seemed to have a protected area in our time as well, under Las Vegas.

Maybe it really was a city inside a giant snow globe buried under Las Vegas.

Again I tried to clear my mind of that stupid thought.

I needed to ask another hundred or more questions, but like everything with this rescue mission so far, most of the questions were going to have to wait until after we got out of here.

If we got out of here.

So I picked the one question that bothered me the most.

"So when we came through the door, we stepped into the future?"

"I believe we did," Helen said, then sighed and slumped in the chair like a kid not getting her way.

The future. That was the key. I had an idea. It wasn't much of one, but it was all I had at the moment.

I stood and started to put my parka back on over my black leather coat. "Stan, could you jump us back to the balcony we came in on?"

He looked at me with that studying look that only the God of Poker could give a person, then nodded and stood and put on his coat as well.

Screamer shrugged and did the same and so did Patty.

"I'll be right here when you get back," Helen said. "I'm still chilled from my last little adventure out there."

Stan just shook his head and a moment later we were standing on the balcony looking through the snow and out over the beautiful city below.

The cold air hit my face with a bite, but actually it felt good and cleared my thoughts even more. The wind swirled the light snow through the buildings and now there seemed to be very few people on the streets below. Whatever the local time was, it must be getting late.

Back in Vegas it wasn't even dinnertime yet.

Patty took my hand and I could feel her calming influence push through me.

I looked at the blank wall behind me where the door from Las Vegas into this city had been.

"So what are you thinking, Poker Boy?" Screamer asked.

I pointed at where the door had been. "We came in level to Freemont Street in downtown Vegas. Right?"

Everyone nodded, so I turned and pointed down. "We have to be a good thirty stories above the street level here. And we know the exit is underground and against the Silicon Sucker's territory."

"So more than likely it's down on the main city level somewhere," Screamer said. "That's a lot of area to look for a door that is more than likely very hidden."

"I agree," I said.

I turned to my boss. "Stan, is it possible in our vision or in our minds, whatever, to overlay a view of Las Vegas from our time over this city? Same scale and everything?"

He looked at me and actually frowned. "We would need to be connected."

"Screamer?"

He nodded and I indicated everyone should step to the metal railing of the balcony and face out over the city. Screamer stood between me and Stan and Patty had my hand on the other side.

Screamer's main power was the ability to hook up thoughts, to see what others were seeing with a touch.

He touched my hand and suddenly he and I and Patty were all together again in my head. We had done this so many times over the last few years, I sometimes wondered if them being in my mind wasn't more comfortable than when they weren't there.

I like it too, Patty thought at me.

Me, not so much, Screamer thought back.

Then Screamer touched Stan and brought the God of Poker into the mix. And instantly a map of Las Vegas formed in my vision. Actually, more than a map, an image of the city as if we were in the air over the downtown area where we had gone through the door.

Rotate it so that the Strip is running along that big boulevard below, I thought to Stan.

He did, and suddenly the two main roads overlaid almost perfectly, only the one in this city kept going out into the distance, right through where the airport had been in our time.

This is a future Las Vegas, Screamer thought, clearly stunned.

"Stan, take us north, keeping the cities lined up, along our Highway 95 where the Silicon Suckers home castle is."

Suddenly we were no longer on the balcony, but instead flying through the snow with an image of Vegas below us overlapping the streets and boulevards of Elysium.

It was even colder up in the air like this. My face and hands were going to take some warming time when this was over. I just hoped my nose didn't freeze off.

I'd still love you anyway, Patty thought.

Knock it off you two, Screamer thought.

Stan took us north slowly until finally I indicated he should stop.

We were right over the edge of the Silicon Sucker's boundary. And clearly they still lived there, since there was nothing but huge mounds of sand and empty spaces over their Territory. The mounds of sand towered into the air over the edge of the new city.

The Silicon Suckers still exist, Patty thought, feeling as stunned as I felt.

I pointed to a wooden shack that had been built against the huge mound of sand. It looked very, very old and weathered. And sand covered the back half of the building. And on the front, facing the city, was a closed wooden door.

Is that the door home? Screamer asked in a thought that felt excited.

I could sense Patty was excited as well.

It might be, I thought back. *It would have been a long ways underground in our time. Stan, take us along the edge of the Silicon Sucker's territory to the west and then back to the east.*

We spent the next five cold minutes drifting through the air, the map of our time imposed over the city below. Then we ended up back over the old shack half buried in the sand.

We had found nothing else touching the Silicon Sucker's territory.

Looks like we might have found our door out, I thought to the others.

Part of me wanted to shout for joy.

And part of me was scared to death that we were wrong.

NINE

AN INSTANT LATER we were back in the warm room with Helen and the wonderful crackling fire.

Screamer dropped his grip on my arm and I was again alone inside my head.

"Any luck?" Helen asked.

"Maybe," Stan said to her. "Get on a coat and gather your things."

She jumped to her feet like an excited child and vanished.

Patty and I moved over in front of the crackling fire, holding our hands closer to the flames in a sad attempt to warm them.

In less than fifteen seconds Helen was back, bundled in a heavy coat with a bag over her shoulder. With a wave of her hand, the fire went out, the lights in the place dimmed, and white sheets covered the furniture.

"Planning on returning?" Screamer asked.

"You never know," Helen said.

An instant later Stan had us standing in the desert in front of the old shack. The wind was blowing harder here and the snow felt like small grains of sand against my cheeks.

Up close the door looked very similar to the one we had come through on the way in. Same rough metal handle with strange inscriptions, same old wood. That made me feel a little more hopeful.

I turned to face everyone and held up my hand for attention. Then shouting over the wind I said, "If this is our door out and we end up in the Silicon Suckers' tunnels on the other side, it is critical we say nothing and calmly walk to the surface."

I looked directly at Helen and she looked back, very puzzled.

She then started to say something and Stan held up his hand. "If you can't agree to Poker Boy's instructions, you stay here."

"And how can you make me do that?" Helen demanded, her eyes blazing as she turned to face her ex-husband.

She was so angry, I had no doubt that the snow wasn't getting near her. I know I wanted to step back, but I didn't.

Stan just kept his poker face and said calmly, "We will go through first and make sure the Silicon Suckers never open the exit again."

"You would do that to me?"

"I would," Stan said. "And I am sure your parents, once they know you are alive and living just fine, would agree with me."

She started to say something and then closed her mouth. She turned her back on Stan, staring at the wooden door in front of her. Her face was bright red, almost matching her hair blowing in the wind.

"It is critical we say nothing and walk to the surface," I said again, looking directly at her and keeping my voice as even as I can. "Please? The Silicon Suckers have opened this tunnel for us. The least we can do is honor their customs in their land."

Finally, she took a deep breath and nodded.

I glanced past her at Stan and he nodded. I had a hunch he was going to make sure she followed the instructions. I didn't want to think of dealing with the Silicon Suckers again if he couldn't keep her under control.

I took a couple steps through the sand and pulled on the door. It didn't move.

Stan stepped up and made a motion and then pulled the door open, scraping back sand as he did.

A dark concrete tunnel led into the mound of sand inside the small shack and again Patty snapped on her flashlight and I led the way, holding her hand.

Screamer followed us, then Helen, and Stan came in last, pulling the outside door closed behind us.

We walked silently for about thirty paces and then around a corner to face another door.

I indicated everyone keep quiet with a finger against my lips, then I pushed the door open.

Beyond the door was a sand tunnel that I knew was dug by the Silicon Suckers. It had the same light that seemed to come from everywhere and the same scraping marks on the walls.

But the question was had we gone back in time or were we just walking inside a Silicon Suckers' tunnel in the future without invite?

Patty instantly snapped off her flashlight and put it away.

I led the way up the steep slope of the tunnel, only glancing back to make sure Helen was still with us and that Stan had closed the door.

There were no side tunnels at all.

The climb had to be the longest in my life. But actually it took us less than ten minutes until the tunnel leveled and I walked out into the evening light and warmth of the desert outside of Las Vegas.

A bright red Ford pickup truck sped past on Highway 95.

As Patty stepped into the evening sun, Laverne and Benny appeared, both looking happy and angry at the same time. I didn't want to think about what this family meeting was going to be like.

As Helen stepped into the light, a bright smile crossed her face as she saw her parents. Then she turned to Stan.

"You can take off the shield now holding me here," she said.

"Not me," Stan said, smiling.

Helen turned to stare at her parents. "Mom?"

"We'll talk," she said.

And with that Helen vanished, and not to a place she wanted to go I would wager.

"Thank you again," Lady Luck said and behind her Benny nodded.

It never got old having Lady Luck thank you.

Lady Luck went on. "After we get family business taken care of, I would love to hear about your adventure on the other side. I'll come join you all for lunch one of these days."

Then she and Benny vanished as the four of us stood there with our mouths open.

An instant later Stan had us back in my office and we were all missing our parkas.

And I had about six thousand questions built up to ask.

Screamer shook his head and looked out at Las Vegas below my office. "Well, that was an interesting afternoon trip. I think there's a steak with my name on it at the MGM Grand."

"Mind if I join you?" Stan asked. "I would love to know how you knew Helen or Sheila, as you called her."

"You drive," Screamer said, smiling, and an instant later they were both gone.

Without answering a single question I had.

"So that leaves just the two of us," Patty said, looking at me with those big brown eyes of hers. "Any ideas?"

"Maybe trying to find out what just happened? And what those keys were all about. And why exactly that city is there. And who did it."

"More than enough time for that," Patty said, smiling. "I'm going to call in and cancel work tonight. I think they can get by without me, don't you?"

I took a deep breath and looked out over the city I loved. I was finally starting to catch her drift. It was time to celebrate being back and being alive.

"I do," I said, nodding seriously.

"Then after I call work I want to take a long hot shower," she said, smiling at me and giving me a quick kiss. "I'm still chilled. Then maybe some dinner."

"Mind if I join you?" I asked, holding her close. "I'm sure they can get along without me at the poker tournament tonight as well."

"For dinner?" she asked.

"I was thinking of the shower to be honest," I said.

"You drive," she said, smiling.

"With pleasure," I said.

And it turned out that with pleasure was a very good description of the rest of the evening.

—

Dee W. Schofield

Not really dead.
Not really alive.
And the man
of her dreams
starts the autopsy.

Mated from the Morgue

A Fun Romance
of Near Death

Not really dead, not really alive. Debbie finds herself one fine day in a hospital morgue and the man of her dreams walks in to start her autopsy.

In just moments her wonderful body will be cut open.

And she can't move to stop him.

MATED FROM THE MORGUE
(Published under the name Dee W. Schofield)

ONE

I'M ON one damn cold metal table, bright lights shining on my naked body, my brand new, enhanced breasts aiming at the ceiling tile of this stupid hospital morgue like they were supposed to. And what do I feel? Annoyed. Just annoyed. Not cold, not embarrassed, just annoyed.

And just a little scared.

Panic?

Sure. That was in the mix as well.

I'm about to be very, very dead if someone doesn't catch a clue real quick that I am still inside this stupid body of mine and very much alive, even though it doesn't look like I am.

Some pimply-faced kid set up a tray of sharp knives and bone spreaders beside my table, looked at my breasts, then my crotch, and left.

This felt like sitting in a dentist's chair getting ready for the dentist to use all his nasty-looking instruments. Only, that tray of stuff was sitting there just waiting for some lowlife mortician to come in and cut me open like a stupid trout.

While I'm still alive and can feel it! Okay, maybe panic was a little closer to the surface than I thought.

Can't any of the idiots out there see that I'm still alive, that some blood was pumping? Otherwise, how could I be lying here on this damn cold metal table thinking that if I ever did get out of this, I was going to kill someone.

Anyone.

From across the embalming room I heard a door open. I sure as hell wanted to turn my head and smile at the person just to give them a shock. I tried.

Nothing.

Not even a muscle twitch.

Suddenly, a hunk of a good-looking guy in a rubber apron and a hairnet appeared over me like an angel. He had flashing dark eyes, longish, dark brown hair under the net, and a smile that just wouldn't stop.

And he was looking right in to my eyes.

"You are far too good-looking to be here on this table," he said.

I tried to shout, *No Shit, Sherlock!*

My mouth wouldn't move. Not even a grunt came out.

He walked slowly down along the table, clearly taking in all my naked assets.

Now I was starting to feel embarrassed. This was not really the way I wanted a hunk of a guy to see me. He looked at the toe tag on my foot, then came back up and checked off something on a clipboard.

"Debbie," he said, smiling at me again. "My name is Mathew. I'm here to try to find out why you just keeled over dead in your tuna salad."

I'm not dead! I tried to scream.

Nothing.

I was facing a young hunk of a doctor who talked to the bodies. Even with that bad habit, I still wanted to jump his bones.

I wanted to jump anything, actually. Getting cut open on a morgue table was not my idea of a good way to leave the planet.

How the hell did I end up here?

And what the hell was a guy like him doing here? He could be modeling for a men's magazine in sweaters with golf clubs in his hands. Instead he was cutting open dead people.

And more than likely a not-so-dead one in just a moment.

I had two degrees in business and ran my own company. He clearly had a medical license of some sort to call himself a doctor. He couldn't be dumb. Maybe, just maybe, he might figure this all out. The idiots in the ambulance and the bitch doctor in the emergency room sure hadn't.

Having yourself declared dead while you are listening is just not a good time. If I got out of here, I was going to need counseling for years.

The door to the room opened again, and Doctor Mathew turned those wonderful, dark eyes away from me.

"I won't need you anymore today, Jim," he said.

His voice sort of echoed, so the room had to be fairly large. More than likely he was talking to the kid with the face-full of pimples, but I couldn't see the kid.

Doctor Mathew disappeared from my limited sight, and I heard the kid mumble something, then the door closed.

And then there was the sound of a lock turning.

Oh, shit!

This might turn even uglier than it was. I just went from a horror sit-com to a full-out horror movie.

TWO

NOW THE PANIC was starting to swell up. I had seen far too many movies where the good-looking doctor was some sort of perv.

My brain told me I wanted to swallow and then scream for help, but none of that was happening.

In horror movies, they always made the poor victim unable to move as well.

The hunk of a man appeared above me again, smiling. At least he was a good-looking monster.

"We're all alone now, Debbie. Just you and me. Maybe we could call this a date. You would be the first date I've had in a year. Since my wife died."

Oh, shit! Oh, shit! I was doomed. I just hoped I didn't remind the guy of his dead wife.

"You remind me a little of Marcie," he said, smiling and checking out my scalp with very tender fingers and a light touch.

Oh, shit! Oh, shit! Oh, shit!

"But she was shorter and had green eyes," he said, "instead of pretty blue ones like yours. She also wanted to have breast enhancements like yours, but was killed in a car crash before she got the chance. Life is so short. Clearly it was for you as well."

He kept working over my scalp, very carefully, like a lost hairdresser trying to pad her bill and find her way to the door by Braille.

"I'm afraid I won't be a very good date," he said, smiling at me and looking right into my eyes. "I just don't think it's been long enough for me since my Marcie left."

He laughed in a strained way and shook his head.

Wasn't it bad enough that I was on a morgue table, thought to be dead, and now some guy was going to get his jollies on my naked body?

"But don't worry," he said as he smiled down at me. "I have always been a complete gentleman on a first date."

I'd believe that if I wasn't as naked as the day I came into this stupid world. Except for the toe tag.

He started to check out my neck with those wonderful hands of his, then he stepped back, a frown on his face. "Your skin is still warm to the touch."

Could he be figuring this out?

He stepped away and I could no longer see him. From what I could tell he was flipping through some sort of paperwork.

"It's been three hours since you collapsed," he said, clearly still talking to me. "Two hours since you were declared dead. And you've been down here on this table for over an hour now. That's just weird."

I should be as cold as a rock. Right? Come on, Doc! Figure it out.

Next I could hear him rummaging through a drawer, and a moment later he was back, a stethoscope around his neck and a small device in one hand.

He held the device in my ear for a moment, then looked at it.

"Weird," he said. "Just weird." He looked into my eyes again. "You are as strange as you are beautiful."

If I could have even blushed I would have right at that moment. Maybe I did, just a little. I couldn't tell.

He put one hand on my chest, right on my brand new, specially-enhanced left breast, and leaned forward, not noticing at all what he was touching. I was still just dead meat to him, like I had been to my first husband for two years of that disaster laughingly called a marriage.

With his other hand he held the cold stethoscope to my chest.

For a moment he listened, then he moved the stethoscope to a location just under my enhancement and held it there. His eyes were distant, intense, as he tried to listen.

I'm in here, Doc! I wanted to shout.

After a moment he pushed down fairly hard on my chest with one hand while listening.

And then he pushed again, right on my breast.

Gentleman, hell!

But I knew he had no real idea what part of my body he was touching and pushing on. And that was damn fine with me. I wanted out of this nightmare—then he could push on my new breasts as much as he wanted. In a nice soft bed at his place or mine.

Suddenly he jumped back as if I had shocked him.

My new breasts were good, but not that good.

THREE

"NOT POSSIBLE!" he said.

Then he was back at my chest, leaning over, breathing gently into my chin as he leaned way down and almost put his ear against my chest with the stethoscope pressed in hard.

He listened and listened and then suddenly jumped back again, knocking over the tray of instruments.

"Oh, hell, Debbie, are you still in there?"

If I could have moved I would have jumped up and kissed him.

Suddenly, he vanished out of my vision and I could hear him grab a phone. He called in some sort of code and unlocked the door. Then he was back at my side, staring into my eyes.

"Hang on, Debbie. Help is on the way."

He took my hand and squeezed it gently.

I just stared into those wonderful dark eyes of his and said nothing. Not like me, but I had no choice.

It was still a very, very nice moment.

What seemed like only a few seconds later the door exploded open and help arrived.

Six of them, including Doctor Mathew, moved me onto a stretcher, put an oxygen mask over my nose and mouth, covered me with a sheet, and banged me out of the room so fast I thought I was on a ride in an amusement park.

Doctor Mathew never left my side as he and two other doctors talked all the way down the hall and up an elevator, clearly headed into more tests than I wanted to think about. I had no idea what they were talking about, but to be honest, it all sounded wonderful. A ton better than having someone declare you dead when you were really just fine.

For the moment my nightmare in the morgue was over. Now if I died, it wouldn't be because I was sliced and diced. It would be with real doctors trying to save me.

They arrived in a place with dozens of people swarming around all seeming to talk at the same time. They hooked me up to a dozen monitors and confirmed I still had a very, very slowly beating heart.

And that my brain was still working.

I knew that, but it sure felt better to have some doctor say that.

"Oh, wow," I heard Doctor Mathew say as someone else announced the test results. "I could have killed her on that table."

Some other male doctor said, "But you didn't. Nice work, doctor."

So after what seemed like only a moment since they shoved me out of the morgue, Doctor Mathew leaned in over me again and smiled.

His smile got more wonderful every time I saw it. And those dark eyes of his could melt an iceberg.

I was almost dead and still in lust. How sad was that? It had clearly been too long since I had been laid.

"Hang in there, Debbie. We're going to put you under while we do more tests and figure out just what is happening to you. But don't worry, I'll be right here when you wake up."

Then he gently reached forward and closed my eyelids.

"Sleep well."

He could do that to me for years if he wanted to.

And that was the last thing I remembered as that little cloud of blackness sort of came in from all sides.

FOUR

AND THEN the blackness pushed back.

Weird. It seemed I didn't want to be knocked out.

Or all of that had been some horrible nightmare.

Around me, I could hear the beeping of machines; and in the background, the sounds of a people talking.

And a television was on, softly going over some sort of news.

I blinked and opened my eyes to the lights of the room.

I was in a very different room than the one the tests had been in. And CNN was on the television. I had a light oxygen mask on my nose.

And holy crap, I had moved my eyelids!

I tried a finger and could feel it move as well.

And then an arm.

And then a leg.

Everything moved!

And I could feel I had a tube stuck in my arm.

And my chest hurt something awful.

And I was beyond thirsty.

"Water?" I tried to say, and I actually think what I managed to croak out sounded like a word.

Instantly Doctor Mathew was standing over me, smiling. He had been sitting beside my bed watching television.

"Glad to have you back, Debbie," he said, again giving me that wonderful smile of his.

He eased a tiny ice cube toward my lips and managed to help me get it in my mouth.

"Just let that melt for a moment."

In all my life, an ice cube had never tasted or felt as good.

Doctor Mathew smiled as I worked the tiny ice chip over like it was a seven-course meal.

"My name is Doctor Mathew Stevens," he said. "I have no idea how much you remember, but you were declared dead."

I nodded slightly, and indicated he should come closer. He leaned in and I somehow managed to whisper. "A weird first date, Mathew. Thank you for saving me."

He leaned back, smiling and blushing, realizing I had heard every word he had said in the morgue. Somehow, with that handsome face of his bright red, he managed to recover a little and go on.

"We had to remove your breast implants," he said. "You had an allergy to them that just shut you down. It would have killed you completely in another few hours. Don't worry, you can get the implants replaced with a different type later."

At that moment I didn't care. Who knew having large breasts could kill a woman? My original, factory-issued breasts weren't that bad in the first place. Dumb idea by me to think they might help me with men.

I just nodded to Mathew, so he went on.

"You've been out for about five days," he said, "in a drug-induced coma so the toxins could clear your system completely. You should be up and around in a few days and feeling back to normal in a week."

He leaned in and gave me another piece of ice, which again felt wonderful.

I sure liked having him close.

"Thank you for saving me," I said again, my voice gaining strength.

"That's what we try to do," he said, nodding and blushing a little again. "You are welcome."

A bashful doctor. Who knew there was such a thing?

I smiled at him.

"You have a beautiful smile," he said. "Glad I could see it."

"So am I," I said.

Then I smiled again. "I understand about your wife, at least what little you told me. But if you are willing to give it a try and are ready, I would be up for a second date. The first one turned out so well."

He stood there just staring at me, then, after a long few seconds, he finally laughed.

"Honestly," I said, "I don't expect you to save my life every date."

"That's good," he said, shaking his head and laughing. "I would love to try a second date. Especially since that was a first date I could never imagine happening. I normally don't date patients."

"Why?" I asked, smiling so hard I was going to knock the small oxygen mask off my nose.

"Because I'm a forensic pathologist," he said. "I only deal with the dead."

"Thanks to you," I said, "I am far from dead."

"Good. Because I only really date the living."

I just sat there smiling, trying not to laugh because my chest hurt too much. It seemed that those larger breasts really had helped me get a man.

∼

Now Available
from all your favorite booksellers
in trade paper and electronic editions.

DEAN WESLEY SMITH

AN EASY SHOT

A GOLF THRILLER

Seattle detectives Craig and Bonnie Frakes wanted nothing more but to enjoy each other's company and their golf vacation in Scottsdale. They needed the rest.

Their vacation plans take a sudden turn when they overhear a conversation plotting a murder.

A fast-paced thriller that I first published years ago under another title and under a pen name. The publishing company died just as this book came out, so I figured it would be fun to bring the book back and give it a second life here.

AN EASY SHOT

Part 1 of 8

———————————

For KKR, always the love of my life.

———————————

PROLOGUE

Monday, April 3rd
11:12 p.m.

CHARLES ROBINS IGNORED the crisp desert air and the star-filled Arizona night as he stepped onto the stone patio of his Scottsdale mansion. His entire focus was on the dark-suited man who leaned against a rock wall, smoking.

Beyond the wall, the lights of Phoenix stretched out across the valley floor. Often, on spring nights like this, Charles would have his after-dinner brandy served on this patio. He loved the view, the lights, the feeling of being above all the masses below.

But not tonight.

At the moment there was much more important business to attend to. There would always be other warm nights and brandy on the patio.

The man dropped the red-tipped cigarette and ground it under his foot as Charles closed the patio door and turned.

The man would fit into most crowds. His dark suit wasn't expensive, but it wasn't cheap either. His face was clean shaven and had nothing really distinctive about it. His hair was short and he was going slightly bald. Charles doubted he would even recognize the man if they passed on the street. Yet the man was one of Charles's most trusted and valued employees.

The man waited, making Charles come to him. No one else could do that. Charles controlled businesses worth a billion dollars, had twenty servants and six body guards in this house alone, and was considered one of the most eligible bachelors in the country. Yet this man just didn't seem to care.

Charles asked him to do special tasks, paid him well, and that was all the man did. He scared Charles by his very coldness. No one else in this world did that to Charles.

In the three years the man had worked for Charles, this was only their fourth meeting. All four meetings had been on this patio, and always alone. Charles didn't even know the man's real name and had no desire to learn it. Charles just called him Bill when he had to call him anything at all, and the man didn't seem to care. Yet Charles knew to the penny how many hundreds of thousands of dollars this man, under a false company name, had been paid for "consulting."

And every penny had been worth it.

The man spoke little, and Charles liked that about him. Tonight there were no greetings. The man, his dark eyes hidden in the faint light, simply stood and waited, his hands behind his back, as if he were in control.

That attitude made Charles feel even less sure about what he was about to do, but at this point he could see no other choice.

"Senator Knight from California will be playing in a pro-am golf tournament here in Scottsdale this weekend," Charles said, keeping his voice low so that it wouldn't carry in the desert air. "Then he will be flying to Washington for a vote Monday morning."

The man said nothing.

Charles went on. "I want you to make sure he doesn't make that trip."

"Never make the trip?" the man asked, his voice very low and deep. "Or delayed?"

"I don't honestly care," Charles said. And he didn't. Senator Kelly had been after him for years. Having the man permanently out of the picture would not be a bad thing. But it was critical Kelly didn't make that vote.

"Understood," the man said, nodding once. "Is that all?"

"Make it look like an accident if you can," Charles said. "But if you can't just make sure it's done. He cannot be allowed to be in Washington on Monday. Understood?"

Again the man nodded once. "This is a United States Senator you are talking about. It will cost you more."

"Of course," Charles said. "Just get it done."

Without even a nod the man turned and started down the rock path beside the garage wall. The night seemed to swallow him. One moment there, the next gone. How the man got past Grant and his men, and in and out of the estate's security system was another question Charles just didn't want to know the answer to.

Charles stared after the man for a moment, feeling uncertain, and very worried, just as he had felt every other time he had talked to him. Yet the man always got the task done.

Charles turned to look out over the lights of the valley below. This mansion, all his property, everything he owned and controlled, was being threatened and he couldn't let that happen.

Senator Kelly was the push behind legislation that would cripple two of Charles's main companies, and lead to investigations that Charles knew he couldn't withstand. If Senator Kelly's legislation passed, Charles would be broke and fighting to stay out of jail in less than a year.

Most of his waking hours—and many of his nightmares—over the last few months had been to fight this bill. He had wrapped up enough votes in Kelly's committee to tie and kill the bill if Kelly didn't vote. But Chairman Kelly's vote would put the bill on the floor of the Senate and from there it couldn't be stopped.

The key to it all was making sure Senator Kelly didn't make that vote.

Charles glanced down the dark path where the man he called Bill had disappeared. He could see nothing.

With a deep breath of the fresh, crisp night air, Charles turned and headed back inside. He had a lot of work to do and work was always the best thing to take his mind off of what he had just ordered done.

If that was even possible.

Friday, April 7th
8:02 a.m.

THE THREE GUNMEN walked into the small apartment of Steph and Danny Baines without knocking. Two wore masks, the third, who was in charge, didn't seem to care who saw him. But

he knew that the residents of the nearby apartments had all left for work. Only twenty-four-year-old Steph Barnes was at home.

The small apartment hugged against the back of a large red rock just above the small valley that held Sedona, Arizona. It had one bedroom, a small living room and kitchen, and a fantastic view of the red-rock country around Sedona from a balcony.

Danny worked as the assistant golf pro for the local country club and Steph taught sixth grade. They were both from Phoenix, had met in college, and were hoping that Danny would get a job this next fall on one of the bigger Scottsdale clubs so they could move back. They both loved Sedona, but it was just too cold in the winter for both of them.

Danny stood just under six feet tall, had sun-bleached brown hair and a smooth-as-silk golf swing. Steph was almost as tall, with light auburn hair and a smile that could melt a sixth-grader. Everyone said they looked more like brother and sister than husband and wife.

Steph had taken the morning off from school to help Danny get ready for the charity tournament in Phoenix. They both had figured that it would be a wonderful opportunity to meet some people who might help them get back into the Phoenix area. And when he learned he was playing with Senator Knight, Danny got even more excited. Steph was going to come down by bus on Saturday and join the group on Sunday. Not only was it going to be a good chance for Danny to make contacts, it was going to be fun as well.

Steph had just dropped a fifth golf shirt into Danny's suitcase when the front door opened. For a moment she thought it was Danny coming back from the course early. Then she heard a strange voice from the doorway.

"Don't scream or nothin'" the voice said. "Just finish packin' for your husband and everything will be just fine."

She spun around to face three men. All were holding machine-gun-like weapons on her.

Somehow she managed to not scream. Somehow.

CHAPTER ONE

Friday, April 7th
9:20 p.m.

THE WARM DESERT breeze wrapped around Craig Frakes as he stopped to look back up the hill at the lights of the Canyon Hotel nestled into the rocks. After the long winter in Seattle, he couldn't believe he was here in Scottsdale, Arizona, getting ready to play an entire weekend of golf. This had to be a dream. He was sure he would wake up any moment to the sound of rain pounding against the bedroom window.

His wife, Bonnie, stopped beside him and took his hand, also staring up at the resort they were staying in for the next three nights. "Beautiful, isn't it?"

Beautiful didn't really begin to describe it. The Canyon Hotel had been built using the massive brown rocks and the desert hillside as a frame. The architect had nestled the rooms into the canyon walls, mixing large timbers and massive boulders throughout. The main area was a combination of stone, wood, and soft car-

pets that felt more like a warm cave and a living room than a hotel lobby.

And the fantastic architecture didn't stop at the lobby. Their room—as the hotel called it—was more like a suite, with a light brown leather couch and chair, a massive bed, and a bathroom larger than some apartments he had rented in college. A switch inside the bathroom door sent a waterfall cascading over rocks and down into a large tub. Craig couldn't imagine how every room in the hotel could be as plush as theirs, but he had a hunch every room was.

From where they stood on the path near the first tee of the Canyon Resort Golf Club, the hotel lights filled the night with a soft glow that felt welcoming and warm, barely pushing back the light from the stars and the small crescent moon.

"You know what's really great about being here?" he asked, looking over at his beautiful wife. Her hair seemed to shimmer in the glow from the hotel and she looked almost waif-like in the white shorts and light blouse.

"What?" she asked, smiling at him.

"It's warm," he said, "it's not raining, and my lips are already chapping from the dryness. What more can a guy ask for?"

She laughed, the sound carrying out over the open fairway and lush grass. "Oh, I can think of a few more things."

She squeezed his hand and pulled him away from staring at the hotel and down the dark, paved golf path that led along the right side of the first hole of the course. "Come on, let's go for a walk."

Now that she mentioned it, Craig could think of a few other things he *could* ask for. And knowing Bonnie, he just might be lucky enough tonight to get one of those wishes.

"Going to be tough to see what the golf course is like in the dark," he said.

"I wasn't thinking of looking at the golf course," she said.

"Oh, I like the sound of that," he said, as they topped over a small rise and headed down a shallow hill that slowly blocked the lights of the hotel.

After the last six months of hard work, they had been looking forward to this vacation. They both worked for the Seattle police department. He was a homicide detective, while she had moved off the streets and now worked special services dealing in domestic violence and runaway children.

Everyone said they made the perfect couple. He was six-one and had just turned thirty-one. She was five-two and thirty. Both of them had dark brown hair, but Bonnie's eyes were a deep brown while his were green.

They had met in college and lived together for years before finally getting married. At some point they both wanted children, but so far their jobs kept them too busy.

He stayed in shape by running and lifting weights, while Bonnie liked swimming more. But they were both avid golfers. Bonnie's handicap was three shots lower than Craig's, and she beat him three out of their four outings, something Craig very seldom let her forget. They loved the game and the good-natured rivalry, and when the opportunity to represent the Seattle Police Department in this charity golf tournament came along, they jumped at the chance to get out of the Seattle spring weather and actually play a round of golf without wearing rain gear.

On top of that, this weekend was going to be the first real vacation they had had in over a year. Craig couldn't believe it had been that long. Being a detective never seemed to allow for much free time. And Bonnie's job wasn't any better. At one point earlier this spring she had had over one hundred active cases of children needing homes, abused spouses, and missing children. He marveled at her strength under that heavy a load.

Now here they were, walking on what seemed to be a perfect-temperature evening in Arizona, the cares of police work a long plane ride behind them.

"You're sure being quiet," Bonnie said as they strolled along the dark path, hand in hand.

They were walking slower than he remembered walking in a long time. It felt great. He could feel the tension draining from his back and shoulders.

"Just relaxing and watching the lights of the valley. And enjoying the company."

"How about enjoying the company a little more closely?" she asked, her voice low and sultry and very suggestive. She pulled him and they bumped hips.

Craig could barely see her smile in the dim light. She was teasing him and he was enjoying it.

"This far from the hotel room?" he asked, teasing back. "I'm afraid I just don't know what you have in mind?"

She laughed. "Six years of marriage and you've forgotten what we used to do on the muni course?"

He would never forget those nights, but instead he said, "Hmmm, how about a reminder?"

As the path crested a small rise near a massive boulder, she pulled him off the pavement and around the rock that towered over the edge of the fairway.

The grass on the other side was lush and soft as she pulled him down beside her. He expected it to be damp and cold, like the grass in the Pacific Northwest always was at night, but instead the fairway was dry and slightly warm from the heat of the day. He was starting to like the desert more and more.

The lights from the valley below gave them just enough light to see what they were doing, yet not enough for Craig to worry about being seen from any distance. And the boulder blocked the view to the path.

"This feels wonderful," Bonnie said, rubbing her hands over the ground as she kicked off her shoes.

"I couldn't agree more," he said, wrapping his arms around her and pulling her close for a long, passionate kiss.

His heart was racing and he was short of breath. For some reason he felt too old to be kissing out under the stars. That seemed like a young person's thing. When had he gotten so old?

He pushed the thought away and let the excitement of the moment take him. After a moment, he started to unbutton her blouse, slowly, carefully, not breaking the kiss.

He could feel her skin under his fingers, getting him even more excited than he already was. But he forced himself to try to take his time. In this kind of situation, that was going to be difficult, at best. It had been a long time since they had done something like this.

Too long.

Finally, after what seemed like an eternity of bumbling, he got the last button undone. It felt like a victory, the same as it had with his first girlfriend back in high school.

Bonnie pulled back. "I see you are remembering just fine."

He ran his hand over her breast, enjoying the soft feel of her skin and the silky feel of the bra. She shivered slightly and leaned into his touch.

"I think it's coming back to me," he said, "but I'm still not sure."

She laughed. "Let's be sure."

She pulled off her blouse and tossed it toward the base of the rock, then as he watched, she lay back, lifted her hips, and slipped off her white shorts, tossing them on top of the blouse.

Just the movement of her body in the faint light made him excited.

And the fear of getting caught. That was exciting him even more.

He glanced around, trying to listen *over* the sounds of his beating heart to see if anyone was coming. As far as he could tell, they were alone.

At least for the moment.

"No grass stains this time," she said.

He laughed. Back on one of their early college dates, they had ended up on the golf course, kissing and touching and having a great time late one night. Bonnie had been wearing white shorts like the ones she had just taken off, and they had gotten ruined from grass stains. And since she had been living at home at the time, it had been very embarrassing to explain to her mother.

"You got to admit, getting those grass stains was fun."

"And this isn't?" she asked, smiling.

"I didn't say that."

They kissed, long and hard, a kiss like they hadn't done in some time. Work had just been so much for both of them that sex had often taken a back seat. His hope, and it seemed to be Bonnie's as well, was that this weekend that would change. Sex would become something they focused on and enjoyed. And this was getting the weekend off to a great start as far as he was concerned.

In the faint light, she was fantastically beautiful. The white of her bra and thin panties was like a light beckoning him to come closer. And he obeyed.

Hell, he *wanted* to obey.

He let his hands brush up her legs, over her flat stomach, to her breasts.

She pulled back. "Wait just a minute. You have too many clothes on now."

With that she sat up and pulled on the bottom of his shirt, helping him take it over his head. It ended up in the pile with her clothes. Then she worked at his belt and unzipped his slacks as he took off his shoes.

He lay back, his butt off the ground, as in one smooth motion she pulled his pants off, leaving him laying in the middle of a fairway on the warm grass in only his white underwear.

It was the most excited he could remember feeling since college.

And the most afraid of getting caught.

He had forgotten what that feeling of doing something illegal was like.

The grass was warm and soft against his skin as he ran his hands over it. What the hell. If they got caught, they got caught. It was their vacation, after all. And they were a long way from home.

"Now you have too many clothes," he said.

"Oh, I like this game," she said, giving him a kiss and then pulling away.

As he watched, she unhooked her bra, tossing it aside with the rest of their clothes. The soft light made her skin seem ultra smooth and silky, as if there wasn't a mole or wrinkle anywhere.

"Like what you see?" she asked, looking down at him.

"Much more than like," he said. "How about love? Admire? Adore?"

"You say all the right things," she said, her laugh carrying into the darkness of the desert and golf course. She lay on top of him. The feel of her breasts against his chest was wonderful.

"Nice," she said, pressing her leg into the hardness of his crotch.

He pulled her tight and they kissed again, moving their bodies slowly against each other. He wanted to touch, to stroke every inch of her. He loved the way she felt against him, her soft skin moving slowly against his.

He kept at it until she finally pulled his head up and kissed him long and hard.

He returned the kiss, suddenly not caring if anyone else was nearby or not. She rolled him over on his back and kneeling beside his legs pulled off his underwear with a frantic jerk, flicking them into the air over her head.

"Oh, I like this," she said, running her hands over him.

"You're not the only one," he said. The sensation was wonderful and much more intense than it had been in a long time.

The warm night, the fear of someone nearby, the grass against his back all seemed to vanish as his body pushed upward. Before she was all the way into position he couldn't help himself and started to move up and down under her.

After a wonderful eternity, they lay panting, sweating, both trying to catch what air they could manage.

That had been intense, and wonderful.

He kissed her neck and she shivered. But she didn't move.

He kissed it again and got the same reaction. Only this time she hugged him, being careful to keep him in the same position.

"Wow," he managed to whisper into her ear.

She squeezed him with her entire body. "Yeah. No argument there."

She carefully stretched out her legs and lay down on him, keeping them together as they rolled over so they were facing each other in a full hug. On one side he could feel her soft skin the length of his body, and on his back grass was sticking to his sweaty body.

With the stars above and warm night air around them, it was a moment he didn't want to let go of.

Clearly Bonnie didn't either.

There was no sound of anyone walking toward them.

The night was quiet, so they just lay there, holding each other, not saying anything.

He couldn't remember feeling this good in a long time. It was an absolutely perfect start to the vacation.

He closed his eyes and let his body completely relax.

CHAPTER TWO

Friday, April 7th
9:46 p.m.

DANNY BAINES TOSSED his bag on the hotel bed and looked around. In all his life he had never felt so scared, so alone, so completely out of his mind.

This all had to be a nightmare and he would wake up very shortly.

He walked into the large bathroom and stared in the mirror.

His eyes were red and he looked like he hadn't slept.

Actually he'd had a good night's sleep last night with Steph and this morning had headed to the course to get his clubs and help get ready for the weekend rush of players before he had to leave for Phoenix.

When he got home, he found his bag packed and sitting by the front door. A man he didn't recognize was sitting on the couch, pointing a gun at him.

Steph was nowhere to be found.

He almost went crazy when the guy said they had taken Steph. He stormed at the guy.

"If I shoot you," the guy had said, pointing the gun at Danny, "I have to kill your wife as well."

That stopped Danny.

And then Danny's blood seemed to freeze as the man laughed. "And she's a looker, too. It would be fun doin' her."

"So why are you doing this?" Danny had asked.

For the next twenty minutes the man had explained exactly why they had taken Steph. And what they wanted him to do to get her back.

Then the man had helped him carry his bag to his car, helped him check the apartment to make sure everything was turned off, and then stood there and watched Danny drive away.

Now Danny was in Phoenix, checked into his room, and going crazy. He couldn't do what they were asking.

He just couldn't.

But it seemed he had no choice.

He headed through the bedroom and out into the main area of the small suite.

The phone was sitting on the desk under a mirror. He moved over to it. He had to call the police. He had to have help.

He picked up the phone, then put it back down, the man's voice echoing in his ears. "Trust me," the man had said, "you call the police and we can kill your wife before you hang up the phone."

Those words echoed through his mind. How would they know if he called the police?

He couldn't take the chance.

The image of Steph's face filled his mind and he moved over to the couch and sat down.

It was going to be a very long night.

And an even longer golf tournament.

CHAPTER THREE

Friday, April 7th
9:53 p.m.

BONNIE'S BREATH was even against his neck, the grass soft under him, and he wasn't sure if he hadn't even dozed a little. Amazing, falling asleep nude in the middle of a fairway. This just wasn't like him at all.

Suddenly he realized what had woken him up.

Someone was coming!

The sound of a deep, male voice in the distance drifted over them.

He pulled back enough to see his wife's face in the dim light. Her eyes were closed and she seemed to be asleep as well. He could feel their skin sticking together.

He leaned in close to her ear. "I think someone's coming," he whispered, trying not to startle her.

"Oh, damn," she whispered back.

Her eyes snapped open and she rolled away from him.

The stickiness on his stomach had dried his skin against hers and it pulled like removing a bandage.

"How long were we asleep?" she whispered as she grabbed her shoes and the pile of clothes and moved over toward the side of the giant boulder that towered over them and the fairway. If they stayed against the backside of it, they wouldn't be seen from the cart path.

He grabbed his shoes and followed her as again the male voice could clearly be heard. At least two people were coming from the direction of the clubhouse, walking along the same path they had walked.

Bonnie, her back against the tall rock, slipped on her underwear, then shorts. He started to do the same, then realized his underwear was still out in the middle of the fairway where Bonnie had tossed them aside.

He eased away from the rock slightly and glanced toward the clubhouse. The silhouettes of two men could be seen coming up the small rise about a hundred yards away. One was smoking a cigarette and the red tip glowed in the dark.

"Shit!" he said, softly.

Craig pointed at his underwear and Bonnie snickered. If he went back out onto the fairway to get his underwear, he would be seen, so he slipped his pants on without them.

"Watch that zipper," Bonnie whispered as she put on her bra. "I don't want that part hurt."

"Trust me," he whispered back, "neither do I."

She laughed softly and they both sat down with their backs against the rock, waiting for the intruders to pass as they put on their shoes. He felt like a kid again, almost getting caught at something he shouldn't have been doing. His heart was beating hard and he was enjoying the feeling as the two men moved toward them.

This was fun.

And for some reason damn scary at the same time.

The sound of their footsteps seemed very loud, echoing over the grass and desert like irregular drum beats. Neither man had said a word for at least fifty paces. Then one with a high voice and a slight New York accent said, "I still can't believe we're doin' a Senator."

Some Classic Dean Wesley Smith Stories
Available at your favorite booksellers.

"Believe it," the other man said.

The second man had a deep, distinctive voice that sounded like a musician's.

"I don't much like the idea of the entire fucking government comin' after me."

The two men were even with the rock and passing.

Craig glanced at Bonnie. Her eyes were huge and she was holding her breath just as he was. Suddenly this had turned from fun to something very serious.

"If nothing goes wrong, no one will be coming after you," the deep-voiced one said. "We just make sure it looks like an accident."

"Yeah, sure," the first man said as the two started down the hill away from Bonnie and Craig. "I better be gettin' paid real good for this."

"Trust me," the deep-voiced man said, "you are. We all are."

"We better," the man said. "A senator. This is nuts."

Craig stared at Bonnie as the two men moved on, clearly headed somewhere out on the golf course. He couldn't believe what he had just heard. And he didn't want to think about what those words seemed to mean.

Bonnie finished putting on her shoes and he followed suit, not saying anything. He stood and made sure the men were long out of sight, then went out and grabbed his underwear off the fairway, stuffing them into his pocket as he turned.

He joined Bonnie on the cart path, headed back toward the clubhouse. After about ten steps he whispered, "Did that sound to you like it sounded to me?"

She put her finger up to his mouth and shook her head. "In the room," she whispered, just loud enough for him to hear.

Then she took his hand and they headed toward the beautiful hotel at a much faster pace than the stroll that got them there.

To be continued…

Some Classic Dean Wesley Smith Stories
Available at your favorite booksellers.

USA Today Bestselling Writer

DEAN WESLEY SMITH

AFTER THE DANCE

A
Dead
Teenager
Story

Billy meets Laura at the dance. She loves to dance. But she has a problem. She died on the night of her first dance.

But when the dance falls on her 16th birthday, she gets to go to the dance again. And this year she meets Billy, a wonderful, gentle boy.

She hopes he will understand.

A dead teenager story about what happens when the song ends.

AFTER THE DANCE

FROM THE MOON-CAST SHADOWS of the night I watch Billy pick up his gray wool sweater from the newly mowed grass of my grave.

He holds the sweater away from him, as if he has never seen it before, let alone worn it to the dance last night.

Those gentle hands of his shake, and even across the darkness of the cemetery, I can see the fear clouding his green eyes. His brown hair is mussed by the night breeze and I can tell he is about to panic and run.

I want to step out of the shadows, to let him kiss me again as he did at my parents' front door, to feel his strength against me, but I know that would send him fleeing, now that my father has told him the truth. I can't have him leave. There are only a few hours before the sun breaks over the tops of the hills and I will be forced to return to my grave. I must act before then.

But at this moment the time is not right.

I stand in the night shadows and watch him hold his sweater. He stares at it and then at my headstone.

I know the words he reads.

LAURA JANE ROBERTS
Born September 22, 1946
Died September 22, 1962

Nothing more. A simple statement of facts.

Even frightened, Billy seems unable to tear himself away from those words that are carved in the cold, smooth stone. He must love me as much as I came to love him in the few short hours of the dance.

I almost laugh out loud, but then stop. That would scare him too, so I hold my hand over my mouth and let the laugh die with the wind in the trees.

Billy sits down beside my grave, his sweater beside him on the grass.

Good. He is not going to leave yet. I can wait a little longer, until the night air chills him and forces him into my arms.

I move to a group of shadows closer to him and stand thinking about my first fall dance twenty-eight years ago tonight.

That night had started out so special.

I went to the dance with my best friend, Donna. I remember my stomach twisting with excitement. The first dance of my sophomore year. And my birthday would start at midnight.

Donna and I had planned to stay out late, until one in the morning, dancing with every boy we saw and celebrating the arrival of my birthday.

Only Donna started drinking. Rum and Coke that some stupid kid from another school gave her.

Before midnight, before my birthday had even started, she was sick. She had ruined everything.

I remember telling her I hated her, yelling at her, calling her names as she threw up time after time.

I stormed out of the bathroom and into the parking lot and the cold night air.

That's where I met Craig.

He was sitting in his blue Chevy, with the radio blaring and the windows wide open. He said he was from downtown.

Looking back now, from the cemetery, the dark shadows, and all the years, I should have known better. But I was so mad at Donna and the cloth seats of his car felt so soft and he liked the same music that I did. After all, at midnight it was going to be my birthday. I had a right to have a good time.

At eleven he suggested we go driving around.

I knew better, but I didn't want to go back into the dance and face Donna, so I said yes.

At first we only went downtown and cruised. But by quarter to twelve, he had driven out to the edge of town and pulled off onto a dirt road next to an empty field.

He stopped, shut off the car, the radio, and the lights.

The darkness seemed to scream in my ears and I was so frightened, my hands were shaking. He tried to kiss me and I wouldn't let him. I told him I wanted to go back to the dance, but he just laughed.

I started to get out of the car like my mom had told me to do, but he grabbed my arm, yanked me back, and hit me.

From that point everything was sort of fuzzy. I think he hurt me real bad with that first hit.

I remember crying and him laughing at me. A high, nervous sort of laughter that I knew didn't sound right.

He kept trying to kiss me and touch me.

Every time I tried to make him quit he hit me.

I screamed once and he hit me so hard I could taste the blood.

Looking back now I mostly remember him laughing. That and thinking about my birthday and how it was ruined.

I guess he finally hit me too hard, because everything went completely black.

The next thing I knew it was years later, the dance was again being held the night before my birthday, I was standing on my grave, looking at my own headstone, and thinking how odd it was to be dead because I didn't feel dead.

In fact, I didn't feel a thing.

Nothing.

I didn't even care what had happened to Craig. I just wanted to meet someone and dance.

Now, four dances later, Billy, my date and dance partner for the evening, is sitting next to my grave. I think he is shivering.

Maybe it is time for me to talk to him.

Maybe now he will listen if I go slow.

Very, very slow.

"Hi, Billy," I say as I move forward, my voice as friendly and as sweet as I can make it in the night air.

He jumps and scrambles to his feet, clutching his sweater to his chest. His eyes are wild and his face is twisted in fear.

I know he is about to run.

"I'm sorry about lying to you about where I lived," I say.

I stop far enough away that he does not feel threatened.

He looks around as if searching for an escape route, then back at me.

I just stand there in the seemingly bright spotlight of the moon, looking as timid as I can, waiting, hoping he will stay without me forcing him to.

After a moment he chokes out a question. "Are you really dead?"

I nod, making my best sad expression, even though I feel no sadness. I know that's what he expects.

"But how..."

He leaves his question open. "I don't know," I say. "I really don't. I just knew I had to go to the dance, maybe to meet you. I don't know."

I give him my best lost-girl shrug. I am surprised at how calculating I can be. I could have never done this while I was alive.

He turns and points at my headstone. "Is that really you? I don't believe this."

"That's really me," I say.

He shakes his head. "No way. Someone is playing a joke on me. That's it, isn't it? This is just a big joke and you set that old man up in the house to tell me you had died. Right?"

I shake my head slowly, thinking back over the night. After Billy and I danced for hours, dream hours, he took me home. On the way to his car I asked to borrow his sweater. I told him I was cold. He took it off and gave it to me to wear. Then he kissed me, softly, and left me at my parents' house.

Down the street he remembered his sweater and went back to get it. I watched from the shadows as my father answered the door. Even after having this happen four times on the anniversary of the night I died, my father does not believe I return.

He refuses to believe.

So four times he has yelled at a boy.

He told Billy, in no uncertain terms, that I was dead and that Billy was rude for doing such a nasty thing to him. Then he slammed the door in Billy's face.

I feel so sorry for my father, but he is part of the pattern and I cannot break it.

Billy, very confused, found his way to the cemetery and to my headstone. I knew he would.

They all did.

"This has to be a joke," he says.

He glances around the night shadows and up and down the rows of headstones.

"All right!" he yells. "The joke's over."

But his call is swallowed up by the darkness and the cold light of the moon. Nothing moves.

No one comes forward.

After a moment he is forced to turn back and face me.

"I don't believe you," he says.

Again I shrug. "There is nothing I can do to prove it to you. I only have a short time. I must leave at sunrise."

"Why?" he asks.

"I really don't know. Anymore than I know how I got here. I just know. Would you stay a little while and talk?"

He glances quickly around. Then it is his turn to shrug. "Why not?"

I smile and move closer to him, to my grave.

He backs away until he sees that all I am going to do is sit down on the grass near where he was sitting. Then, slowly, he comes back and joins me, keeping his distance.

I smile at him and after a moment of studying me, he shakes his head. "You don't look dead."

I laugh softly. "I don't feel dead. I enjoyed the dance. The decorations were wonderful. Especially how they made the gym look like the insides of a space ship."

He nods. "I had a good time," he says. "But this is a strange way of ending it."

I sigh and shake my head. "I had it worse."

His face becomes serious, as if he suddenly believes that I am dead. "What happened?"

I shake my head. "It was too ugly and it no longer matters."

Of course, that's a lie. But I cannot tell him so. And I could never tell him what happened. He would never understand.

"How often do you come back?" he asks. "Every year?"

He is unlike the others. They refused to believe right up to the last moment. He is asking questions as if he truly believes that I am dead. Maybe the world is changing.

"I only go to the dance when it falls on the night before my birthday."

That is the truth. I find it funny how I can mix the truth with lies and make them both sound so convincing.

Billy nods. "That makes sense."

Now it is my turn to be amazed. He is the first one who has been so understanding. I hope he has not guessed what I have planned for him. I might not be able to hold him if he knew.

I do not let my worry show.

Instead, I turn the conversation to questions about him, about his life, about the world he lives in. The same world that was taken from me and that now I only get a few hours every few years to see.

As the others did, Billy follows my lead and gladly talks about himself.

After an hour he has relaxed.

Behind him the eastern sky starts to fill with light. My time is very short.

He notices me looking at the sky and he stops.

Then he asks the question the three before him asked in one form or another. "What happens next?"

I smile at him. "I have to go back."

I point at my headstone.

Now Available
from all your favorite booksellers in trade paper and electronic editions.

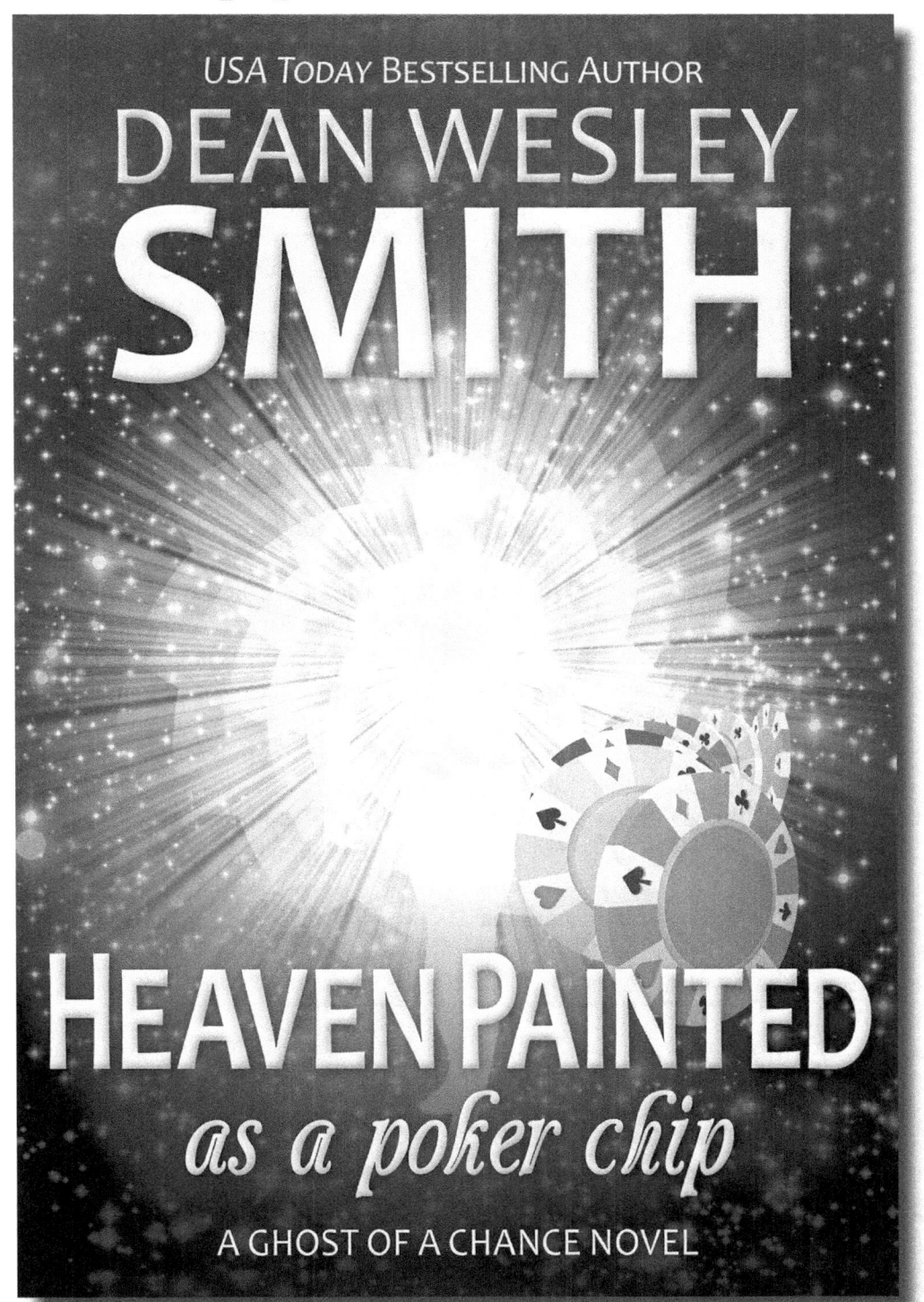

USA TODAY BESTSELLING AUTHOR

DEAN WESLEY

SMITH

HEAVEN PAINTED

as a poker chip

A GHOST OF A CHANCE NOVEL

"But why did you come out in the first place?" he asks. "I don't understand."

"Because I'm lonely," I tell him. That is partly the truth.

The sun is about to top the horizon. I glance up at it and he sees me look. I think he sees the fear and the sadness in my eyes.

"My night is almost over," I say as I stand and he stands with me. "Thank you for being so kind."

He shakes his head and takes a step toward me.

They all did.

They all wanted to hold me, to not let me go.

"I have no choice," I say. I make my voice sound helpless, sad.

The sun is at the edge of the horizon.

I can feel the pull of my grave.

Now is the time.

I step toward him, gently, eyes down.

"Thank you," I again say. "You are very kind."

He steps close to me and I turn my head up as I did on my parents' front step for him to kiss me good night.

His lips touch mine.

It is a wonderful kiss and I wrap my arms around him just as the sun casts its first rays among the stones and the trees. The pull is hard, but it only lasts a moment.

Then I am back on the soft padding inside my coffin, still kissing Billy. Still holding him with my dead arms.

Still pressing against him.

I try to make the moment last.

It takes Billy a few seconds to realize what has happened.

Then he starts struggling and screaming.

His kicking messes up the crowded insides of the coffin.

He is choking because there is no air. It had all been used up years ago by Henry and Don and Brian. There is none left for Billy and I feel sad because I wish Billy would last a little longer, as Henry did.

But there is no hope of that.

My coffin is a very small bed.

So Billy realizes where he is, feels the bodies of my lovers, feels my body wrapped in his embrace, feels the thickness of the smell press over his face, feels his lungs gasp for air.

He screams and struggles.

But soon he too is dead.

I adjust his body so I can hold him and still touch the bones and dried flesh of my other lovers.

My soft coffin is now very crowded, but I don't mind. I'm sure that by the time I awake again the worms will have guaranteed that there will be room for one more.

Good night, my loves.

Sleep tight.

~

Now Available
from all your favorite booksellers in trade paper and electronic editions.

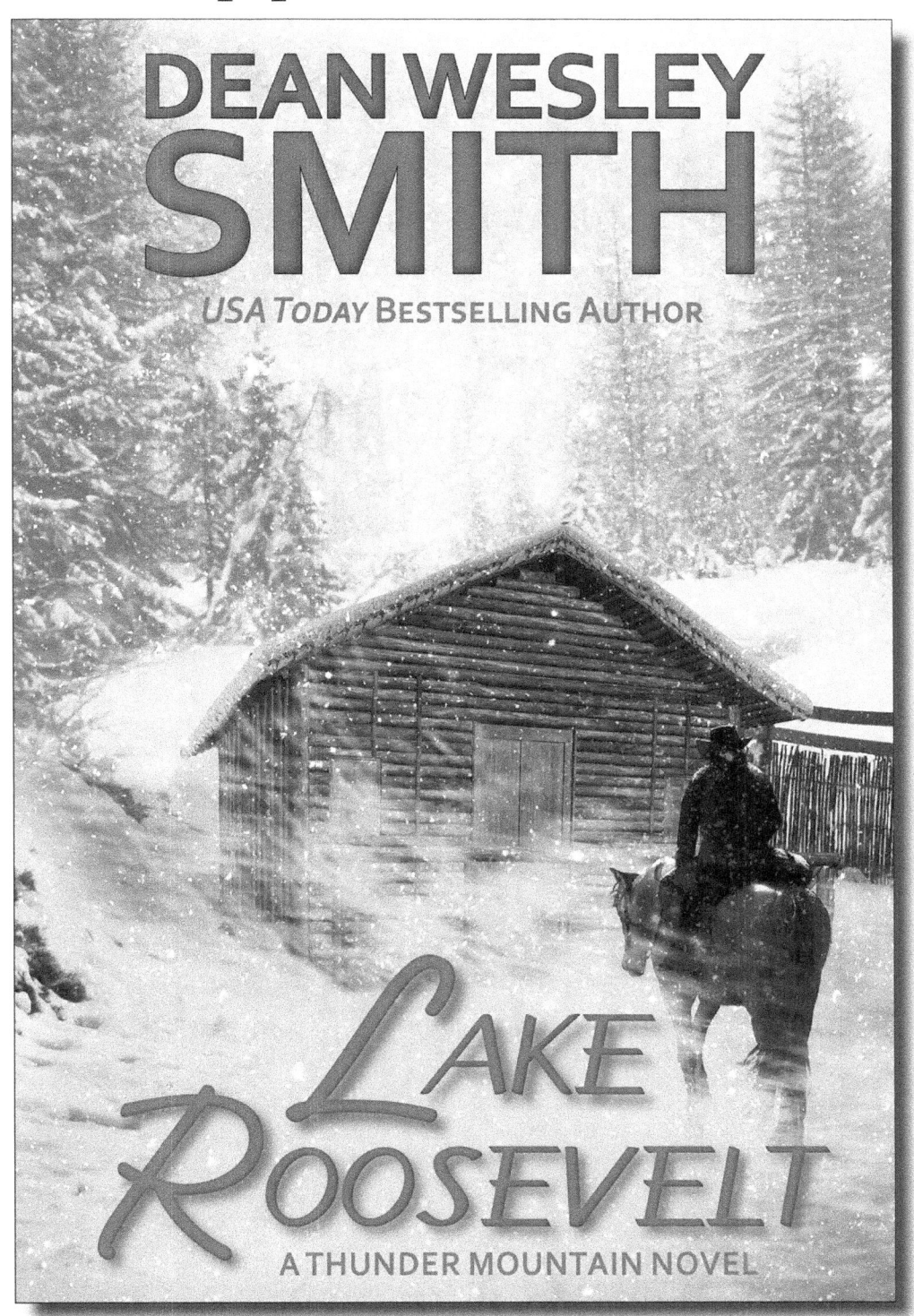

DEAN WESLEY
SMITH
USA Today BESTSELLING AUTHOR

LAKE ROOSEVELT
A THUNDER MOUNTAIN NOVEL

Dean Wesley Smith

USA Today **Bestselling Writer**

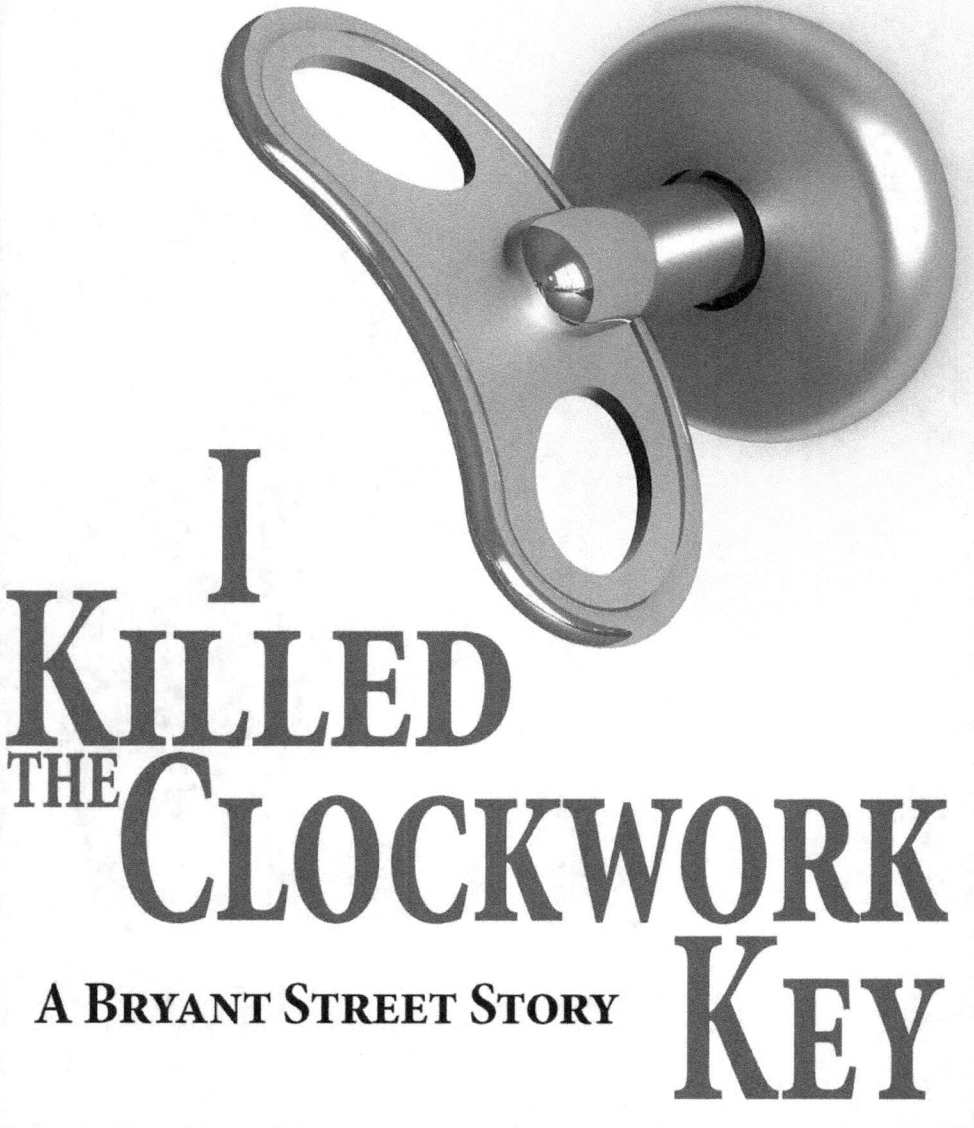

I
Killed
the Clockwork
Key

A Bryant Street Story

We are all born and raised with an image of a perfect life, an American Dream illustrated by a simple subdivision street called Bryant Street.

But in chasing and holding the American Dream, we often forget why we are in the race.

For those of us living on Bryant Street, I thought I just might get you wondering why.

I KILLED THE CLOCKWORK KEY
A Bryant Street Story

THE EARLY MORNING on Bryant Street seemed like any other early spring-morning day in a subdivision that looked like most other middle-class subdivisions in America. Young trees, well-kept green lawns watered by automatic sprinkler systems, clean sidewalks, and a dozen for-sale signs every two blocks.

Half the houses along Bryant Street were bank-owned, and most of the other half had huge mortgages that would never be paid off and would soon also become bank owned.

Barb's and my place was no exception. The Bryant Street subdivision was a small, but beautiful subdivision that might as well be a ghost town.

And I was one of the only remaining ghosts. A ghost of past times on Bryant Street just as any ghost was from a past where life had once existed, but had been killed in a brutal and ugly fashion.

Tuesday had arrived. Monday was finished. The week stretched ahead of me like a dull highway across a flat desert. Or at least I thought it did, until I killed the Clockwork Key, the thing inside of me that wound me up and kept me moving along the same path, in the same circle day after day after day.

We all have Clockwork Keys, but most of us never notice we have them or seem to care.

When I killed my Clockwork Key, I was halfway to my sixty-three-payments-left black Lexus. All normal, until Barb came out of the front door.

"Ram!" she shouted.

She called me Ram because of my days playing football in college where we met. It had been my nickname and she still called me that, even though my real name and the one I liked was Raymond. To her calling me Ram reminded her of better times, better nights of sex and lots of drinking and laughing and throwing parties where kids threw up in garbage cans and behind hedges and called it the "good old days."

I turned, not really caring what she had to say. We had gone through the morning routine. I had kissed her at the door, she had said she thought she was going to have better luck today finding a job. I had told her I thought she would as well.

All simple morning lies to keep us walking along in our circles and not thinking about anything in our life or how we would eventually have to leave Bryant Street and her dream house that we had paid far, far too much to build back when "times were better" as people said.

I'm not sure I remember those times, but people do tell me they existed.

"You forgot your briefcase!" Barb shouted, as if I couldn't hear her in the complete silence of the early morning in a mostly-empty subdivision. I was usually the first out of the subdivision these days of the few people that actually left, since I was one of the few on the street who actually pretended to still have a job.

She held up the black briefcase and instead of coming down the sidewalk to bring it to me, she just stood there, waiting for me to come back to her to get it.

And I just stood there waiting for her to bring it to me.

We had a marriage standoff.

Barb and I had had many such standoffs over the years.

But back in the "good old days" or when "times were better," I usually was the one to break the marriage standoff. Now I couldn't care.

I had walked down the sidewalk, I had done my bit to keep the morning moving, to stay in my routine, to continue to pay for the house and the cars and the food for as long as I could, even though we were within six months of being out of money.

She had done her bit to cook the breakfast and to make small talk and to pretend she was preparing to go looking for a job even though we both knew there were no jobs to be had and she would never leave the house or get out of her bathrobe.

We had both played our parts perfectly, just as we did every morning.

Now, standing there on that wide sidewalk with the carefully manicured edges so that the grass wouldn't touch the pavement, neither Barb nor I knew what to do.

We did not know, in our perfectly ordered world, who had the responsibility for the briefcase.

A marriage standoff.

Sure, the black briefcase was supposed to have my job paperwork in it, paperwork I brought home to work on every night, but never did, because I hadn't had a job for over a year.

And in a year of looking, I had found nothing.

And had never told Barb I had lost my job. It just hadn't been worth the problems telling her would have caused me every day. We had long before stopped acting as partners.

And the last thing I had wanted to do was stay in the house with her all day long. I felt bad enough about losing my job and not finding a new one. I didn't need that kind of punishment as well.

My former job was nothing more than crunching numbers to determine who would be laid off next. I assigned numbers, calculations, statistics to people, real people, and then gave those special living numbers to my boss who pretended to check them and then give them to his boss and so on up the corporate ladder until someone decided to act.

Because of my numbers, a certain person or numbers of people each week had been laid off to keep the company profitable (on paper) for the shareholders who continued to send the stock higher and higher making everyone happy who owned the stock.

At first I had felt remorse for the people that my calculations had caused to lose their job. But then, after a few years of doing the same thing every day, every week, I no longer cared about the faces and the lives destroyed behind those simple numbers.

And then one day I had become a number as well. Someone above me had figured the numbers for me and I had been laid off.

Now in our marriage standoff, Barb, once a good-looking woman with brown hair and good teeth, stood there in her blue bathrobe and blue matching slippers on the brown welcome mat in front of our

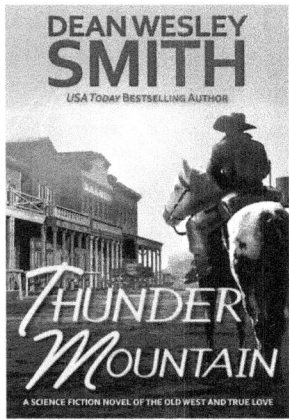

brown and tan home, smiling and holding the worthless lie of a briefcase that contained nothing of value in it.

My life had become nothing of value, either.

It seemed logical I should carry a briefcase that carried nothing.

I stared at her and she smiled at me, holding the briefcase.

And I smiled back and made no movement toward her.

The morning sun felt warm against my back, and I realized that in all the years of mornings I had walked from the house to the car I had never noticed any feeling about anything.

Now I felt warmth.

And the smell of the freshly-mowed grass suddenly caught my attention.

And the sounds of birds chirping in the young trees almost distracted me from staring at Barb.

Slowly, her smile faded.

"Ram, don't you need your briefcase?"

I turned my back to her and looked around at the neighborhood.

It was a perfect neighborhood, a perfect, Hollywood-version of a neighborhood, as if some screenwriter had written in a few words at the beginning of a script, "Standard Subdivision: Well-kept and manicured."

I had not really, really stopped and looked at Bryant Street and the homes along the street for a long time. And now that I had stopped, thanks to the marriage standoff, I could actually see what I had missed.

The paint on a few of the empty homes was starting to show weathering. The shrubs on a few homes hadn't been trimmed in years and had grown too large for the yards.

Windows on two of the closest bank-owned homes were dirty, and the drapes in one window were torn and looked faded.

And as I watched, a woman's face appeared beside the torn curtain, staring at me with sunken eyes and hair that looked like it hadn't been combed in weeks.

A ghost of a former resident, maybe.

I recognized her after a moment. DeAnna Sterling. Or what was left of DeAnna Sterling. She used to be a large, almost obese woman. Now she looked more like a model for a bad fashion designer.

Her husband, Dan had been laid off two years ago and the bank had foreclosed on their home over a year ago.

That home had been DeAnna's dream home, and she and Barb used to be best friends.

I had a vague memory of Barb telling me DeAnna had had a breakdown and had refused to leave her home.

Now I understood why our grocery bill had grown higher. Barb did the shopping, telling me about the inflation. The inflation was that we were feeding DeAnna.

I looked down the street. I wondered how many other ghosts were in these empty buildings and what they did when I was working.

DeAnna ducked back into the darkness of her home.

I turned back to face Barb who had that "worried look" I knew so well on her face. She had not expected a marriage standoff either this fine morning. More than likely she was missing her morning program and her second cup of coffee, and that was not right.

Or more likely she was worried that I had seen DeAnna.

I stared at my home. I had somehow managed to continue making payments on this "perfect" home. I had started to do the yard work myself when I could no longer afford a gardener, and I drained most of the remains of my estate from my parents to keep walking this routine.

To keep pretending that I was living a life I wanted to live.

I was nothing more than calculations and statistics and numbers as well. My entire life consisted of walking the same routine, doing the same thing, trying to find a job that didn't exist to pay bills I didn't want to pay so that I could keep doing the same thing again and again and again.

And now, because of a briefcase and a marriage standoff, I could see clearly for the first time what I had been doing.

I had broken the cycle.

I had broken my Clockwork Key.

I reached up and undid my tie because I was getting warm standing there on the sidewalk in my black suit.

Barb's "worry look" switched to her "puzzlement look" mixed with her "slight-panic look." I knew all her expressions. I knew how she thought at every moment of every day.

I dropped my tie on the grass I had mowed yesterday after I had gotten home from my pretend job.

"You keep the briefcase," I said to Barb.

"Ram!" she shouted, her voice rising to the level I hated, the level that made her sound like a record had spun up just a little too fast while she spoke. "What are you doing?"

"You keep it all," I said, waving at the home I had come to hate and the neighborhood I had never really looked at in years.

"Ram? What's wrong?"

She had still not moved off the porch, and was now clutching my briefcase against her chest as a symbol of the life she didn't want to lose. An empty briefcase that meant far more to her than I ever did.

"Nothing's wrong," I said, smiling at her. "I've got to go. You keep it. You keep it all. You win."

With that I turned and walked the short distance to my car and got in.

She still stood there in front of the worthless home, in her blue bathrobe with perfectly matching blue slippers, my empty briefcase clutched against her chest.

I still had enough savings left to get a divorce, give her the house in the settlement, pay off my car, get a nice, cheap apartment in some other town where there were still a few jobs to be had, and maybe eat for a year or more.

After all, I was a numbers man and I knew the numbers. I had lived those numbers for years now, walking in clock-like service to a life I did not want with a woman I had grown to hate.

I pulled out of the driveway and stopped in the middle of Bryant Street, giving it one more look.

Barb clutched my briefcase, staring at me.

I smiled at her, a real smile for the first time in years. Not a pretend smile, but a smile I actually felt.

I waved at her. Then, with my hand solidly planted on the horn, I drove down Bryant Street for one last time, letting the loud sound of my leaving echo off the ghost-like remains of my former life.

～

Dean Wesley Smith

USA Today Bestselling Writer

Me and Beans and Great Big Melons

A Grocery Store Romance

When Innis went shopping to get ready for the Packers-Rams game, he never expected to meet one of them aliens.

But he also never expected to meet a woman who ate beans either.

A strange supermarket romance. Are there any others?

ME AND BEANS
AND GREAT BIG MELONS

I HAVE NEVER THOUGHT, wondered, or even pondered the idea of having a supermarket love affair. If I had, I certainly wouldn't have thought it would start and end in front of the green beans. I'm the kind of guy who really doesn't eat green beans, red beans, black beans, or any other color bean. I'm not prejudiced in my bean selection. I pretty much just hate them all equally.

And I flat don't understand how anyone could even eat the things.

I met my supermarket lover as I tried to figure out which Hamburger Helper would work for the night. I was an expert in Hamburger Helpers and all the different incarnations of the stuff. I could almost make it without looking at the box. Almost.

"Excuse me," a soft, husky voice said.

I jerked around, realizing that my cart and my body had made an effective roadblock in the aisle. And I hadn't even set up any detour signs.

A woman stood there with one of those yellow baskets for small amounts of stuff. Just like me, she was wearing jeans and a blue tee-shirt, but unlike me she also had a brown purse over her shoulder.

The purse, oddly enough, accented the wonderful color of her hair. I wondered if she had bought the purse because of that, or changed the color of her hair to match the purse. It was a question I would never think to ask any woman, even a woman I didn't know.

But yet, for some reason, she had made me think of it. I made a note to myself mentally to write down the weird supermarket moment. I hoped to be a writer in the future, when I could find the time, and often made notes about things that might come in handy in a story some day.

I found myself attracted to this woman wanting to get past me, and I did an instant inventory of her appearance.

Before I was laid off down at Sears, I had done lots of inventories of the warehouse, and had become known as "Innis, the Inventory King." I had decided one day to practice the same craft on women I met, and grocery stores were great places, full of inventory.

Using my skills, I instantly looked her over while moving my cart out of her way. She wore a loose blue tee-shirt with nothing written on it, tight jeans, and expensive tennis shoes. Total inventory cost of two hundred bucks. She had on no jewelry at all, not even an earring. She was an easy inventory subject.

Miss Brown-Hair-Yellow-Basket: Two hundred bucks.

"Sorry," I said, as I finished my inventory and cart moving at the same time, leaving the cart in front of the green beans, never thinking that she might actually be trying to get to that area. If I didn't eat green beans, no one else did I was sure.

My first wife had called that self-centered-universe attitude my defining characteristic. I had considered that a compliment and still do.

"No problem," the brown-haired, two-hundred-dollar-woman said, giving me a wonderful, bright smile as she moved past me. The aroma of fresh soap caught me and I stared at her from behind for a moment, first watching her long hair move against her matching purse, then her ass under her tight jeans.

I had always been an ass man, staring at woman's asses before any other body part if the chance arose. This woman had a stareable ass, of that there was no doubt. Really tight.

A stareable tight ass wasn't worth anything on my inventory list, but it should be.

She walked a few steps and stopped, looking at the canned vegetables.

I went back to trying to decide which Hamburger Helper to pick to eat while the football game was on tonight. Packers against the Rams. Could be a real shouter.

"Sorry to bother you again," she said from behind me.

I turned around to look into the deepest green eyes I had seen in a long time. If all women had eyes like her, I would shift to being an eye-man instead of an ass-man.

She pointed at the bean section that my cart was blocking.

"Oh, sorry," I said, moving to pull the cart out of her way for the second time. "I didn't think anyone ate that stuff."

She laughed. "Usually I like my beans fresh. But when I can't get them fresh, I make do with canned."

Usually I'm not real honest with the women I meet, but this woman ate beans and had annoyed me by making me move my cart twice in the middle of my Hamburger Helper shopping. So I said the first thing that came to mind.

"I'm that way with women," I said. "When I can't find the fresh stuff, I resort to the canned as well."

She stared at me for a moment.

I returned her stare.

The faint store music went away; the sounds of the other shoppers went away. It was a movie moment.

Of course, I had no doubt this movie moment was going to end with the woman walking off in a huff. At least then I could watch her ass and get back to my shopping.

But she surprised me.

Suddenly her smile returned, followed by the richest, deepest laugh I had heard in a long time. It echoed off the cans of corn and surrounded me, pushing me back against the shelf of Hamburger Helper.

"Now that's an opening line I've never heard before," she said after she caught a breath from the laughter.

"Opening for what?" I asked.

She smiled. "My legs."

I looked her right in the eye. "Now tell me why I would want to get between the legs of a woman who eats beans?"

Again I was serious, and again she stared at me, stunned into a second movie moment right there on aisle four.

Then she damned near lost a lung laughing that wonderful laugh of hers. I guess to her I was a real laugh-a-minute kind of guy.

She finally caught her breath and stared at me, her bright smile lighting up everything.

"Well?" I asked. "I'm waiting for my reason."

"Because," she said, "beans go well with franks at a picnic."

She stepped forward and grabbed my crotch, never letting her green-eyed gaze drop from mine.

She rubbed me through my jeans a few times as again we were having a movie moment, only this time it was a sex scene right there in front of the Hamburger Helper. I doubted I was ever going to be able to eat Hamburger Helper without a hard-on again.

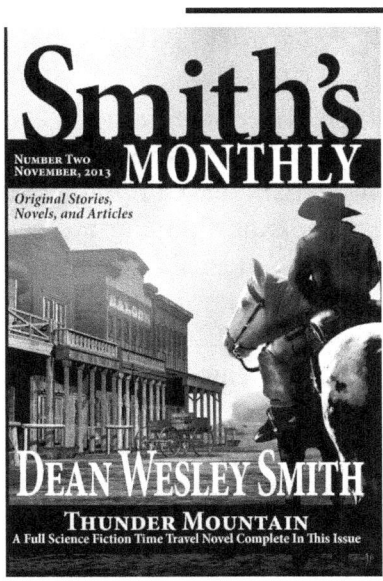

Don't Miss an Issue!

Subscribe to Smith's Monthly

Electronic or Paper Subscriptions Available.
For Full Subscription Information Go To:

www.SmithsMonthly.com

"I assume little Frank here wouldn't mind a picnic in the park."

"His name is Ben," I said as she kept rubbing. "Big Ben. And he likes melons on his picnics."

"I think that could be arranged," she said, rubbing one small, tight breast against my arm. Whatever she had thought, that wasn't a melon. More like an apple.

"Any other menu items?" she asked.

Any man with a woman rubbing his crotch on aisle four of a grocery store might have trouble answering a question like that. I didn't. "A television to watch the game while I eat."

Her hand came away from my crotch like Big Ben had lit a match and burnt her. She stared at me, then said, "My ex-husband would have rather watched television than make love to me."

"Did he like Hamburger Helper?" I asked, adjusting Ben a little to ease the tension of tight underwear.

"Yeah," she said, clearly upset at my request for a television at her picnic.

"Figures," I said.

Now she was starting to get angry. A moment ago she was offering me a picnic, basket, apples, and all. Now she was mad. I had never had a woman mad at me on aisle four in a grocery store before. Two things new in one day, both on the same aisle. I would really have to write this down for the story I would do some day.

"And why does it *figure*?" she demanded, as if I owed her an answer just because she had given Big Ben a quick rubbing.

I shrugged. "You eat beans."

She made a choking sound, grabbed two cans of green beans, held them up for me to see like she was giving me the fin-ger, put them in her little yellow basket, and walked off.

I watched her ass until she turned the corner and disappeared toward aisle five. Because her ass was so nice and tight, and her hand had felt so good on Big Ben, I thought for a moment about following her. But I knew there was nothing I could say to her to calm her down.

Besides, she ate beans. I hated beans, and no amount of Big Ben rubbing was going to erase that difference.

Also, if I spent time dealing with her over on aisle five, it might carry on to aisle six, and then even into the frozen food section on aisle eight, and if that happened I might miss the opening kick-off.

No bean-eating woman with a nice ass was worth missing the kick-off to a Packers-Rams game. Even if she had offered Ben an offer he had trouble refusing.

It seemed that my supermarket love affair had started and ended on aisle four.

I went back to trying to figure out which Hamburger Helper to get, finally picked up just the standard, and headed for aisle two where the Pabst Blue-Ribbon Beer lived and breathed and waited for me. No Hamburger Helper football game dinner was complete without Pabst.

I turned the corner onto the aisle. There was a short woman with a nice ass and short red hair parked right in front of the Pabst. She was studying the beer on the other side of the aisle as if reading labels would make the stuff any better.

I knew right off she was an alien, off one of them big ships from some other planet that had landed a year or so ago. All the alien women that I had seen on Fox News had short, bright-red hair and great bodies.

Now Available
from all your favorite booksellers
in trade paper and electronic editions.

There had been hundreds of thousands of them, and all the countries of the world welcomed them to live. After awhile, they weren't even headlines anymore unless one of them got drunk and punched a cop or something.

The aliens had said they had come in friendship and just wanted to learn about us, but I had read stuff, and I knew better. More than likely they were going to kidnap us all and take us away and make dinner out of us.

But still, alien or not, she was standing in front of the Pabst and I had a game to watch.

"Excuse me," I said.

She turned to look at me, a puzzled look on her very human but very alien face.

Her dark eyes were like magnets, swirling pink and orange and brown. They held me with some unseen force. She was dressed in jeans and a blue tee-shirt, just like I was. Just like Miss Brown Hair had been. Only instead of apples in the tee-shirt orchard, she sprouted the biggest melons I had ever seen, especially for an alien as short as she was.

I did a quick inventory. Same as Miss-Brown-Purse. Two hundred bucks. It seemed it was two-hundred-dollar-woman-day in the supermarket.

"Yes?" she asked. "Can I help you?"

Very formal, like the secretary at my doc's office. But oh, Miss-Alien-With-Melons' voice could melt grease in a cold frying pan.

I pointed to the beer. "Hamburger Helper and a hand job are never complete without Pabst."

For some reason it was my day to be honest with women. And aliens it seemed. Maybe someone had put something in the grocery store air to make me

do it. Or maybe it was the excitement of a good football game that was causing it. I would have to think about it later, after the game, if I could stay awake long enough to do so.

She kept staring at me, then slowly smiled as she moved aside. "Aren't you forgetting one thing?" she asked.

"What's that?" I asked, figuring an insult to be next out of her mouth. Something about the rudeness of humans in social situations and that we all needed alien training or something. I grabbed my half case of beer and placed it next to the Hamburger Helper.

"A good Packers-Rams game."

Now it was my turn to stare at her like she was a winning lotto ticket. I didn't know alien women watched American football. Fox News had never mentioned anything like that. Maybe there was hope for all of us after all.

So, with that encouragement, I went ahead and asked the all-important question.

"Do you eat beans?"

She made a face. "Are you kidding? No human or alien should eat those things."

"Good," I said. "How's your ass?"

She turned around to show me, then said, "Engineered to be as tight as they make them. How's your big fella?"

"Big," I said.

She smiled and I smiled back.

I loved those alien eyes.

Then after my third or fourth movie moment of the shopping trip, this time right there in front of the beer, I stuck out my hand. "I'm Innis. I count things and hope to write stories."

She took my hand, her smooth skin sending wonderful warm sensations through my body right there in the cold beer section.

"Here on your planet, in your language, I'm called Melody," she said. "I'm not from around here. I rub things and hope to paint things. And if we don't hurry we're going to miss the kick-off. How big is your screen?"

Her eyes seemed to swirl and she smiled with that question.

"Sixty inches," I said, proud of the moment I could say that to an alien woman.

She smiled even wider and then reached down and touched Big Ben through my jeans. "Sixty inches, huh? Mind if I join you? I'll buy the hamburger."

"Deal," I said, enjoying the fact that Ben was getting a work-out right there in the supermarket.

She put a second half-case of Pabst in my cart, left her empty cart in front of the other beer, and helped me push mine to the meat section, letting one of her wonderful large melons rub firmly against my hand.

It pleased me that she hadn't intended on sharing my Pabst. I really had to know a woman, or an alien for that matter, before I let that happen. Even if she was sharing her melons.

On the way past aisle six, we passed Miss Brown-Hair-And-Matching-Purse, who gave me a very, very long and angry look.

"Wow, what is her problem?" Melody asked, turning with me to watch the angry woman walk away. "Besides the fact that she has a tight ass."

"Very tight," I said, agreeing. "But she hates football and eats beans."

"Oh, that explains it," Melody said, shaking her head. "One of my people's biggest puzzles about your planet is how anyone could eat beans. They are poison to us. It may be a mystery we will never solve."

I was starting to really like these aliens.

"Let me know if you do," I said.

"The moment we figure it out," she said, laughing a high laugh that sounded very off-worldish. With that, me and my first alien supermarket lover headed for the check-out counter and a Hamburger Helper football game.

~

Some Classic Poker Boy Stories

Available at your favorite booksellers.

73

USA *TODAY* BESTSELLING AUTHOR

DEAN WESLEY SMITH

CALLING DEAD

— A COLD POKER GANG NOVEL —

Las Vegas retired detectives in the Cold Poker Gang worked hard to solve cold cases. Sometimes those cases brought back personal nightmares.

Deciding to tackle one of the coldest cold cases in the files, retired dectives Lott, Julia, and Andor uncover far more than simple murder, but maybe the worst serial killer ever.

A twisted mystery that will keep you reading to the last page.

CALLING DEAD
A Cold Poker Gang Novel

For Kris.
Thanks for all the positive support while I battled this to the end.

All characters and places in this novel are fictional.
Any resemblance to any person living or dead is purely by chance and not intended.
Calling Dead is when a poker player calls a bet
that the player has no chance of winning.

PART ONE
The Deal

PROLOGUE

August 7th, 2000
9:30 A.M.
In the desert outside of Las Vegas, Nevada

DETECTIVE BAYARD LOTT stood in the old mine tunnel, staring at the eleven dead women sitting in a neat row on the dirt floor in front of him. Lott had his hands on his hips and was doing his best to keep his breathing level.

And failing.

Not easy. Not easy at all with such a horrific sight.

The tunnel was supported by square and rough wooden pillars about a foot or so apart and not much more than six feet over the hard-dirt floor. The timbers looked old and very dry and some had visible rot on the edges. Dirt and dust filtered down in around the timbers with almost every sound.

It felt to Lott as if the entire thing might come down at any moment. He had always hated enclosed, tight spaces, and this mine was not helping that hatred in any way.

In fact, what he wanted to do was just turn and get out of there, but the bodies in front of him made that impossible.

He was only ten paces inside the boarded-up entrance. The light from the bright day outside helped his flashlight illuminate the scene clearly, while at the same time casting strange and odd-shaped deep black shadows that made the dead women seem even more horrific, if that was possible.

The heat had to be over a hundred inside the tunnel and the air felt used and contaminated with the death he faced. He was sweating, even though the August day outside hadn't gotten that hot yet. It would, later in the afternoon. He couldn't imagine staying in this mine very long now, let alone in the high heat of the desert summer day.

He knew that going deeper underground was cooler, but not this close to the surface in this kind of intense desert heat. This felt more like the interior of a closed-up car.

The smell was like a musty dry cloth that had gone sour. The stench clogged everything in Lott's senses, which was part of why he was breathing through his mouth instead of his nose.

Beside him, his partner, Detective Andor Williams, took slow, loud breaths through his mouth as well.

Andor was shorter than Lott's six feet by five inches, but was a bit wider. Standing side-by-side, they almost touched both sides of the mine walls with their shoulders. Lott's head was only a few inches under the closest timber holding up the dirt above and he had walked bent over to just get this far inside.

Now, seeing what was in here, neither one of them had wanted to take a step farther than what they had already done.

On the dirt floor in front of Lott, sitting with their backs against the left wall of the tunnel, legs stretched out on the dirt, were the eleven dead women. The women were mummified in the heat after clearly being in here for some time, their faces contorted and sunken-in with wrinkles that made them look ancient.

Lott had no doubt that the heat and the tunnel environment was going to make it hell to determine how long these poor women had been in this mine.

It might have been only weeks, but it could have been years. After decades of working as a cop in Las Vegas, Lott had seen heat do some amazing things to a dead human body, so the physical condition of the bodies was no surprise to him.

But what they wore was what surprised him.

Each woman had a black clutch purse on her lap, and her mummified hands covered the purse. Each woman was fully dressed in identical black skirts and white blouses, just sitting with their backs to the wall.

If that wasn't strange enough, they all had long dark hair, trimmed to exactly the same length and in exactly the same style. That, combined with the schoolgirl look of all of them, made the scene look more like a bunch of large wrinkled dolls sitting there instead of women.

Thankfully, all had their eyes closed.

"This is one sick mother who did this," Andor said softly.

Lott could only agree. He had no doubt this sight was going to give him nightmares for a very long time.

"Let's back out of here until forensics can clear the place," Lott said. "If we're lucky, we can just work off the pictures they take."

More than anything, he wanted to be out of that closed-in space and away from the dead women. As a detective, he had seen a lot of death and he had never gotten used to it.

Andor nodded and turned to head back to the mine entrance ten steps away.

"Let's just hope the sick bastard who did this left the identifications of those women in those purses."

Lott took one more look back at the eleven dead women, their skin mummified, all dressed like a class of schoolgirls from a very strict school with a uniform dress code.

Horrific didn't begin to describe the scene.

He turned to follow his partner back out into the warm and cleansing desert sunshine. He had a hunch that nothing about this case was going to be easy.

And that hunch proved to be very accurate.

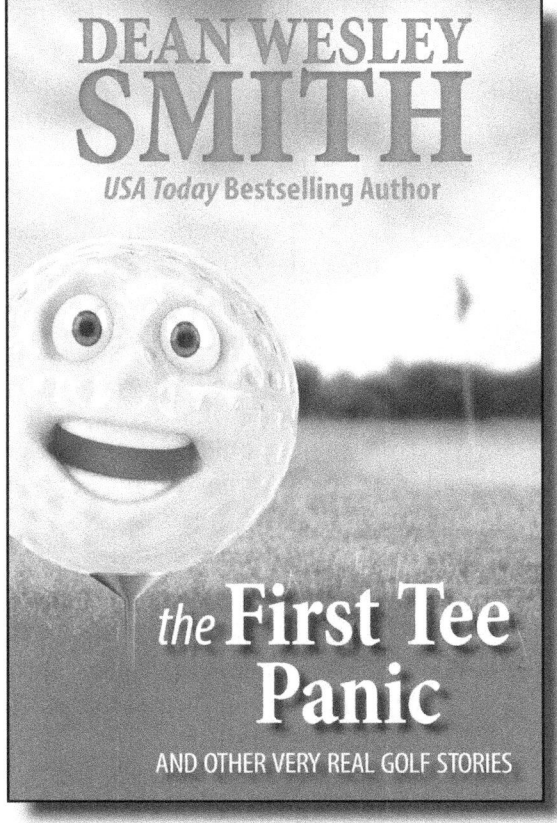

CHAPTER ONE
Fifteen Years Later…

August 6th, 2015
5:30 P.M.
Las Vegas

RETIRED DETECTIVE Bayard Lott sat at his wooden kitchen table working at a piece of Kentucky Fried Chicken. He loved the legs and always ordered extra legs when he picked up a bucket of KFC for dinner before the weekly poker game he held in his basement poker room. The open bucket now sat in the middle of his table smelling wonderful.

For Lott, there was nothing like fresh KFC. It made the daily exercise he did to keep his sixty-three-year-old body in shape worthwhile to be able to eat KFC like this regularly.

He would have the chicken for dinner tonight, lunch tomorrow, and maybe a snack or two over the next few days before buying another bucket. His fridge was never without KFC for long.

Across the table from him was his former partner, retired Detective Andor Williams. Beside Andor was retired Reno Detective Julia Rogers. Both Andor and Julia were working at the bucket of chicken as well, making sure Lott didn't have that many days of snacks from this particular bucket.

Tonight, Julia had on a white blouse with a running bra under it and light tan slacks and tennis shoes. Her long brown hair was pulled back and tied off her face and her green eyes seemed to light up with every bite off a chicken wing.

Lott had on a short-sleeved golf shirt and jeans and tennis shoes. Andor wore what he always did, a long-sleeved shirt with the sleeves rolled up and tan slacks and brown dress shoes.

They each had a paper plate, a stack of napkins, and both Andor and Julia had grease on their faces at the moment. Lott had no doubt he did as well.

Julia looked wonderful, even with grease on her face. She exercised as much as he did, if not more, just so she could eat what she wanted as well.

The newly remodeled kitchen echoed the sounds of the three of them working at the dripping, Original-Recipe KFC. The rest of the groceries and snacks for the Cold Poker Gang poker game tonight in the basement were forgotten for the moment on the new granite counter.

Chicken had to come first, especially if it was fresh KFC. That was the rule in his house.

Lott loved the Thursday night games when five or six retired detectives got together to play cards in his downstairs poker room. While playing, they also worked on and talked about cold cases for the Las Vegas police department.

Even though they were all retired, a few years back the chief of police had given the Cold Poker Gang special unit status. That was because the Cold Poker Gang had solved some of the city's most puzzling cold cases.

All of the gang could still carry their guns and badges, but they didn't get paid and weren't officially on the force.

But that was enough for all of them to feel valued. And after closing so many major cold cases, everyone on the force, including the chief of police, gave them all a lot of respect, which Lott liked more than he wanted to admit.

Sometimes in retirement, all you had to live on was respect. Past or present.

He would take either.

And they all knew they were lucky. Even after retirement, they got to continue a job they all loved and had lived their lives to do. But they didn't have to do all the paperwork or report at certain hours. They worked at their own pace and on their own time and money.

Julia called it "Retirement with benefits."

Lott's daughter Annie, also a former Las Vegas Detective, had found that extremely funny, but the humor had just gone right past Lott. Julia had promised she would explain at some point, which made Annie laugh all the harder.

As far as Lott was concerned, this was a perfect job, even though he didn't get paid for it. The job had value, made him feel valued, something that didn't come easy in retirement.

He had been forced to retire early, at fifty-nine, before he had wanted. He had decided to be with Carol, his wife, during her last year of sickness. She had now been gone for four years, and Lott was finally moving on with his life, thanks to the Cold Poker Gang, his daughter, Annie, and Julia beside him.

Julia had been forced to retire from the Reno police department at the age of fifty-five when a bullet shattered her leg. She barely had a limp, but the injury had been too much to allow her to continue working, so she had moved to Las Vegas to be close to her daughter, Jane, and play some poker.

It was during a poker tournament out on the Strip that Julia had met Annie and learned about the Cold Poker Gang. Julia was the only woman in the gang at the moment.

But Lott knew that two of the best women detectives still active on the force were thinking of retiring soon, and both wanted to join the gang. It would be great to have them in the game.

And to help with the cases.

Julia and Lott had hit it off almost at once after she joined the game just over a year ago. They were slowly building a solid relationship. He now often spent the night at her condo and loved waking up beside her in the mornings.

She and Andor made it a habit to come over early on game nights and help him eat KFC and set up the downstairs poker room.

It was during the game that Andor presented cold cases he had gotten from the chief of police for the gang to work on. They only got a new case when they had solved an earlier one, or had given up on one.

Actually, they never gave up on a case, they just put the file "on the bar" near the poker table downstairs to be reviewed every week. They were all very proud of the fact that in over two years of doing this, only five files were "on the bar."

They had closed a lot of very cold cases.

"So what's the new case tonight?" Julia asked Andor, giving him a smile that could melt most anyone. She blinked her large green eyes at Andor who just shook his head.

"Nice try, Rogers," Andor said, then took a bite on another piece of chicken.

Lott laughed. Andor always kept the cases secret until after an hour into the game. Then he would present them like presenting a gift to a royal court. She asked him ahead every time there was a new case, and he never told her. It was a little dance they both seemed to enjoy.

Andor was a bulldog of a human being. He never walked anywhere. He stormed. He had a heart of gold, but a bull exterior. Julia was thin and not much taller than Andor. She moved around him like a butterfly around a stump. Sometimes that drove Andor crazy, but Lott knew Andor really liked and admired Julia.

Andor had also had been forced to retire early to take care of his wife, who had died just six months after Carol had died. Lott and Andor had spent a lot of those months after Andor's wife died sitting in bars drinking.

It did neither of them any good, but it was the only thing they could think to do at the time.

The Cold Poker Gang had gotten both of them back to work, and they loved it.

"All I will tell you about the new case," Andor said, licking off his fingers and dropping the bones of the chicken on his plate, "is that today is the fifteenth anniversary of the day Lott and I originally caught the case."

Andor glanced at Lott and shrugged, almost an apology before going back to work on yet another piece of chicken.

Lott stared at his former partner.

Fifteen years would make the year of the case two thousand. Early August. What cases had they done at that time that went cold? They hadn't had that many cases go cold over the years. Maybe ten major ones was all and they have already solved a couple of those with the gang.

Then Lott suddenly realized which case Andor was talking about. And why he had given him that apologetic look.

"You are kidding, right?" Lott asked.

Andor shook his head. "About damn time we give those eleven women some justice, don't you think?"

Lott dropped the drumstick on his plate, wiped off his hands and sat back. He hated this idea.

He hated it more than he wanted to think about.

He had hated that case more than any other case they had caught over the years. It had given him nightmares for years, and there hadn't been a clue that seemed to lead them anywhere to who had killed the women.

He had woken up Carol on more than one night by screaming in a nightmare when that case was active.

It was the coldest of the cold cases they had.

Julia glanced at him, clearly seeing he was upset.

"That bad?" she asked.

Both Andor and Lott nodded.

"A case of nightmares," Lott said.

"In more ways than one," Andor said.

"Damn, I hate this idea," Lott said.

"Yeah, me too," Andor said. "But we need to do it."

CHAPTER TWO

August 6th, 2015
11:30 P.M.
Las Vegas

THE TWENTY-FOUR HOUR café at the Bellagio was busy, but not so crowded at almost midnight that they couldn't get one of their favorite booths tucked back in a corner and surrounded by tall green plants. The sounds of the slots in the casino was nothing more than a background noise. The low murmur of people talking and laughing filled the air.

Julia loved casinos, loved the energy, loved the feel. And she flat adored the food in this café. Anything she wanted to eat at any hour of the day or night, and top quality at a decent price. Didn't get better.

Especially after a long night of poker.

She enjoyed coming here after the Cold Poker Gang games with Lott. And tonight she had asked Andor to join them. She had really, really wanted to get more information on the cold case he had brought to the table tonight. And since Lott and Andor had been the two lead detectives on the cold case fifteen years before, they knew more than anyone.

The case had been called "The School Girl Murders" because of the way the woman were dressed and placed in the cave. To Julia, the entire thing sounded grisly and yet fascinating. She could not have imagined walking into that mine with those bodies like Lott and Andor had done.

But the entire case had the feeling of something far, far larger. And she didn't know why.

Lott had come into the casino near the poker room to tell his daughter, Annie, and her boyfriend, Doc Hill, that he and Julia would be in the café.

So she had managed to beat Lott to the booth by only a minute and Andor was yet to be seen.

"They still in the tournament?" Julia asked as Lott slid into the large booth beside her and took his cloth napkin and put it on his lap. She knew that Annie and Doc played in a major tournament here every week. Annie was also a retired Las Vegas detective, but she had retired to play poker full time and was now considered one of the best female poker players in the country.

Doc was considered the best no-limit hold'em tournament poker player there was. Period. Julia considered herself a good player and had won her share

of small tournaments, but compared to Annie and Doc, she was still a beginner.

"Both still in the tournament," Lott said, taking a sip of the glass of water the waitress had brought. "Annie has a stack and Doc is short-chipped, but I have a hunch that won't last long. Three tables left, so they have a ways to go yet."

Julia nodded.

At that point, Andor joined them, sliding into the booth across the dark-colored table to face them.

"Hungry," he said, grabbing a menu from where the hostess had left them on the front edge. Not hi, nothing.

After they finished deciding what to order and gave the smiling waitress with blonde hair tucked up on her head their order, Julia looked first at Lott, then at Andor.

"All right," she said. "What's not in that file you two aren't talking about?"

Andor just shook his head and beside her Lott sighed.

Then Lott said, "We had eleven women, all in their mid-thirties, all with long black hair cut to the same length."

"And all dressed the same," Julia said, shuddering a little and glad they were in the bright, alive casino. Those pictures Andor had brought with him had been just like a bad horror movie.

Andor nodded, so Lott went on.

"We found the identities of nine of the eleven women," Lott said, "as was in the file. They were abducted about one per month for almost a year. The best anyone could figure, they had been in the cave for two years. We never did find information about the other two I'm afraid."

"And no connection at all between the women?" Julia asked.

"None that we could find," Andor said. "Except that they all had natural black hair. And the school uniforms they were dressed in were standard and could be bought anywhere in the country at the time."

"File says no DNA," Julia said. "Any chance fifteen years and better technology would make a difference on that?"

Andor shook his head.

"All the women were cleaned perfectly," Lott said.

"How did they die?" Julia said. "I didn't see that in the file."

Andor glanced at Lott, then looked at Julia. "We kept it out of the file to use if we needed it."

Julia knew that was standard. Every department did that.

"They basically died of dehydration and heat," Lott said.

"Slowly," Andor said. "There was no indication that any of the women struggled at all, so more than likely they were drugged and then died from the heat."

"In the cave?" Julia asked, shocked.

Lott shook his head.

Andor stared at the table.

"They were left to die somewhere in the heat?" Julia asked. She didn't know what she felt about that. Only a true monster would do that.

"Not really, no," Andor said. "They weren't just left in the heat."

"They were baked," Lott said

"Baked?" Julia asked, turning to stare at the very troubled face of the man she had come to love over the last year. Baked made no sense at all. How could you bake a human being?

Lott nodded.

"Best we can figure," Andor said. "They were slipped into a huge oven on some sort of surface that would not conduct heat. Then they were baked, first on one side, then on the other. Slowly."

"Very slowly," Lott said, clearly disgusted. "Not hot enough to blister the skin, but hot enough to dry them out like a raisin over time."

"Oh, my god," Julia said. She was having trouble even trying to imagine such a thing, or one human doing that to another.

"Then the sick bastard dressed them, trimmed their hair, and staged them in the cave," Lott said.

Julia shook her head, trying to push the image of a naked woman baking in an oven out of her mind. "That's going to give me nightmares."

"Welcome to the club," Andor said.

"And that's not the worst part," Lott said.

"There's something worse than baking a woman alive?" Julia asked, now really, really sorry that she had been interested beyond the game earlier.

Andor stared at the table in front of him, then he said simply, "The guy liked flank steak."

"Rump roast as well," Lott said.

"Yeah," Andor said. "All the good parts."

CHAPTER THREE

August 7th, 2015
12:30 A.M.
Las Vegas

THE FOOD CAME at that moment, the waitress carrying a large round tray on her shoulder and putting it down on a stand beside the table. Lott was glad that they had all decided to not talk about the cold case while eating. That case was just not good dinner conversation.

The possibility of cannibalism just put most sane people right off their food.

By the time they mostly finished eating, Annie walked up. She was frowning and had what Lott recognized as a "bad beat" cloud over her head.

She had on a dark blue blouse and jeans and had her brown hair pulled back off her face. Like her mother, Carol, Annie was tall and thin and always walked with a purpose.

She slid in beside Andor, shaking her head.

"Thought you had a large stack," Lott said. "What happened?"

"Pair of nines cracked my aces," Annie said, "and then I couldn't get ace-king to hold up."

"Ouch," Lott said.

"Yeah, double ouch," Julia said. "Doc still in?"

"He is and it's a thing of beauty to watch at times," Annie said, shaking her head. "But after those two beats, I needed to get something to eat."

"Well," Lott said, smiling at his beautiful daughter, "we're happy to have you."

A moment later the waitress came to take some of their dirty dishes and Annie's order.

"So what's the new case tonight?" Annie asked. "A fun one?"

"Not so fun tonight," Andor said.

"Gross, actually," Julia said.

"The School Girl Murders," Lott said. "We're giving that case another run."

Annie looked at him surprised. "The cannibal case? Really?"

"We don't know the guy was a cannibal," Lott said.

"We don't even know it was a guy for sure," Andor said. "In fact, we flat know nothing."

"Fifteen years and not a clue has surfaced," Lott said. "Cold as a dark day in the winter in Antarctica."

"Wow," Annie said. "So refresh me on the case and let's set a plan of attack."

Lott laughed. "You want to help on this one?"

"I was still a patrol officer when this one came in," Annie said. "Always sort of held a fascination for me."

"Gave me nightmares," Andor said. "But glad to have any help on this monster."

So for the next few minutes they went over again what was in the file and the knowledge that wasn't common, such as the slow baking of the bodies to kill the women, and then the removal of some of the body's meat.

Lott was feeling a little more settled about taking on the case again. He was putting it back into perspective. This all was done by a sick serial killer who needed to be caught and punished if he was still alive after all this time.

"So let's list the clear points we have to go on," Julia said, pulling out a notebook from her purse and opening it to a blank page.

"School girl obsession," Andor said. "Those uniforms were mostly used for grades seven through twelve. Usually in Catholic and some private schools."

Julia nodded and wrote that down. Then she looked at Lott. "You said the women were abducted at a pace of about one per month?"

"They were," Lott said. "Two years before we found the bodies."

"Nothing at all similar with the women. Some were rich, some single, some married. All had black hair."

"So black hair a certain length is an obsession as well," Julia said, writing that down.

"I wonder why the killer stopped at eleven," Annie said. "Is there something about the number eleven that might be a lead?"

Lott nodded as Julia wrote that down as well. He remembered that he and Andor had thought of that, but could find no connection at all. But never hurt to look again.

"So how could a human body be baked?" Julia asked. "Was one side or the other burned?"

"No burns," Lott said. "Just really slow baked and the fluids drained off."

"We tried to figure that out as well," Andor said. "The bodies must have been put on something that wouldn't transmit heat, some sort of pad or something, then put in a very large oven."

"Actually they were still alive when put in the oven," Lott said. "But drugged. Since all the blood was gone when we found them, basically either drained out or evaporated from the heat. Add onto that the two years that had passed in the cave and we never did determine what that drug might have been."

That stopped the four retired detectives cold. Standard for this case. No real leads at all.

Julia wrote in her notebook, but Lott didn't try to follow what she was writing. She was good at sometimes putting pieces together that others didn't see. This case was going to take a miracle of pieces and some real luck to solve.

After a few moments, the waitress brought Annie her Denver omelet with white toast and coffee. Even though Lott had just eaten a Chef's Salad, the omelet smelled good.

Lott wasn't convinced he could eat and talk about this topic, even though it had been years and he was working to get some distance on the topic.

"So after they were baked," Julia said, looking at the paper in front of her, "the killer cut off slices of meat from each woman?"

Lott nodded.

"So the assumption was that the killer was a cannibal," Julia said.

"That's where all the jokes around the force went," Andor said. "But we have no evidence of what the killer did with the cuts of meat from the bodies. He could have fed them to zoo animals for all we know."

"I can't remember," Annie said, working at the omelet. "How did you find the bodies in that old mine? Wasn't it boarded up?"

Lott laughed. "A psychic called it in, saying she was having nightmares, seeing a class of girls sitting in the heat in an old mine."

Julia looked at him. "You're serious?"

"Betty?" Annie asked.

"Betty," Lott said, smiling at Julia. "We used her all the time, off the books, of course."

"She was damned good," Andor said. "But never quote me on that."

Julia just shook her head. "Can this case get any stranger?"

"We just started investigating it again," Lott said. "So who knows?"

"Oh, great, just great," Andor said. "I may never sleep again."

CHAPTER FOUR

August 7th, 2015
1:00 A.M.
Las Vegas

"SO WHAT KIND of oven would be large enough to bake a human body without burning it?" Annie asked between bites of her omelet.

Julia nodded and quickly wrote that question down as well. She liked how Annie thought. Actually, she liked Annie period. She was an amazing woman, and very accepting of Julia being with her father. She seemed to know that Julia would never try to replace Annie's mother.

"We figured it was a commercial bread oven," Andor said.

"Or a pizza oven," Lott said. "We checked the bread ovens and they pretty much have a crew on them twenty-four-seven. Pizza ovens were another matter."

"I think we found something like sixty-five pizza ovens in the Las Vegas area," Andor said, "all large enough to hold a human body full inside while on some sort of protective padding."

"Nothing came of that, I assume," Annie said.

"Nothing," Lott said.

Julia wrote that down as well. Something was bothering her and that bit of information finally brought it out. "So why go to the bother of baking the women before taking the meat? Wouldn't that just dry the desired meat out?"

Lott shrugged. "We asked ourselves that same question."

Andor laughed. "Lott even had Carol put in a roast and bake it at a slow

temperature without water like a pizza oven would bake it."

"Dried up so bad," Lott said, "that when I cut it, it was so dry, I just marinated the strips I cut and put it into the food dehydrator to make jerky."

"You never told Mom the reason you were doing that, did you?" Annie asked, looking shocked.

Julia and Andor laughed.

"I never said a word as to why," Lott said. "I promise. But she thought I had lost a marble or two for wasting a perfectly good roast like that."

"So back to my question," Julia said. "Clearly baking the women has some meaning to our killer, just as the clothing and the number of victims does. He decided to actually kill them by baking them. That has to mean something."

"I'm betting it does," Annie said.

"And maybe the mine shaft as well," Lott said.

"We didn't even look much at that angle," Andor said. "The mine was owned by a mining corporation that was as surprised as anyone to discover what their closed mine had been used for."

Julia nodded and wrote that all down. Lots of pieces, no idea what the puzzle even looked like. But there was something else really bothering her, so she just blurted it out.

"Why did this killer stop?"

Beside her Lott shrugged and Andor shook his head.

"We're not sure the killer did stop," Lott said. "For years after finding the bodies, which was two years after they were put into the mine, we searched for any references to anything similar anywhere. Nothing came up."

"So we need to do that search again," Annie said. "I'll get Fleet and his team of computer experts on that. They should be able to easily find any sort of reference to this kind of thing if it came up anywhere in the world."

"Thanks," Lott said. "That will help."

Fleet was Annie's boyfriend's best friend. Doc and Fleet had been partners since they had both been in college, with Doc earning massive amounts of money from poker, and Fleet making very wise investments and building a vast corporation of holdings. Right now they were both so rich, they almost felt embarrassed to talk about it.

But Fleet had a computer crew that could get any information without being caught or seen. Annie had met Doc when Doc and Fleet were after the man who had killed Doc's father, and eventually would kill the White House Chief of Staff. That case had forced them to set up a very deep network of computer experts, and they had kept the team together.

Doc and Annie and their team now helped the FBI a great deal on different cases, including one that Lott and Julia had been involved in just lately, stopping one of the worst serial killers of all time.

"My nightmare," Andor said, "is for the last fifteen years, this killer has just continued in this area unchecked."

"That many women haven't gone missing in Las Vegas, have they?" Annie asked.

"Not in Las Vegas," Andor said. "But the women we identified in that cave were from five different states."

That made Julia's stomach twist hard. A killer who went out to get his victims was even harder to trace.

Julia hoped the killer was long gone. Because if not, a lot of woman had died an ugly death over the last fifteen years.

She looked over at Annie. "Can you have Fleet and his computer friends do one other search?"

Annie nodded, her eyes dark and very serious. "You thinking he should look for more black-haired women who have gone missing around Nevada and in all the neighboring states?"

"Exactly," Julia said. "Make the search pattern the entire western half of the country."

"Damn I hope you are wrong about that being possible," Lott said.

"So do I," Julia said. "And I'm sure I am. But we got to check."

CHAPTER FIVE

August 7th, 2015
10:45 A.M.
Las Vegas

LOTT SAT at Julia's small wooden kitchen table, sipping coffee and trying to wake up after a restless night. The kitchen window beside the table looked out over the condo complex's lawn and pool and was very calming. There was no one in the dozen lounge chairs around the pool at the moment.

Bringing back the case had certainly made sleeping difficult, even with Julia beside him. But the sun of mid-morning streaming in the window was helping some, along with the coffee.

Julia's condo's kitchen was small, but functional and comfortable. It was partially open to a larger dining room over a granite counter, but he and Julia liked the small wooden table tucked off to one side of the kitchen in front of the window.

The view out the small kitchen window was calming, if calming was possible when dealing with this case. Lott figured he would take anything he could get when it came to calm at the moment.

The coffee he had made was a French roast and tasted rich. It was Julia's favorite kind, and he had a hunch she was going to need it. She had tossed and turned more than normal during the night, and looked tired when she kissed him good morning and headed for the shower.

He had already showered ahead of her and made coffee and now worked at a bowl of Raisin Bran. But he couldn't finish it all. The dried raisins just kept bringing him back to how those poor women's skin looked while sitting in that mine.

He had hated this case when they had caught it the first time. He was starting to hate it just as much with this second look. And they hadn't even been at it for a full day yet.

Just as he pushed the half-finished bowl of cereal aside, Julia came in looking refreshed, her skin glowing from the shower, a faint smell of lotion around her. She had on a thin white blouse with a sports bra under it and jeans.

He watched her, marveling at how lucky he was to have met her as she poured herself a cup of coffee and put in some toast before kissing him good morning and sitting down beside him. She was the most beautiful woman he had ever met, of that he had no doubt.

After Carol died, he had never figured he would ever move on. Carol had been the love of his life and his partner in life for decades. But now, four years later, he wasn't replacing Carol. He was just starting something new with Julia.

"Long night?" he asked.

"Up twice to make some notes," Julia said. "If that pervert is still out there, we have to stop him."

"I agree," he said, smiling. Detectives just never let a case go. Carol used to complain that he couldn't stop working on a case even at breakfast. Now clearly, Julia was the same way he was.

"So what did you think of that got you out of bed?" Lott asked.

"The mine," she said, turning around and grabbing a small notebook from the white counter top that separated the small kitchen from the dining area. "That mine bothered me last night and it is bothering me still."

Lott leaned forward watching as she took a sip of coffee and then sighed at the wonderful taste. If it was possible, she became more beautiful when focused.

"You think the mine company has something to do with this?" he asked. "Andor and I just didn't spend that much time on it, to be honest."

At that moment, the toast popped up and she stood to get it and put some butter and strawberry jam on the two pieces.

"The stuff with my ex-husband made me realize that often mining companies can hide some pretty amazing things."

"Very true," he said. "And Nevada sure has no shortages of old mines to hide things in."

She brought her toast over and sat down, taking a bite before looking at her notebook. Then she said, "My second idea was that maybe there was a mine tragedy at some point where eleven girls in a class were killed. Did you try to research that?"

Lott sat back, surprised. "No, we didn't, but I'll call Annie and have her get Fleet and his wizards on it."

At that moment Lott's cell phone buzzed in his shirt pocket. He had turned off the ringer for the night. He pulled the phone out.

"Speaking of Annie," Lott said, holding the phone up to the smiling Julia.

He clicked on the phone, glad that Annie had called. "Up early this morning, daughter."

"Got some bad news," Annie said, her voice sounding about as serious as it could be. "It didn't take Fleet and his crew more than a few hours to track over three hundred missing women who matched the profile of the women in the mine. He ran the search from two years before you found the women to now."

Fleet felt his stomach twist into a tight knot. "Three hundred?"

Julia's eyes across the table grew wide in a look of horror.

"Afraid so," Annie said. "Fleet has his people running advanced programs on all of them to see if there are similar details among them besides the initial look. Or if there was a more likely reason they went missing. He's also looking for any similarities, such as a make of a car seen close by or things like that. But that's going to take some time."

"How wide an area did he search?" Lott asked.

"All of Montana, Colorado, New Mexico and every state west," Annie said.

"All basically a two day drive from the Las Vegas area," Lott said.

"Pretty much," Annie said. "Not all of these women who are missing will be involved, of course. But if our killer did eleven women a year for the last fifteen years, that's over a hundred and fifty women."

Lott had no idea what to say to that. Nothing at all.

"We've got to find this sicko," Annie said.

"We will," Lott said. "We're not letting this one go. Two more things that Julia came up with to have Fleet research."

"Fire away," Annie said. "After finding that number this morning, Doc and Fleet are all in with this investigation. Whatever we need, they are willing to throw time, money, and resources at this."

"Good to hear," Lott said. "First off, have Fleet and his people do deep background on the mining company that owned that first mine. Find out how many other mines they own that are closed up around the Las Vegas area and where they are and so on."

"Got it," Annie said.

"And see if Fleet can go back in time and find an incident when a group of school kids died in a mine, or some sort of heat accident. Basically eleven of them, all girls. Something triggered this behavior."

"Tell Julia those are great ideas," Annie said. "Talk with you soon."

She hung up and Lott sort of stared at his phone before turning the ringer back on and putting it in his shirt pocket again.

"Over three hundred?" Julia asked.

Lott nodded. "Fleet searched the years since we found the first mine from Montana south to the Mexican border and everything west of that. And with very strict parameters."

Julia just sat there in the warm sun basking the kitchen table, shaking her head, the last of her toast forgotten.

Lott had no idea what to say. There was nothing he could say.

Finally Julia asked, her voice soft, "What have we stumbled into here?"

"A nightmare," Lott said. "Actually a lot of nightmares for a lot of innocent women and their families."

CHAPTER SIX

August 7th, 2015
1:45 P.M.
Las Vegas

JULIA AND LOTT had talked with Andor and decided to meet for lunch back at the Bellagio Café. Annie said she would meet them.

That way they could all get something decent to eat and plan the next steps in the case. Julia figured they were all going to need to have some good meals while this was going on.

Even with stopping past Lott's place for a change of clothes, Julia and Lott got to the restaurant first, with Lott driving his Cadillac SUV and the air conditioning working at full. The day's temperature had already climbed past 105 and Lott gave the car to the valet so they were only in the heat for less than thirty seconds.

Lott had on jeans, tennis shoes, and a light short-sleeved golf shirt. Julia had pulled her hair back and tied it away from her face. On summer days like this in Vegas, anything extra around her face just made her feel even hotter.

Lott had admitted to her last night that both he and Andor had had nightmares for years about the fact that they had not stopped the killer. And that the killings had been going on.

Now it seemed that nightmare might have been the truth.

They managed, with only a short wait for the table to be cleaned, to get their favorite booth tucked back among the plants along the back wall of the cafe.

Andor joined them five minutes later after they both had iced tea in front of them.

"Do we have a permanent reserved sign on this booth?" Andor asked as he slid in across from them. He had a gleam of sweat on his face and took a napkin and wiped it off. Julia knew that even though he had more than enough money, Andor would never pay for valet service, even on the hottest days.

Both Andor and Lott had lived their entire lives here in Vegas, so they understood the heat. But as Lott had told her a month ago on a really hot day, understanding the heat and liking it were two different things.

Annie joined them a couple minutes later, sliding in beside Andor and putting a gray folder on the table in front of her.

"Where's Doc?" Lott asked.

"He flew up to Boise this morning," Annie said, "after we got the first count on the missing women. He wants to help Fleet and the rest at their corporate office headquarters in the research. Plus, knowing him, he's going to be pulling in favors from law enforcement agencies everywhere if needed."

Julia was very glad to hear that Annie and Doc and Fleet were working on this so hard. They had basically unlimited resources, knew every cop and FBI agent in Idaho and Nevada, and weren't afraid to skirt the law when it came to computer discovery methods.

Annie pushed the folder toward her father. "Fleet and Doc just sent me this. They just found it."

To Julia, Lott looked like he was almost afraid to open it, but he did.

From what Julia could see as she scooted over slightly closer to look at the same time, it was a newspaper article with a picture of a bus stuck on a dirt road among some desert rocks.

"Nineteen eighty-eight," Annie said. "A bus taking a small class of sophomore girls from Saint Mary's, a local Catholic High School, on a desert field trip had engine troubles about thirty miles out in the desert north of here. They were in a small canyon, hidden from view for the most part."

Julia stared at the newspaper article as Annie went on giving a summary of what had happened.

"The missing bus and students became a firestorm over the two days it took to find them, since they were not where they were supposed to be going for the day."

Julia glanced at the article, then decided to wait to read it. She wanted to hear what Annie had found.

"The reporter made some assumptions," Annie said. "The teacher, an older woman, was notoriously deathly afraid of snakes, and more than likely wouldn't allow the girls to leave the bus."

"Oh, shit," Andor said. "On a hot day in the sun, that bus would quickly become an oven."

Annie nodded. "The bus driver and his fourteen-year-old son went for help, but they were turned back by the heat and lack of water. The reporter and police reports believe that by the time the father and son made it back to the bus, the eleven girls were all passed out. The older-aged teacher was dead."

Julia could feel her stomach twisting just listening to this horror story.

"Somehow," Annie said, "the report believes that the father and the son managed to carry the girls out of the bus and up a small hill to an old mine. The mine was a little cooler and they put the girls in there, sitting up against the wall of the tunnel."

"Eleven school girls all dressed the same in a mine," Andor said, shaking his head. "Now we know where all this started."

"There's more," Annie said, looking grim. "The father left the boy and went for help. The father didn't make it, passed out near a highway and died. It was a full day before anyone found his body, and then found the girls. They were all dead. Only the boy survived. He was on the verge of death."

"I'll bet," Andor said.

Annie took a deep breath and then said, "He had removed all the girl's panties and had them in his pocket."

The silence at the table was so intense, Julia wondered if the casino had shut down around them.

Finally Andor said, "So we're looking for the kid. If he was fourteen in 1988, he would have been twenty-six when we found the bodies."

"And over forty now," Lott said.

Julia forced herself to take a deep breath and then sip her iced tea. At that moment, the waitress came by, a woman with a high voice, a big smile, and artificially built-up breasts under her white uniform blouse. She took Annie's and Andor's drink orders, then all of their food orders.

That time allowed Julia to get back centered after listening to that horrid story. Sometimes, even as a detective, stories got to her, and the image of eleven school girls baking to death in a school bus was going to be hard to clear from her mind.

"So what's the kid's name?"

"It used to be Kirk Wampler," Annie said. "But it seems his father was his only relative and when the father died,

Kirk was put into the system and just vanished."

"Vanished?" Andor asked before Julia could. "It was damn hard, if not impossible for a kid to vanish into the Child Protective Services in this state. Run away, yes, but not just vanish.

"That's what Fleet and his people call it," Annie said, "but they are looking and we have a few family names to go visit here in this area that he was put with right after his father's death. They might be able to give us some hints as to what happened to Kirk."

"So we're looking at Kirk to be the one for this?" Lott asked.

He glanced at Andor, who nodded.

Then Lott looked at Julia.

"I think he's our best lead at the moment," Julia said.

Lott smiled. "I could hear a 'but' there."

Julia was impressed. Lott was already getting to know her more than anyone before had ever done. And she was letting him and liking it, honestly.

Julia tapped the folder with the story in it that Annie had relayed. "I believe this incident, if it happened as reported here, started all this. We have to make sure this actually happened as reported. Seems to me there is a lot of guessing in this report."

"A hell of a lot," Andor said.

"Fleet and his people are working on that," Annie said, nodding in agreement.

"I'll get in touch with the chief and pull the official reports on the case and on the search," Andor said. "See if anything was left out of the official story that we would need to know."

Julia nodded. "What bothers me is that this just seems a little too pat for my tastes, all aiming directly at Kirk. There

are a lot of others who were hurt by this incident. For example, all the parents, all the brothers and sisters who lost a family member. And so on. Something like this could knock anyone over an edge."

Lott nodded and smiled. "Looks like we have a ton of work ahead of us on this."

"But at least we have some leads now," Andor said. "Damn that feels good after all these years."

And with that, Julia could only agree.

CHAPTER SEVEN

August 7th, 2015
3:45 P.M.
Las Vegas

LOTT PARKED his Cadillac SUV just down the block from the home that had taken Kirk Wampler after the accident and his father dying. Lott left the car running for a moment to keep the air conditioning pouring cool air over them. Outside the official temperature had climbed to over a hundred and seven. No telling what it was on this street.

Beside him Julia sighed, but said nothing. She clearly wasn't looking forward to this any more than he was.

It seemed Kirk had gone into some treatment after the accident at a hospital for a few months before being released to this family. It was amazing any family would take him after his history and at fourteen.

The house was a sprawling, single-story brown stucco that needed some tender-loving care and a new coat of paint. The lawn was not only completely brown, but looked like it had gone to dirt years before. Two large green garbage cans sat near the closed garage door, both overflowing.

It didn't look much different, actually, than the other houses along this street off the old Boulder Highway. This neighborhood had seen much better days, of that there was no doubt.

No trees or even small shrubs were around the house or any of the closest homes. The drapes in every home were pulled tight. One barren and lifeless place, that's for sure.

Lott knew the look of this home. More than likely this family took the kids in the system just for the money. And they did just a good enough job with the kids to keep getting more. Any kid tossed into the foster care system never really got much of a break.

Kirk had vanished from all records after being with this family for just under a year. Lott hoped he and Julia might find some sort of trace of where he had gone.

"Ready?" Lott asked Julia glancing at her. The air conditioning was blowing slight wisps of hair back from her face and she had a very worried look.

"Is anyone ever ready for this kind of thing?" Julia asked, staring at the home they were going to visit.

"Never," Lott said, smiling.

"Then let's go," she said, opening her door and climbing out.

He laughed and shut off the car and climbed out into the blast-furnace heat, moving to the front of the car to stand beside her. On the pavement like this, the temperature had to be well past one hundred and ten and climbing.

At a decent speed, they headed for the home's front door. Both of them were armed and Lott had his badge ready as well to flash.

They banged on the front door since it was clear the remains of an old doorbell were long past working.

After fifteen extremely hot seconds waiting as the heat not only radiated from the porch, but off the side of the building, someone pulled the door open.

"Yeah," the woman who answered said from the shadows. The smell of bacon hit them through a rough screen door as well as some hints of cooler air.

Lott flashed his badge, holding it up for the woman to see. "Detectives Lott and Rogers. Mrs. Mitchell, we would like to talk with you for a moment about a boy you once fostered by the name of Kirk Wampler."

"You're kidding, right?" the woman asked. Then she pushed the door open and indicated they should come in.

Inside the door was an entry area with empty hooks on the wall. Just beyond the entry was a big living room that looked to be an organized zone of clutter. Toys for small kids were scattered near a large wooden toy box, but not much distance from the box. A card table with a puzzle half put together was in front of a couch facing a large-screen television. And the entire place was dark and cool, something Lott very much appreciated at that moment.

Mitchell was a thin woman, not much taller than five feet, with gray hair pulled back into a bun of sorts, and an apron covering jeans and a dark blouse. From what Lott could find out from a quick call, she and her husband, a dentist, had been fostering kids for over twenty years and seemed to be good at what they did and clearly didn't need the money from doing foster care even though their home looked like they did.

She had on flip-flops and far too much make-up. She didn't indicate that they should sit down, so the three of them stood there on the scarred wooden entrance floor.

"Why you interested in Kirk after all this time?"

"His name came up in a cold case we were working on," Julia said, giving the woman a smile. "Just trying to figure out what happened to Kirk after he left here. He seemed to have vanished from the system."

Mitchell laughed, a sort of rough laugh that had no warmth at all to it.

"I suppose that case is about what happened to his dad and those poor girls in that mine, right?"

Lott nodded.

"It is," Julia said.

"Poor kid never really got over that, even after a couple months with professional help," Mitchell said.

Lott was surprised. Mitchell actually sounded sad.

"So what was he like?" Julia asked.

Mitchell shrugged. "Kept to himself, quiet, didn't much like school. Real depressed. Not a damn thing my husband or I could do to change that and let me tell you, we tried. Near the end here the doctors from the hospital had him on some anti-depressants of some sort, but it did no good."

"See any signs of other problems with him?" Lott asked.

Mitchell shook her head. "Stayed in his room all the time when not forced to come out and eat or go to school."

"So you have any idea where he went after here?" Julia asked.

Mitchell kind of jerked back, then shook her head. "The doctors said they were going to keep it quiet, guess they did."

Lott wasn't liking the sound of this at all. "Keep what quiet?"

"Kirk killed himself," Mitchell said.

Lott could see the hurt in her eyes. This woman actually did care for the kids she was trying to help.

"How did he do that?" Julia asked, her voice soft.

"He stepped out in front of an empty school bus. He's buried beside his mom and dad up in the Palm Cemetery off the beltway."

Lott felt like he was going to be sick. It was a school bus trip that had gone horribly wrong and killed his dad and those girls. And it had ended up killing Kirk as well.

They thanked Mitchell and apologized for bothering her and headed back out into the heat.

Their best lead was dead.

And now all Lott could ask himself was what next?

CHAPTER EIGHT

August 7th, 2015
4:45 P.M.
Las Vegas

LOTT HAD DECIDED that the news about Kirk required a fresh bucket of KFC for dinner, even though there was some cold KFC still in the fridge from last night.

Julia liked that idea. She wasn't sure why the news that Kirk was dead had rocked her so much. With so many women missing, she had just hoped that the answer to this craziness would be simple.

But it now looked like it was going to be far, far from simple. They had no leads at all. None. Maybe a hundred possible suspects, but no leads.

While Lott headed them back toward his place through downtown traffic, Julia called first Andor and then Lott's daughter, Annie, and told them of the KFC plans at Lott's house.

"Perfect," Andor had said. "I was starting to grow roots in that booth at the Bellagio."

Annie said she would be there, but she didn't sound upbeat in the slightest. And Julia did not tell her or Andor about Kirk being dead.

They desperately needed some sort of break in this case.

Lott headed into the drive-through at the nearest KFC to his home. They hadn't talked much during the twenty minutes it had taken them to get across town. Not much to talk about, since they were both focused on the case.

But as they waited, Lott turned to her. "From what Mrs. Mitchell said, Kirk had a lot of doctors. I think we need to see if we can get his medical records."

Julia nodded. "I agree. But at this point I'm not sure what good it will do."

She was convinced that the records would show that Kirk was destroyed by survivor guilt and depression from what had happened to his father and those girls. She had seen survivors of some major tragedy or another kill themselves more times than she wanted to admit.

"Those girl's underwear being found in Kirk's pocket bothers me," Lott said, rolling up the window after the woman gave him his change and said it would be a minute.

"Maybe part of the survivor guilt that killed him," Julia said.

"Might be," Lott said, nodding. "Or they were planted there."

Julia was surprised at that statement. "Why would you say that?"

Lott looked at her, his dark eyes clear and intense. "The eleven women we found in the cave also didn't have underwear on. We paid little attention to that fact because of the hunks of flesh gone from the legs and butts of the women. We figured it was just part of the killer cutting them up. But maybe we should have paid attention to the missing underwear."

"Signs of sexual assault at all?" Julia asked, shocked.

Lott only shrugged. "None after the woman were baked. But I was told that kind of baking and mummifying process would pretty much clean out any sign of sexual activity unless the sex was rough and caused damage."

Julia turned and sat back, thinking. "I wonder if the girls in that mine with Kirk were sexually assaulted before or after they died?"

Lott shook his head. "I honestly don't know. Annie didn't say anything about that, but that kind of information would have been withheld."

"I'll call Andor and see if he has managed to dig up the entire file on that case." Julia said. "Every damn hidden detail of it."

Lott nodded and she was on the phone when Lott took the bucket from the woman in the take-out window and the wonderful smell of fresh KFC filled the car.

Andor said he got it all, including all the autopsies of all the girls and the father. Then he asked, "Got the bucket of chicken yet?"

"Sitting between us as I speak," Julia said.

"I knew I could smell something," Andor said and hung up.

She laughed, then glanced at Lott as he turned them toward his home about a half mile away.

"He's got all the files there are on the first case," Julia said. "And he sounds hungry."

Lott laughed. "Haven't you noticed he's always hungry?"

"This time I think we should have gotten a bigger bucket," Julia said.

Lott indicated the bucket of chicken between them. "I figured as much, so I got the largest one."

"Smart man," she said, laughing.

Damn that chicken smelled good. She was hungry as well. And it was everything she could do to watch the road ahead instead of digging into the bucket.

Everything.

And if the drive had been even a half-mile longer, her self-control would have collapsed.

CHAPTER NINE

August 7th, 2015
5:30 P.M.
Las Vegas

LOTT SAT THE large and very warm bucket of KFC on the table and turned to help Julia dig out napkins and paper plates. The wonderful scent from the chicken filled the kitchen like a soft padding, making it feel even more like a home.

He had also gotten some mashed potatoes and some corn for all of them, so he also got out forks.

Julia got them both a bottle of water from the fridge, then poured them both a glass of iced tea as well from a pitcher of tea he had made the day before.

This remodeled kitchen felt wonderful to Lott. It made him feel almost rich with the granite counters and new cabinets and brand new fridge and stove. Carol would have loved what he had done with the place.

They had the table set when Annie came in carrying a small file and headed for the fridge to get a bottle of water. She grabbed a second one and held it up as Andor followed her in the back door.

He took it from her without a word, dropped a large file on the table out of the way of the chicken, and took his normal place with his back to the front door.

Andor had sat in that same chair when Annie was a baby in a high chair and Lott and Carol had first bought this place. Now the kitchen was remodeled, Annie was an adult, Carol was gone, and Julia sat in Carol's spot.

All the while Andor remained in his same place and Lott remained in his same chair. Strange how things changed, and yet remained the same in so many ways.

They made small talk about the heat and the smell of the chicken as they dug in and got through their first pieces. For some reason, that first piece of KFC just calmed him down, made him feel like he was on track, no matter what was going on in the world. That response had only happened since Carol's death, and he had no intention of trying to change it or cut back on the chicken.

After finishing the first leg, Lott decided it was time to tell Andor and his daughter about Kirk.

He and Julia explained what Mitchell's home looked like and what she was like, then told them that Kirk was dead.

"Seriously?" Andor asked, stopping halfway through a bite of his second piece of chicken. "Can we be sure of that?"

"He's dead," Annie said, nodding. "Fleet and his people discovered that about two hours ago and double-checked everything. Ruled a suicide. Photos of his body and everything in there if you want to check them out."

She pointed to the folder she had brought, but didn't pull it closer. Lott sure didn't care to look and no one else asked for the file either.

Kirk was just a tragic kid, swept up by a horrible accident. It was amazing he lived as long as he did after the events in the cave and on the bus.

Lott also wasn't surprised that Annie had come up with the same information he and Julia had found. Doc and Fleet and their crew were really amazingly efficient.

"So our one suspect was dead before someone murdered the women we found in the cave," Andor said, shaking his head. "This damn case is something."

Lott had to agree with that.

"The kid has no relatives that we could find in any record," Annie said, "so that side of things is a complete dead-end."

"What about all the abductions?" Julia asked. "Anything coming together from all of them?"

"Fleet and his people are eliminating numbers of the ones we found in the first pass," Annie said.

"That's good," Julia said.

Lott could only agree with that.

"Down to just under two hundred black-haired women who have gone missing over the last seventeen years in the western part of the United States."

Two hundred! That number still felt like a kick in the stomach to Lott. An impossible number of women vanished and families destroyed.

Annie went on. "The only detail that is standing out as slightly similar on a number of missing person's cases is a brown panel van seen near where some of the women were before their disappearances. No license plate was ever taken, or description of any driver."

"And the news just gets better," Andor said, wiping off his hands from the chicken grease. "So why, if Kirk is dead, were you wanting every detail of the school bus tragedy?"

Julia took another piece of chicken and nodded for Lott to tell his former partner his idea.

"The underwear off those girls," Lott said. "I'm betting Kirk claimed he didn't do that."

Andor nodded. "He continuously claimed that, over and over in the records I got here." Andor pointed to the thick file.

"So the eleven abducted women in our mine were not wearing underwear either," Lott said.

"Because the meat on their butts and legs had been trimmed away," Andor said. "But I see where you are going with this. Someone else got into that cave with those girls and Kirk, more than likely before the rescue, but after he was passed out."

"Maybe after the girls were already dead," Lott said. "So do any of those reports from the detectives or doctors have Kirk claiming he had visions of ghosts in that cave?"

"Visions that would have been discounted as heat stroke," Julia said.

"Exactly," Lott said. "And since that was just a massive tragedy with no crime involved, no one would be thinking someone else might have been in there and not reported it at once."

"Never looked for that," Andor said, pulling the file closer and opening it. He quickly divided the large stack of papers into four piles and they all went to reading, trying not to get too much chicken grease on the papers as they went.

Finally, Lott decided he just didn't have the room and stood and picked up the bucket of chicken and moved it to the countertop. He didn't feel like he was finished eating yet, but they could finish later.

Julia and Annie handed him their plates and he took Andor's and dumped them all in the garbage.

Then he sat back down and kept reading, letting the silence fill the kitchen.

"Got it!" Annie said after just a minute. "Kirk told one doctor he was sure he had seen someone in the mine as well. He says the kid gave him a sip of water, said help was on the way, and then left."

"So that's why Kirk survived and the girls didn't," Andor said. "Did Kirk identify the kid?"

Annie shook her head. "Kirk said here he didn't know who it was. The doctors didn't believe Kirk. Chalked it up to the heat since no one came forward and reported being in there."

Suddenly, Lott had a horrid thought. "We need to find out if Kirk went back to the same high school while staying with the Mitchells. And we need to really look at the file on Kirk's death. What time of the day and was he alone?"

"Oh, shit," Andor said. "You think?"

All Lott could do was shrug. "If the guy that took those girl's underwear off suddenly realized Kirk would recognize him, I wouldn't put anything past him."

Annie grabbed the file on Kirk's suicide by bus that had been ignored and opened it.

"Ten at night," she read. "A dark stretch of Tropicana. Bus driver was a woman who said she never even saw Kirk until he was suddenly in front of her bus and she hit him."

Lott watched as Annie read on silently, then shook her head. "No one else was with him, supposedly. And there were no witnesses at all."

"Which means our perp might have been there," Andor said, "and just took care of the only surviving witness to the first panty raid."

"Very possible," Lott said.

And he had a hunch they had just gotten a lead. Not much of one, but a start.

And right about this point, they needed a start.

CHAPTER TEN

August 8th, 2015
6:30 P.M.
Las Vegas

JULIA SAT ACROSS the wooden table in Lott's kitchen and watched as Annie called Fleet and Doc in Idaho.

"We need the class list of anyone in the same high school as Kirk. His year and the two years ahead."

"Thanks," she said after a moment. "Kick them through to my computer and Dad's computer. We'll get back to you on some search parameters as we figure it out, but in the meantime, could you also send through if each person from the classes is still alive and what they do for a living and where they live? And also a list of the other girls in the Catholic girl's school where the victims went?"

Again, Julia watched as Annie nodded and then said, "Thanks."

Annie looked at the table. "They are going to also search to see if any of them have a panel van."

Julia was impressed. "Great thinking."

Annie shook her head. "Fleet and Doc are both so upset by all this, they are going at this full tilt. That many women being missing has them both upset beyond anything I have seen in a year or more."

"Not exactly making us all happy," Andor said.

Julia laughed. "Got that right."

The silence filled the kitchen and Julia was about to stand to get the chicken so they could all have more when a thought crossed her mind.

"Black hair," she said.

The other three turned and looked at her.

"How long was that school bus missing?"

"Two days," Lott said, looking at her puzzled. "The file I read had everyone searching for it, but in the wrong area of desert."

Andor nodded. "The governor thought of pulling in the guard to help in the search at one point."

"That's what the newspapers said as well that I read," Annie said. "Headlines for days."

"What about black hair?" Lott asked, looking puzzled.

Julia looked intensely at Annie. "What grade were the girls in?"

"All of them, including Kirk, were sophomores at Saint Mary's School for Girls," Annie said.

"They still had that kind of dress code for kids around here in 1988?" Andor asked.

Julia was surprised at the same thing.

"The girls all went to a small Catholic girl's school," Annie said. "Kirk went to just a regular public school."

"So what's the connection?" Lott asked Julia, his dark eyes trying to see what she was thinking. And at times she was convinced he managed just that.

She smiled. "Black hair. The women in your mine all had black hair. Which one of the girls in that first tragedy had black hair?"

"And did she have a boyfriend?" Andor asked, smiling.

"Exactly," Julia said and watched Lott nod.

"The bus and girls were missing for two days," Annie said. "Everyone in the city would have been out searching for them, and if this ghost that Kirk saw found them first and the girls were dead, including his girlfriend, that would twist any kid up real bad."

Julia nodded to that. "We need to check the file on the first tragedy. How many girls' underwear were found in Kirk's pocket?"

They all quickly went back to the pages on the table in front of them and it was Lott who found the reference first in his part of the report.

"There were ten pairs there," Lott said.

"Eleven girls," Annie said.

"So our killer keeps the women's underwear as trophies," Andor said. "And I'm betting he was in that mine with Kirk."

"Sure looking that way," Julia said. "Now all we have to do is figure out which kid in three classes of high school kids was dating a black-haired Catholic girl who died in the tragedy."

"Andor laughed. "No footwork there at all."

"That's what they pay us the big bucks to do," Lott said.

"Yeah, I wish," Andor said, as everyone laughed and Julia got back up to bring the bucket of chicken back to the table with more plates. They still had a dinner to finish.

PART TWO
The First Hand

CHAPTER ELEVEN

August 13th, 2015
10:30 P.M.
Las Vegas

LOTT WAS NOT pleased at all that yet another poker night had come and gone and they hadn't made much progress on the mine murders. It had been one of the longest seven days that he could remember, and he had nightmares every night, sometimes waking up Julia.

She looked tired as well, and he offered to stay at home some night to allow her to get some sleep and all she had said was, "Don't you dare."

It seemed she was having as rough a time with this horrid case as he was.

Over the week, Doc and Fleet had narrowed down the list of missing to about eleven women with black hair per year that had gone missing since 1998. And they had found out the identities of the two unknown women in the mine that the Las Vegas police could never identify.

He and Julia and Annie had spread out all over the entire area, interviewing anyone who might have known the two girls in the mine with black hair. But there were some classmates that were dead, others just had no memory from school in 1988.

Now they were all headed once again after the poker game for the café at the Bellagio Casino, just as they had done a week before.

Over the game, the five attending retired detectives all brainstormed on various ways to come at this case.

Nothing at all came out of that.

Just more questions.

Why eleven per year?

Why the black hair?

And the question that bothered Lott the most was where were the missing women and why in fifteen years had no others been found?

As the leads with the students seemed to be fading, Doc and Fleet were digging deeper into the mines involved, both the one above the broken down school bus and the one they had found the women in. There was no connection at all between the two mines, but the one with the murdered women seemed to have a somewhat shady past.

Of course, for mines in Nevada, that was not at all unusual. But it was taking time even for Fleet's miracle computer people to dig through the layers of ownership on that mine.

Lott and Julia dropped his car in valet parking and stepped quickly through the heat and into the coolness of the casino. The sounds of machines and bells and people laughing and talking seemed almost comfortingly normal as Lott and Julia took their spot in a back booth at the cafe, neither saying a word.

A minute later, Annie joined them, followed by a sweating and red-faced Andor. He had clearly parked out in the lot. Even though it was after ten and the sun had just gone down an hour before, the temperature outside still topped one hundred and twelve degrees.

"I had an idea on the way over here," Andor said as he slid into the booth and took a cloth napkin to wipe the sweat off his face. Then he dipped the napkin in a glass of ice water and put it on his neck.

"So what's the idea?" Lott asked.

"We're going about this wrong," Andor said.

Julia laughed. "No kidding."

"We need to focus on why those women were cut up like they were," Andor said, the red flush in his face slowly fading.

"We are pretty convinced it started in the bus tragedy," Annie said. "But nothing in that tragedy leads to harvesting flesh."

"Exactly," Andor said.

"We think the ghost that Kirk saw in the mine is our perp, right?" Andor asked. "The one that gave Kirk a little water, took off the women's underwear, and then left."

All three of them nodded. Lott had learned a long time ago that when Andor had an idea, it was just better to not say anything and let him run with it.

"So what did our perp learn to do that forces him to cut off the meat from his victims after he roasts them?"

Lott understood where his partner was going. "And how does he bake them?"

"Exactly," Andor said, pointing at Lott as he often did when Lott had something right. "We looked into that some back in the day, but this baking has, in theory, been going on now for another fifteen years. Which one of Kirk's classmates owns either mines or something that could bake a person?"

"Or both," Annie said.

Annie grabbed the phone and a moment later was explaining to Fleet what they wanted. Doc had stayed in Boise to help out and had been calling in favors all over the West investigating some of the women's disappearances to try to get any little detail that would help. So far he had come up empty, but he was still going at it.

The petite brown-haired waitress took their drink order and their food order at the same time just after Annie finished.

"None of the men in Kirk's high school has any interest or family in mining at all," Annie said. "They had already done that search. They are now going after ovens and class members."

"Damn," Andor said. "So why, beyond some strange sexual thing I have never heard of, would a guy cut off a woman's butt and large muscles in her thighs?"

"Steaks, roasts, maybe jerky," Annie said.

"Damn dry steaks and roast," Lott said. "From my little experiment. But jerky makes sense if the flesh was going to be eaten."

"How much was taken from each body?" Julia asked.

"A lot," Andor said. "Maybe twenty pounds or so from each woman if I remember the autopsy reports right."

"That's a lot of jerky every month," Lott said.

"So we let Fleet and his people do the searches and see what they come up with."

Everyone nodded and then sat there silently, just letting the casino sounds wash around them.

Lott felt the frustration of the week climbing back. Just so many odd details and none of it was fitting together. He knew it had to be the mines that were at the center of this in some fashion or another. He just couldn't figure out how.

He turned to Julia. "You up for a trip to visit a couple of mines tomorrow while we wait for Fleet's search to be done?"

"Not really," she said. "But I see where you are going and I think I need to see them as well."

"I'll go with you," Annie said. "I've been feeling that the mines are the key to this all along, just don't know how."

"I'm in," Andor said. "But I'm going to be bringing a cold pack for my neck."

Lott laughed. "Field trip."

"Let's hope it turns out a bunch better than the field trip those girls in the bus took," Andor said.

"We're bringing cases of bottled water," Annie said, "cell phones, and telling Doc and Fleet exactly where we are every hour."

"Where's the adventure in that?" Andor asked, shaking his head.

"Thank you," Julia said, smiling at Annie.

Lott could only smile at his daughter as well and say the same thing.

CHAPTER TWELVE

August 14th, 2015
9 A.M.
Outside of Las Vegas

WHERE THE BUS had gotten lost was surprisingly close to Las Vegas city limits, yet it felt remote and very isolated.

But in the intense heat of a summer's day, close was still a death sentence without protection.

Lott took the Cadillac SUV expertly along the narrow dirt road up the rocky canyon. He could only imagine a bus up here in this kind of heat. It was well over a hundred already outside and would be climbing as the day went on.

That kind of heat got very deadly very quickly.

Lott had on a light long-sleeved shirt with the sleeves rolled up and suntan lotion all over his arms, face and neck. He smelled more like a coconut than he liked, but he also didn't spend much more than a few minutes a day in this sun and he wanted to be prepared.

He had also brought a wide-brimmed hat.

They all wore jeans and hiking boots and both Julia and Annie had on tank tops with a light open jacket over that to protect their arms some and wide-brimmed Panama hats.

Andor had on a dress shirt with the sleeves rolled up and a ton of lotion smeared all over his arms and face and neck as well. He had on a baseball cap and a wet towel over his neck that he planned on dipping in iced water from a cooler before he got out.

They had a couple cases of bottled water and some food in the back, plus a cooler full of ice and water bottles. They were about as ready as four detectives without any desert experience could get to go look at some mines in hot desert heat.

Lott decided to come into the canyon from the top of a slight ridge, the same way the bus had gone. From the top of the ridge, it took him only a few minutes going along the winding, one-lane dirt road of the canyon before he found where the bus had broken down.

He pulled the car over and stopped, letting it run and the air conditioning working to keep the inside of the car cool. The car blocked the dirt road completely.

On the left side of the car were steep rock walls. The mine was up a brush-covered slope on the right and still in operation, from what it looked like from the fresh dirt. A rough dirt road twisted up through the brush toward the mine tailings.

No cars or people were in evidence.

Lott was surprised at how far up the hill the mine was from the road.

They had expected that the mine would be in use, but it still sort of surprised Lott. It had actually been in operation when the girls died in there, but the owner had been out of town.

"We need to get a complete background check on the owner of this mine," Andor said.

"Fleet already has it," Annie said, handing Andor the file. "The guy that is working this now is an attorney from Las Vegas, working the mine on weekends. He bought it from the guy who owned it when the girls died. Seemed the guy could never go back into the mine after all the death in there and it took him five years to find a buyer."

"What happened to that guy?" Andor asked a moment before Lott could.

"Died seven years ago," Annie said.

Lott nodded. Figured that would be yet another dead end on a case full of them.

Lott glanced at Julia, then around at Annie and Andor behind him. "Anyone have any desire to walk up there and look around?"

"Not a bit," Andor said. "That's a pretty good hike."

"I can't see a reason to now that I see it from here," Annie said.

Julia nodded. "Carrying those girls up that road must have been almost impossible."

"Especially for two men who had just tried to go for help in heat like this," Annie said.

Silence filled the car.

Lott stared at that road. Impossible described the feat. Kirk and his father could not have done it. Not after trying to go for help and getting turned back by the heat.

Lott swung around and looked at his old partner in the back seat.

Andor was staring up at the mine and frowning.

"You thinking what I'm thinking?" Lott asked.

Andor nodded. "No chance in hell Kirk and his dad carried those eleven girls up that hill. More than likely they got back to the bus after trying to go for help and just passed out with everyone else."

Julia frowned. "So who carried them up there and why?"

"And then why not admit it?" Annie asked.

Lott shook his head. "More questions. No answers."

"This damn case is driving me crazy," Andor said.

Lott and Julia nodded together, both staring up the hill at the mine.

"Let's see the other place, Dad," Annie said. "Maybe we can see something there that will make sense of this."

Lott nodded and with one last look at the mine up on the hillside, he put the car in gear and headed down the dirt road.

About a quarter mile down the winding narrow dirt road, he glanced at Julia.

"What in the hell was the bus full of kids doing up here anyway?"

"I didn't see the answer to that in the file," Andor said. "They were supposed to have been up between Boulder City and the dam on the other side of town. That's why it took so long to find them out here, on the north side of town."

"There's a ton more to this tragedy than what is in that record," Annie said.

Lott could only agree with that.

"There sure is," Andor said. "And I think the chief of police can help me get to the bottom of it all this afternoon."

Lott smiled. He knew that tone in his old partner's voice and no way in hell was he going to take no for an answer.

"I'm going to get Fleet and Doc digging as well," Annie said, pulling out her cell phone.

"Good idea," Andor said. "Usually when I smell this much fish, there's an ocean nearby."

Julia and Annie laughed and Lott just smiled and shook his head as he kept working the SUV down the canyon and back toward the city. He had heard Andor use that phrase a bunch over the years. And when he did, there had always been something very wrong about a story.

Always.

And Lott had a hunch, this time would be no exception.

CHAPTER THIRTEEN

August 14th, 2015
9:45 A.M.
Outside of Las Vegas

JULIA WAS SURPRISED when Lott pulled off the paved highway and headed along a straight dirt road toward some low hills, dust billowing up behind their SUV.

After leaving where the bus tragedy had happened, Lott had wound his way back to Highway 95, gone only about two miles back toward Vegas, and turned off again.

"These two sites are very close together in the scheme of things," Julia said.

"They are at that," Lott said. "We didn't know about the bus tragedy fifteen years ago, so this didn't seem odd."

"It seemed like a long damn ways out in the desert," Andor said.

The dirt road went into a narrow canyon and Lott slowed down, moving up through the curves slowly until the canyon seemed to open up and there, beside the road, was an old mine entrance.

This one had no climb to get to it at all. Hauling bodies from a van or truck or car and getting them into the mine would be easy.

"Well, this brings back nightmares," Andor said.

Lott had stopped the SUV directly across from the mine and was sitting there, just staring at it.

Julia eased her hand over and put it on his leg for support as she too just stared at the mine entrance.

"Boarded up just as we found it," Andor said. "Shit I hate this place."

Julia understood that. She had seen the pictures of what those women in there looked like. She could only imagine finding them.

Lott glanced at Julia. "I think I'll wander over there and chase some demons away."

Julia squeezed his leg and nodded. "I'll go with you."

"You don't need to," Lott said.

"But I do," Andor said as he opened the cooler between him and Annie and dunked in his towel in the ice water, then put it around his neck.

"We'll all go," Annie said. "We're here to look for something, anything, that might give us a clue to move forward."

Lott shut off the car as Julia opened the door and stepped out into the heat. It felt like putting her head in an oven. The air off the dirt and rocks was so hot, it just seemed to radiate from everywhere.

"We can't be out in this too long," Annie said as she got out and moved to the side of the road with Julia.

"Luckily that mine is only about thirty paces off the road," Andor said.

"Think that fact might be important?" Annie asked.

Julia nodded. "It could be."

With Andor walking ahead of them in his normal bullish fashion, Julia followed with Annie and then Lott right behind her. There was a rough path to the mine, but nothing really. More than likely still left from fifteen years ago.

And she knew it was far, far too hot for snakes to be moving around, but she watched the shadows along the path anyway.

The mine opening had been dug between a large rock outcropping. A massive sign was faded, but plastered across the wood covering the mine entrance. It said, "No trespassing. Dangerous Conditions!"

"This is exactly how we found it," Lott said. "Same sign and all."

Julia touched Lott's back for comfort. This had to be almost impossible for him to come back to.

"We were about to not open it and just ignore the psychic," Andor said, "but Mr. Nose here thought he smelled something."

"I still smell it," Lott said. "That memory is so damn strong."

Julia frowned and glanced at Annie, who was also frowning.

"A musty smell, like something had gotten wet in a closed-up garage?" Annie asked.

"Yeah, that's the smell," Lott said.

"I'm smelling it now," Julia said.

"So am I," Annie said.

Lott had a panicked look in his eyes that Julia could never imagine the man she loved having.

"That smell can't still be here," Lott said.

"But it is," Annie said.

Julia watched as both Lott and Andor went at the side of the boards.

They pulled them and the sign off without so much as a grunt. That was not a good sign. That meant this mine had been entered a bunch of times and the boards put back up.

The smell hit them all hard the minute the mine opened up.

Julia just sort of held her ground. She had smelled a lot of smells over the years as a detective, but this one seemed to just clog every pore of her body in the heat.

All four of them pulled out their phones and turned on their lights.

Lott turned to Annie. "Stay out here. One of us has to call for help if this thing collapses."

Julia saw Annie start to protest, then nod.

Lott stepped into the smell of the small tunnel first, followed by Andor.

Julia followed, bracing herself for what she would find just as she had done all the time when on full duty.

The thick overhead wooden beams were low and Lott almost had to duck.

Julia was right behind Andor, but she couldn't see much ahead of them since the tunnel was so narrow.

Ten feet in both men stopped, side-by-side in the narrow tunnel, holding up their lights to illuminate what was in front of them.

Julia moved up and looked between them, gently touching Lott on the shoulder to get him to lean a little out of the way.

Eleven women, dressed in schoolgirl uniforms, were sitting against the mine wall on the left. All had black hair, cut and trimmed exactly the same.

All were mummified completely.

It was the most horrific sight she had ever seen.

Ever.

And with the thick smell of dried death clogging her every sense, she had no doubt that she would ever be the same.

CHAPTER FOURTEEN

August 14th, 2015
10:45 A.M.
Outside of Las Vegas

LOTT SAT BEHIND the wheel of the SUV, letting the air-conditioning blow directly on his face.

They had managed to talk Annie out of going into the mine after they came out and had just gone back to the car to call for help.

Annie was about to call 911 as they got out of the intense heat and into the car when Andor stopped her. "We need to get the chief out here and only a few detectives he can trust."

Lott had turned to look at his partner as he wiped down his face with the iced towel, then put it back on his neck.

Julia was looking as if she was in complete shock.

"Why?" Annie asked, still holding her phone.

"The last thing we want to do is force this sicko to go to ground at this point," Andor said. "This creep has been thinking he can get away with this for fifteen years. We need him to keep thinking that for just a few more days while we track him down."

"You think we're closer now than an hour ago?" Julia asked.

"I do," Andor said and Lott was starting to understand what Andor was talking about.

"We now will have the entire force back on this case," Lott said. "Combine all those resources with the resources of Fleet and Doc and the four of us and we might stop this guy if we keep this discovery silent for just a day or so."

The car was filled with only the sounds of the blowing air-conditioning. More than anything, he wanted to get home and take a long, long shower to get the smell off, but he knew that wasn't going to be possible for some time now.

Andor started to dial his phone. "I'll get the chief out here. And he's going to have to pull some strings with the State Police as well to keep this under wraps, if he agrees."

Lott nodded. Beside him Julia nodded as well.

She had been supportive of him going into this, now he eased his hand over and touched her leg to offer his support in return.

She smiled and put her hand on his and then nodded that she would be all right.

Lott knew she was one damn tough cop. She would be affected by what she had seen in that mine, but she would be all right in the long run.

"At least we have closed eleven missing persons' cases today," Lott said softly, "and given some families some closure."

Julia nodded and took a deep breath of the cool air pouring over her.

Lott glanced back over at the mine. They had left it open, the boards pulled to one side.

He really wasn't looking up at the mine, just at it across a small distance from the road.

And he suddenly had another idea.

He turned in his seat to look at his daughter as Andor waited for the Las Vegas Chief of Police to come on the phone.

"Can you get Fleet and Doc to search records of abandoned mines in a fifty mile radius of Las Vegas," Lott asked.

"They have already done that," she said. "There are upwards of five hundred."

"Have them sort the mines for elevation to the nearest road," Lott said, pointing over at the mine. "Use this mine as a baseline."

Julia looked at him. "You think our perp doesn't like to carry bodies up hills?"

"That's exactly what I think," Lott said as Annie smiled and pulled out her phone. "I think he did that from that school bus and never wants to do it again."

"I'm going to tell Doc and Fleet what we found," she said, nodding. "I'll tell them we're going to try to keep it under wraps for a day or so."

Lott nodded and about that point Andor got on the line with the chief.

Annie climbed out into the heat and closed the door quickly.

"Chief," Andor said. "The gang has something and it ain't pretty. No announcement to anyone, just grab a few detectives you can trust to keep their mouths shut and a couple of forensic boys and get out here."

Andor nodded. "Chief, just trust me. You need to see this and we need to keep a lid on it for a day or so if we're going to catch this bastard."

Andor nodded at what the chief said, then said. "You know the cold case we are working with the eleven dead women? We're at the same mine. Directions are in the file."

Andor then hung up and nodded to Lott, who had turned and watched him talk to the chief. "He'll be here in thirty minutes without fanfare. He said he'll look at the situation and decide."

At that moment, Annie climbed back in. Just less than a minute in the sun had her sweating.

"Fleet's people are running the mine elevations in relationship to nearby roads now and will text the results to me shortly," Annie said.

She dug into the cooler for a bottle of water. "Both Doc and Fleet will be on their jet and headed this way in an hour and will be in town in the middle of the afternoon."

"Good," Lott said. "We're going to need as much help as we can get very shortly."

Julia frowned. "Why do you say that?"

Lott pointed over at the mine. "There were eleven women in there. One year's worth if this sicko is doing what we think he's doing."

"It's been fifteen years," Julia said softly.

"Shit," Andor said.

"There are fourteen more mines full of bodies," Julia said, her voice gaining strength with each word.

Lott nodded, trying not to let the image of those eleven mummified women in that mine come back to his mind.

"We need to find those other mines," Lott said, "and then put it all together and stop this. And fast."

CHAPTER FIFTEEN

August 14th, 2015
11:30 A.M.
Outside of Las Vegas

LOTT HAD MOVED the SUV off to a wide area in the dirt road and just down from the mine entrance by the time the three other cars arrived.

All four of them got out of the car, and moving slowly in the intense heat, went back up the road as Chief of Police Dan Beason, a thin man with bright eyes and a disarming smile, climbed out of one of the unmarked cars.

Lott liked the chief more than he wanted to admit.

Chief Beason stood a good six-three and just towered over everyone around him. He had thick, dark-brown hair and had taken off his jacket coat to show he was wearing suspenders with bright red stripes over his blue dress shirt.

Lott had never seen him without a jacket, so the look was startling and seemed to give the chief even more power.

"Detectives," the chief said, nodding to all of them as they walked up along the dirt road. "What's the discovery?"

Andor pointed at the mine. "Fifteen years ago we found eleven women all dressed like school girls in that mine."

The chief nodded and said nothing.

"Our theory," Andor said, "is that the perp has been taking women at eleven per year for the last fifteen years from around the country, baking them, cutting meat off them, and staging them like a class of school girls in mines."

"Shit," the chief said and two other detectives who had come up beside him went pale.

Lott didn't know them other than by reputation. Jones and Schmidt. The top team working at the moment. Lott and Andor used to hold that spot before they had decided to retire to take care of their dying wives.

Andor pointed at the mine. "We came back here today wondering if we could find some clues or see something we had missed the first time around and smelled that same damn sick smell of musty death, so we opened up the mine."

The chief glanced at the open mine only about fifty paces away. "Are you serious?"

"Don't go in there if you want to sleep for the next month," Lott said.

At that, the chief and the two detectives and three others all turned for the mine.

"No point in standing in the sun," Andor said.

They all turned and headed back to the SUV and Lott got it going and the air-conditioning on full.

They all watched in silence as the two detectives went in first, somehow convincing the chief to stay in the sun from the animation of the conversation.

After about two minutes, both came out, shaking their heads and not looking happy.

Two of the other cops went in and less than fifteen seconds later one of them came out, stepped off to the side of the mine entrance, and lost what must have been a pretty good lunch.

Lott remembered doing that himself on his first real death scene with a body that had been rotting in the sun for a few days. Nothing at all compares to that sickly odor of human death.

At that moment the chief just turned and started back toward the road.

"Better move the cooler out of the way and scoot over, Annie," Lott said.

Andor put the cooler over the seat and into the back and, as the chief approached their car, Annie opened the back door and moved over closer to Andor.

The chief crawled in, slammed the door and then let out a huge sigh. "Oh, thank you."

Annie handed him a bottle of cold water and he drank half of it. Then he said, "So you think we can catch this bastard if we hold this information for a day or so?"

Lott had turned around to face where the chief was sitting and Julia had done the same from her seat.

"I do," Lott said. "Doc Hill and his partner, Fleet, have been using all their resources to track missing women with black hair from around the western states. They have found just under two hundred and Doc has all the law enforcement offices in those areas combing the files for clues that we can put together into a large picture."

"Two hundred missing women?" the chief asked, his eyes large.

Lott remembered that feeling as well. A stunning number.

"The guy seems to take them at eleven per year," Andor said. "He was somehow involved in the old bus tragedy near

another mine where eleven school girls died when their bus broke down."

"We don't know how, yet," Annie said, "Since the only survivor was killed, a fake suicide we think, about a year after the initial tragedy."

"Shit, just shit," the chief said, shaking his head.

Lott could not have agreed more.

"We think our perp," Andor said, "was the one who carried all the girls from the school bus up to the mine. We think one of the two with black hair in those girls might have been his girlfriend or something like that. We're digging on that now."

The chief nodded. "Glad you have Doc and Fleet with you on all this."

"So are we," Lott said.

"There might even have been more than one who carried those girls out of that bus tragedy," Annie said. "But that's the key to all this, we are convinced."

Lott couldn't imagine how it felt to suddenly have all this information being tossed at the chief, but the guy was smart and was known for making solving crime more important than politics.

"Also a key," Julia said, "is the baking of the women. That takes a pretty large oven and we're searching those, trying to cross-reference anyone from those girl's age who owns an oven large enough to roast a woman without really burning the flesh."

"And what is our perp doing with the large amounts of flesh he cuts from every woman?" Andor asked. "Major question."

"He bakes them and cuts them up?" the chief said, looking startled. "Sorry, I haven't read this old cold case."

Andor nodded. "The perp harvests the meat from the women's butts and legs after he bakes them into what looks like a mummy. He drugs them, but the baking is what kills them."

The chief looked like he might be sick and Lott didn't blame him in the slightest.

Andor went on. "Then he dresses them in school girl costumes, trims their hair all the same exact length, and stages them in a mine just as the eleven girls were in the first bus tragedy, all without underwear."

"When we caught this case back fifteen years ago," Andor said, "we didn't know about that original bus tragedy back in 1988."

"Never put it together until now," Andor said.

The chief just sat there, shaking his head.

At that moment, Annie's cell phone chirped like a lost bird. She glanced at it, then she said, "The mine information is in from Fleet."

She looked at it and then glanced up at Lott. "There are two dozen closed up old mines this close to a road. All are owned by the same company that owns this mine. Fleet and his people are digging at the company, trying to find out who is behind it."

"Where is the closest?" Lott asked, not really wanting the answer, but needing it.

Annie glanced at her phone. "Just over a mile from here."

"Hang on," the chief said, "I'm coming with you."

He opened the door and went back to the detectives cooling off in the cars behind him. Then he returned to their car and got in.

"I got three of them staying here until we decide what to do," the chief said. "Jones and Schmidt are coming with us."

Lott nodded and with a quick motion buckled up his belt and headed the car down the road.

"Give me directions," he said to Annie.

And less than five minutes later they pulled up across from another old, boarded up mine. The mine was similar to the last one, just off the road, with a cliff face on one side of the dirt road and the mine cut into an area between two rock faces.

Lott flat didn't want to know what they would find as all five climbed out into the intense heat. But he had no choice.

They had to look.

CHAPTER SIXTEEN

August 14th, 2015
12:30 P.M.
Outside of Las Vegas

JULIA WALKED BEHIND Lott and the chief of police along a small dirt path toward the mine. Lott was leading and carefully watching the shadows in the brush and rocks for any snakes. There were a certain type of rattlesnake that lived in this kind of area, but the heat would force them down into the rocks.

As they approached the mine, the ground around it cleared of brush and Lott and the chief walked right up to the wood nailed securely over the entrance.

A huge sign the size of the entrance covered the wood warning of no trespassing and danger.

Andor glanced at Schmidt and Jones. "You two want the pleasure."

"Haven't got my stomach back from that last one," Schmidt said.

Andor glanced at Lott and Lott nodded.

They moved up near the mine and both of them shook their heads, then stepped back.

"Same smell," Lott said.

"Damn it," Julia said.

"I'd step back," Andor said. "The first wave out is pretty bad."

The chief and the two active detectives stepped back.

Julia stayed next to Lott until he indicated she should move back as well. "No point in taking this."

She nodded and stepped back next to the chief and Annie about four paces from the mine entrance.

Both Lott and Andor took deep breaths of the hot desert air, stepped to the wood and at the same time, yanked it off.

It came down as easily as the last mine wood had come loose. Clearly it had been taken down and put back up numbers of times.

Both Andor and Lott ducked to one side, coughing.

Then they both clicked on the light on their phones and headed inside.

The chief stepped forward and Julia took his arm. "Trust me, you do not want to see this. The pictures will be bad enough. There is honestly no reason to."

"She's right, Chief," Schmidt said.

"Those two found the original group of women fifteen years ago and have been having nightmares for years about it," Annie said. "You don't need those nightmares."

The chief nodded, but clearly didn't like not going in. Julia liked that about him. Actually, she was liking a lot about the chief in the short time she had known about him and now met him.

She could see Andor and Lott go in about five paces, both of them moving carefully and slowly and ducking to stay under the large timbers that still held the mine up. Then they both stopped, stood there for about ten seconds before turning and coming back out.

Lott looked haunted and wouldn't look at her. "This is one of the oldest ones. Those women have been in there a very long time, I would say over ten years."

"The Cold Poker Gang just solved another eleven missing persons cases," Andor said as he and Lott pocketed their phones.

"Same set-up?" Julia asked, her stomach clamped down into a tight knot.

"Exactly the same," Andor said.

Lott nodded. "Now we got to find the mine that isn't full yet."

The chief looked at him. "Not following you."

"By what Fleet and Doc have found in computer searches of missing persons that match these women's descriptions," Annie said, "Our perp takes women from January through November, one per month from somewhere around eleven western states, taking December off. There have been no missing women in December in the eleven western states that fit this profile in sixteen years."

"So somewhere in this desert we have an old mine with only seven or eight bodies in it," Andor said. "We need to find that mine and get it staked out, which is why we wanted you to keep this all silent."

The chief nodded, his face sweating. Then he turned to look at Annie. "What time of the month do the women normally go missing? Any pattern there?"

"Damn," Annie said, grabbing her phone and hitting a key.

"She's going to find out," Julia said, smiling at the chief. "Great question. One we had not thought of."

The chief turned to the active detectives. "Who else can we trust to not blab their faces off about this?"

"The three at the other mine," Schmidt said. "The rest I wouldn't trust as far as I could toss them to not talk to the press."

The chief nodded. "Get a hammer and then board that mine back up just like it was. Those women will be fine in there for the moment."

Schmidt nodded and turned for his car.

Julia watched as Annie clicked off her phone. "A black-haired woman by the name of Missy Andrews just went missing yesterday from outside of Missoula, Montana. A brown, 1990s panel van was seen close by at one point. No plates or real description."

"So we either get lucky and stop him on the road," Julia said, "or we find where he is baking these women and stop him there."

Lott nodded. "And we do it in the next twenty-four hours to save that woman's life."

Julia just felt her stomach clamp up at that.

"No pressure," Andor said.

"Yeah," the chief said. "No pressure."

CHAPTER SEVENTEEN

August 14th, 2015
4:30 P.M.
Las Vegas

LOTT CAME OUT of Julia's shower feeling much better. He had left a number of changes of clothes at her condo at her suggestion, since he often stayed there, and was now glad he did.

He had soaped and scrubbed his skin and hair more than he had done in years to make sure that smell was completely gone. The memory wouldn't leave, but at least the smell would.

He had just finished dressing in jeans and a light blue dress shirt with the sleeves rolled up and was combing his hair when Julia came in. She was wrapped in a towel and her face was red from all the sun.

"I put our clothes in the wash machine," she said. "That might be a smell that will never come out."

He didn't honestly care. He might throw those clothes away even if the smell came out. Anything he could do to not remind himself of seeing that much death in one day would be a good thing.

She turned on the shower, checked the temperature, and then dropped the towel and climbed in while Lott watched.

In his opinion, she was one of the most beautiful women he had ever known. And if they hadn't just spent the day finding more dead bodies than he wanted to think about, he might have offered to scrub her back right at that moment.

But he had a hunch she was as focused on this case as much as he was. And on saving that one woman they knew was headed in this direction and to a certain horrible death if they couldn't stop it.

"I'll be in the kitchen getting a snack," Lott said to the showering woman.

"I won't be long," she half-shouted back.

He headed out of the bathroom, feeling almost human again.

The plan was that they would head for the Café Belagio after showering and getting changed to meet Doc and Fleet and Annie and Andor and plan what to do next.

In the last four hours, they had found all but one of the mines with women's bodies. Schmidt and Jones had taken some of the mine locations, the chief and the other two detectives had taken part of the list. Lott and Julia and Annie and Andor had stayed in Lott's car and taken another third of the list Annie had gotten from Fleet.

The four of them had found three more mines full of bodies.

It had been the chief and the detectives riding with him that had found the one only half full to the south and east of the city.

The chief had set up very discrete watching posts on both entrances to that canyon, hidden completely from view. No way that killer would get out of that canyon if he went in there.

The chief was also going to get officers in the State Police working the highways coming down from the north, watching for any sign of a brown panel van.

And his men were stationed, without knowing why, at all the major entrances to the city watching for the same thing.

And he had promised that nothing would be broadcast at all over any police channel.

Lott got into clean jeans, a long-sleeved white dress shirt, and put on new tennis shoes. More than likely after that smell, he was going to have to toss his favorite tennis shoes.

While he waited for Julia, he took out his small notebook and pen and sat down at her kitchen table overlooking the trees and lawn and pool common area below and started to write a list of things they didn't know yet.

First, what was the connection between the original bus tragedy and the perp? There was no doubt in his mind there was a connection, but they hadn't been able to find it yet.

Second were the unknown factors all the victims had in common besides black hair. He had a hunch there was more. There had to be.

Third, the question of the ownership of the mines. Did someone in that company have anything to do with this? And if so, who?

Fourth, where were the victims taken and how were they baked to death?

Fifth, why were the victim's harvested for meat? Where did cannibalism come into play in this? Or was it even cannibalism? Was the women's flesh being used for something else?

He stared at his list, his eye continuing to go back to the first question. The real key to locating this sick killer was that bus tragedy. If it really was a tragedy and not done on purpose. Why had that bus been so far away from where it had planned on going?

Julia came in while he was staring at the list and wrapped her arms around him and put her chin on his shoulder. She smelled wonderful, with a slight peach scent from the shampoo she used. She had on a light green blouse with a sports bra and jeans and new tennis shoes as well.

"Am I missing anything?" he asked, showing her the list he had been making.

"Underwear," she said. "And why did Kirk need to be killed?"

He wrote both down, nodding.

"A lot of questions, that's for sure," he said.

"Let's hope we don't have to answer them before this sicko is in custody," Julia said as Lott stood.

He looked at her as she stepped away and he stood, putting his notebook back in his pocket. "You think that has a chance of happening?"

"Not a chance in hell," she said, shaking her head. "The person who has been doing this without getting caught for over fifteen years isn't going to be pulled over in a standard traffic stop."

"You think the brown panel van is stored up north somewhere?"

"Of course it is," Julia said. "No chance a van that might be linked to an abduction is going to be driven right to this guy's home and parked."

"I was thinking the same thing," Lott said as they headed out and Julia locked the door behind her.

"So it's up to us to save that woman's life," Julia said. "Because by the time the killer takes her to the mine and gets caught that way, she will be very, very dead."

"The chief can't sit on this long enough for even that to happen," Lott said as they headed down the stairs. "There are a lot of crime scenes in that desert at the moment and he doesn't dare hold this down for more than twenty-four hours. Even that long might cost him his job."

"And when all that hits the papers," Julia said. "We lose our latest victim and any chance of finding this creep."

Lott knew she was right.

They had to crack this case and crack it quick. Time was not on their side.

Or the side of that poor woman from Missoula.

CHAPTER EIGHTEEN

August 14th, 2015
5:30 P.M.
Las Vegas

LOTT AND JULIA didn't talk much as it took a while for Lott to get them through rush hour traffic and to the valet parking at the Bellagio. The heat on the few steps from the car into the casino seemed even worse than normal. More than likely that was because they had been in and out of it all day.

"We're going to need more water," Julia said as they got inside.

Lott nodded. "Felt that."

He let her lead the way toward the café, winding between people and families ambling down the wide tile hallways.

The sounds of the casino wrapped around her and calmed her some. She loved all the people enjoying the machines and the gaming tables and just having wonderful vacations. She seemed to take energy from just being in a casino. It was why she enjoyed the poker tournaments around town at times and coming here for lunches and dinners.

Plus the food was good, with lots of choices, and the staff was always friendly.

Doc, Fleet, and Annie had already secured a round table tucked off in a back corner surrounded on three sides by tall plants and flowers. Almost like a private office right in the middle of the casino.

Julia hugged both Doc and Fleet. Fleet was rail thin and tall, with a slight pot belly. He always wore a silk vest and suit and tonight was no exception, the gray silk making him look dashing and rich. He had lost the tie, something she very seldom had seen him without.

Doc wore jeans and a light dress shirt with the sleeves rolled up, just as Lott often did. Doc was about six feet tall and as solid muscle as a human being could get. He was also about as tan as they came and had just spent most of June and July guiding rafts on the rivers of central Idaho. He had only come out a week before and planned on going back into the River of No Return in three days.

He and Annie made a stunning couple, right off a magazine cover.

Julia had no doubt that if this case was still active in three days, Doc would not be leaving it for Idaho rafting. He took the work he did with Fleet helping the FBI and other police networks very seriously.

Doc and Fleet and Annie always worked behind the scenes, but so far their team had really been instrumental in solving some major crimes. It seems Doc and Fleet had friends in just about every area of police and federal governments, all the way up to the President of the United States.

Julia was constantly impressed by what they could do, all the while seeming to enjoy life and play poker. And, on top of that, Fleet was raising a family of two kids in Boise.

A couple minutes later, Andor came in, leading Chief Beason. Andor was sweating, but both of them had changed clothes and the chief wore jeans, a UNLV tee-shirt, and a baseball cap. No one would recognize him, Julia was sure.

She was surprised that the chief had come along. He clearly felt this group was the best chance at catching this killer.

Doc and Fleet both stood.

"Great seeing you again, Chief," Doc said, shaking the chief's hand.

It was clear to Julia that Doc and the chief liked and respected each other.

"We really appreciate the work you and the gang here have done to break this ugly mess open," the chief said, pulling up a chair with his back to the room.

"We're not done yet," Fleet said.

Everyone nodded to that.

After a moment of small talk about Doc and Annie's summer on the rivers in Idaho, it was Doc who turned the topic back to the case. Julia was always impressed by Doc and now was no exception.

"So where do we stand?"

The chief quickly outlined what he was doing and how long he could hold this silence before all hell broke loose.

"Maybe thirty hours at most," the chief said. "I have two friendly reporters from local stations and one from the Sun Times coming in tomorrow night, after the late news and press time on the paper, to talk with me. I'll have to give them the full story that we have at that point. They won't be able to hold it."

Julia felt her stomach twist and she forced herself to take a drink of water. That was not a lot of time to catch a serial killer who had been working and killing women for over fifteen years.

"You going to be able to handle that many bodies and crime scenes?" Lott asked.

"I have help coming in already from California, Reno, and Salt Lake," the chief said. "I'm talking with the FBI tomorrow afternoon, since this is all across state lines. And at that point I'm going to have to bring in the State Police, since most of this is in their area. But they can't even begin to handle it any more than we can. Between the three agencies and outside help, we'll deal with it."

"I'll give you a list of the women we think are victims," Fleet said, "to contact their families when the time is right to get DNA samples to match."

"Thanks," the chief said. And then he turned and looked directly at Lott, Andor, and Julia. "And thanks to you three for being willing to dig at this. If nothing else, we'll stop this and save some lives."

Julia just nodded, as did Lott and Andor. She felt slightly embarrassed. Detectives were not used to being thanked for doing their jobs. Even if they were retired and still doing their jobs for free.

CHAPTER NINETEEN

August 14th, 2015
6:00 P.M.
Las Vegas

THEY HAD ORDERED and the waitress had just turned away when Lott decided it was time to get things organized. He was feeling the time pressure more than he wanted to admit. "I made a list of what Julia and I think are the major questions we are facing that might get to this sicko."

"You don't think our surveillance on the roads will catch this guy?" the chief asked.

Lott shook his head. "It needs to be done, but this guy isn't going to be that stupid. I'm betting that panel van is in a storage unit somewhere in Idaho or Utah or Northern Nevada."

Lott was worried the chief would be angry, but instead the chief just nodded, as did everyone else at the table.

"And once this breaks," Andor said, "the guy is going nowhere near that mine or any mine in this area."

Again everyone nodded.

"So I got six areas of questions," Lott said. "Let me skip the first one because I think it holds the key and see if we can cover these other five and add in what we are missing before going back to number one."

"The bus tragedy number one?" Andor asked.

Lott nodded.

"First," Lott said, turning to look at Fleet and Doc, "besides the black hair, is there anything at all these victims have in common?"

Fleet shrugged. "All normal. Almost without an exception, they had decent jobs of one level or another. Nothing common between the jobs or financial status at all. About half were married or separated. A quarter of them had children, some raising the kids as single mothers. All were between the ages of twenty-two and thirty. And a large percentage of them were outwardly gay. Numbers of them were married to their partners."

"Gay?" Andor asked, sitting forward.

Lott felt the same thing as clearly did the chief, since they both sat forward as well.

"Were these women forcibly abducted, or did they just disappear?" the chief asked.

"They all seemed to have just disappeared," Fleet said. "Almost all had gone out for the night, some with friends, some on their own. They just never returned. It sometimes took a full day or two before someone would report them missing."

Lott made himself take a deep breath and just try to think.

"So how did we get this last report on the Montana woman so fast?" Andor asked.

"The woman only went for some groceries around nine in the evening and was due back within thirty minutes," Fleet said. "When she didn't return, her partner tried to reach her and the victim's cell phone had been shut off. The woman's car was still in the store parking lot with a flat tire."

"No security cams?" Julia asked.

"Nothing in that area of the parking lot," Fleet said. "But through other cams in the area we got a brown panel van leaving the neighborhood right after the abduction."

"So our killer offered to help her with her tire problem," Andor said.

Lott was staring at Julia, who was looking stunned.

"Who would you trust in a parking lot at nine in the evening that you didn't know?" Lott asked Julia.

"Another woman," Julia said softly.

"Damn it all to hell," Andor said. "We've been assuming this was a guy all this time."

"I have a hunch we were wrong," Lott said, feeling as stunned as everyone at the table felt.

Then Fleet pulled out an iPad and clicked up a file as the silence of the table let the casino sounds of laughter and bells ringing flood back over them.

Then Fleet turned the iPad around to show everyone a picture of a middle-aged attractive woman posing for what was clearly a professional picture. She had long blonde hair pulled back off her face and wore a silk business jacket and an expensive blouse in the picture. To Lott, the woman's dark eyes looked dead and piercing.

"Who is that?" Julia asked a half second before Lott got the same question out of his mouth.

"Her name is Karen West," Fleet said. "She is the CEO and President of Roso Industries Inc., a major investment holding company based here in Las Vegas with upwards of forty different corporations under the umbrella. She has a lot of money."

"Let me guess," Lott said. "One of those corporations owns all the mines."

Fleet just nodded.

"I've met that woman a number of times at fundraisers for different charity events," the chief said. "Are you thinking she might be the killer here?"

"Let's find out where she is right now," Lott said. "I would call her a person of interest at the moment."

The chief nodded.

Lott wasn't sure if she was anything more than a person of interest. So far everything about this case twisted into dead ends. More than likely this would as well.

Fleet flipped the screen around, then grabbed his phone.

"Find out where she went to school as well, would you?" Lott asked Fleet, who nodded.

"Any bets?" Andor asked.

"No bet," Lott said. "But if she is the one, the question then becomes that with her money, how do we pin it on her and make it stick? We have no concrete evidence at all, remember?"

"And how do we save the woman she has with her now?" Julia asked.

Lott just nodded.

Damn he hoped this hunch was the right one. He was tired of going back to square one on this case.

PART THREE
Playing the Hand that is Dealt

CHAPTER TWENTY

August 14th, 2015
6:30 P.M.
Las Vegas

THEY HAD QUICKLY worked their way through Lott's list, spotting nothing else that made sense. Before they could get back to the bus tragedy, the food started arriving. They were all almost finished with their salads and soup when Fleet got the reply from his people.

Julia had been working on a wonderful hazelnut-dressing dinner salad with extra tomatoes. Even though it tasted wonderful and she knew she was hungry, she was having to force herself to eat. She had no idea how long she would be awake tonight, and she knew she needed to eat and drink water to make sure she was fully recovered from the time in the sun and heat this afternoon.

"Karen West took a week of personal time this last week," Fleet said after hanging up his phone. "She does that most every month it seems. I have my people trying to track down what sort of vehicle she is driving, but my sources tell me she talks to no one about what she does during that week every month."

"That's pretty damning," Andor said, shaking his head.

Julia could only agree with that. Not proof by a long ways, but damning. And

one thing detectives tended to know was when all arrows pointed in a certain direction, chances are that direction was the right way. And right now a lot of arrows were starting to turn and point to Karen West.

"She also went to the same Catholic girl's school and was the same age as the girls on that bus," Fleet said, his voice low against the sounds of the casino around them.

He again pulled up an image on his laptop and turned it for everyone to see.

It was clear to Julia it was a young version of Karen West, dressed in the same uniforms as all the women found dead in the mines.

The final arrow.

Julia had no doubt at all now who had killed all the women.

"I think she just moved from a person of interest to the major suspect," the chief said. "I'll get everyone looking for any of her registered cars, or her company's registered cars, coming into town, see if we can spot her that way."

"If we don't catch her in the act, how do we prove she is the killer, assuming she is the killer?" Annie asked. "I'm betting anything these crime scenes in the mines are as clean as the first one Dad and Andor found."

Julia had to agree.

Everyone sat silently, thinking. With a woman of that kind of power and money, that was going to be very difficult at best, unless she had made a major mistake and Julia doubted this Karen West had done that.

"So what the hell happened in that bus tragedy?" the chief asked, breaking the silence.

Julia and Lott quickly went over all the details of the tragedy for the chief as their main meals arrived. She was having a filet of cod, sautéed in butter. Asparagus spears filled the plate, also sautéed lightly in butter.

She worked at it slowly, letting herself savor the taste as everyone got on the same page with the bus tragedy, including their suspicions that it had not been a complete accident.

"So you think this Karen West was the ghost in the mine?" the chief asked. "And carried all those girls up to the mine herself?"

"Not possible," Julia said, and beside her Lott nodded. "She had to have help."

"I'm betting it went down like this," Lott said. "Karen West and a friend somehow managed to give the driver bad directions as a prank, change the destination. I don't think they ever figured the bus to break down. More than likely they were doing it to annoy the teacher."

"I agree," Julia said. "I think the driver and his son, Kirk, went to try to find help, but the father collapsed and died and Kirk turned back to the bus, where he passed out with the girls."

"Then," Andor said, "after the bus had been missing for a day or so, West and her friend decided that was enough and went to where they knew the bus had gone. There they found the teacher dead and most of the girls and Kirk almost dead. They got the girls up to the mine, took most of the panties off all the girls and stuffed them in Kirk's pocket to focus the attention on him, and went to try to let someone know without revealing they were at fault."

"They didn't get the word out quick enough and the girls died," Julia said.

"That had to mess them up something awful," Andor said.

Julia agreed with that completely.

Fleet picked his phone back up, ignoring the half-eaten prime rib in front of him.

The table went silent, listening to his side of the conversation.

"Find out who was Karen West's best friend in school the year of the bus tragedy," Fleet said. "And see if she is still alive or not."

He nodded and then hung up.

They all went back to eating and Julia forced herself to pay attention to the wonderful, light fish on her plate and enjoy the taste. She had a hunch things were going to get really stressed and harried before this was all over.

A moment later Fleet's phone buzzed and he answered it. He listened and nodded as everyone at the table watched him. Then he said, "Thanks," and hung up.

"Her girlfriend's name was Bettie Lynch," Fleet said. "She and Karen West were married a few months back in California."

Suddenly Julia wished she hadn't just eaten that dinner. Her chest and stomach had clamped up so tight, she could hardly breathe.

Around the table the rest of the group sat silent. Some had their forks over their meal, frozen in mid-air. Fleet was looking puzzled at that response.

Finally it was Doc who broke the silence. "Mind telling those of us from Idaho why that was so shocking?"

"Bettie Lynch is a well-known figure here in Las Vegas," Lott said, calmly pushing his plate away.

Julia forced herself to take a deep breath and focus on being calm.

"Lynch has a chain of stores," Andor said.

Suddenly Doc's very tanned face went completely white. "Are you talking about Lynch's Jerky and Treats?"

"The same," Lott nodded.

The chief of police sat there for a moment in the silence, then pulled out his cell phone and called his office. He ordered an emergency meeting in thirty minutes. "Everyone. Get them out of bed."

Then he stood. "We may not have enough evidence to convict, but we're going to get some court orders and search a house and close down some stores. What do I owe for dinner?"

Doc waved him off. "Just catch those two."

"Oh, we will," the chief said. "And first thing we are going to do is test some of the products in those shops."

Julia watched the very angry chief of police storm off through the casino. Then she turned back to the silent group.

"So who thinks he's going to get West and her partner?" Julia asked.

"I wouldn't put money on it," Doc said. "Even though he and other major agencies are going to do their best."

Lott and Andor both nodded.

"So it's up to us. What do we do first?" Julia asked.

"Tomorrow morning at sunrise," Fleet said, "we check to see if that last mine was being watched."

"Because if it was," Doc said, nodding, "those two killers are going to be nowhere near Las Vegas."

Julia agreed.

Now, somehow, after all this today, she needed to get a few hours sleep. She doubted that was going to be possible.

CHAPTER TWENTY-ONE

August 15th, 2015
5:15 A.M.
Las Vegas

ANDOR HEADED to the police headquarters while Julia, Annie, Doc, and Fleet came with Lott in his SUV to the last mine, the mine only half-full of bodies. The sun wasn't up over the east hills yet and the air still felt warm, meaning the day would be another hot one.

Julia sat in the front seat beside him as he took the SUV up the narrow dirt road to the east of the city, working carefully along rocks. He loved having her beside him. It just felt right.

Annie, Doc, and Fleet were in the back seat, with Annie in the middle.

"Snakes will be out this time of the day," Doc said.

Annie punched him with her elbow in the ribs.

"I do not plan on leaving the road," Fleet said.

Julia glanced back. "Some snake issues?"

"No issue," Fleet said, his voice very serious. "I hate them, fear them, and will not go near them, so there is no issue."

Lott laughed, as did Doc.

Julia just shook her head, smiling.

Lott stopped the SUV in the middle of the narrow dirt road beside a mine entrance about a hundred paces to the right just slightly up a slight gully. The mine opening in the dark morning shadows looked old and abandoned and had a large sign on it warning no trespassing and danger.

If they had to move up that gulley to that mine, there was no doubt there would be snakes this time of the morning.

They all sat there staring at the boarded up mine, knowing there were women in there who had met a very sudden and horrid death. Lott didn't want to think about it. All he could think about was stopping these two crazy killers and saving that last woman from Montana.

"Stay put for a moment, everyone," Lott said.

He climbed out into the shadows and warm air of the early morning and held his badge up in the air for the cop watching the mine to see. He had no idea where the cop watching this mine was stationed, but he didn't want to take a chance.

"Up here, Detective Lott," a voice said. "I got the heads-up you were coming."

Lott turned to look up through some rocks as a man in a light jacket stood and waved. He had to be a good hundred paces up through the rocks. No chance the guy could have been seen up there if West and her partner had come here.

Lott could only imagine how hot it got up there during the prime of the day.

"We're here to see if this thing was bugged," Lott said.

"Anything I can do, just shout," the cop said.

"Thanks!" Lott said. "The way things are moving, I doubt you'll be here much longer."

"Good to hear," the cop said.

Lott turned and nodded that the rest could get out.

Annie and Julia got out and waved to the cop on the hill.

Doc moved around and opened up the back of the SUV.

Fleet climbed out slowly, looking around before moving to the back of the SUV with Doc and opening up some equipment.

It didn't take him long studying a hand-held device that looked more like an early version of a heavy cell phone before he nodded.

He turned slowly, nodding.

Then he handed another device just like it to Doc. "Go up the road about twenty paces and aim that at the hill above the mine. I'll triangulate the location."

"Is there something here?" Julia asked.

Fleet nodded as Doc headed back up the dirt road twenty paces, then turned and aimed the device at the rocks and dried brush above the mine.

"Twenty paces above the mine and to the right in those rocks," Fleet said, pointing. "There's a camera broadcasting a signal on two minute intervals."

Lott could see exactly where he was pointing. From that spot, the camera could see both the road and the opening of the mine. Lynch and West had watched everything yesterday.

"Can the signal be traced?" Annie asked.

Fleet shook his head.

"So the two women know they have been found," Annie said, her voice low and angry as Fleet motioned for Doc to come back down the road to join them.

"They know," Lott said. "And more than likely they have a very good plan on what to do next."

He was angry, more angry than he wanted to admit even to himself. And now he had no idea how they could ever save that woman from Montana, let alone even find the two women who had killed so many. The two killers had

money, they were smart, and they had a head start.

Even with every federal, state, and local law enforcement officer in the western part of the United States looking for them, Lott had no doubt they wouldn't be spotted.

Fleet put the two devices back in a silver case and shut it.

Silently, they all got back into the SUV.

Lott headed the big Cadillac back toward Las Vegas.

"Now what?" Annie said as Fleet dialed the chief of police's number to tell him the bad news.

Not a one of them had an answer.

CHAPTER TWENTY-TWO

August 15th, 2015
7:00 A.M.
Las Vegas

AS IF THEY all needed comfort food, they headed back to what was turning out to be their meeting headquarters, the café at the Bellagio. Julia rode in silence in the front seat, just doing her best to figure out what to do next.

Annie had called Andor and told him to meet them.

Then, until they reached the area near Las Vegas Boulevard, they continued to ride in silence. Julia could feel the pressure of the anger and the feelings in the car, compounded by the frustration. This group, including her, were not used to having someone beat them.

And at the moment, Lynch and West appeared to have beaten them.

"This is going to explode over every television station and news source in just an hour or so," Annie said. "No point in Chief Beason trying to keep it under wraps now. They might be able to hold most information until later in the afternoon. But no doubt it will be a national firestorm that's going to descend on this city."

"The chief will keep us out of it," Lott said.

"I got my people tracing all of the two women's assets," Fleet said. "Second homes and so on."

"Not worried about us being involved in the media side," Annie said. "I just have no idea how those two women could even think of going underground with this kind of press and manhunt that will happen."

"Let alone with us, and every federal agency," Lott said, "being able to track their every asset and move."

Julia looked at Lott, who was pulling them into the valet parking area of the Bellagio near the café entrance. Around them dozens of cars sat waiting to either be put away or picked up by their owners. All were modern cars like Lott's Cadillac. No telling how many of them were rentals.

A hint of an idea was forming and she let it.

Around her, all the people moved in their own worlds, some with luggage, some just going into the casino. All handing cash to the attendants as a tip to take care of their cars or a thank-you for helping with luggage.

Cash.

Massive numbers of people.

Julia suddenly knew exactly how these two women would escape notice and capture.

Exactly.

Lott put the SUV in park as Julia smiled. "I know how I would escape this in Lynch and West's positions."

Lott's head snapped around to look at her, his wonderful green eyes looking intent.

"I need some real breakfast, though," she said, smiling at him and climbing out of the car.

From the back, Annie laughed.

"Now that's just mean," Doc said, laughing.

They all headed through the warming air into the air conditioning of the Bellagio and to the café. As Julia watched, Lott slipped the attendant a five-dollar bill to take care of the car.

Julia nodded, letting the idea form even more.

Their regular booth was open in the back, so she waited until they were all seated and the hostess had left and then just smiled. "Lynch and West aren't going anywhere."

Lott just shook his head. "West was already out of town."

"She'll come back here," Julia said, becoming more and more sure of her theory the more she thought about it.

"So what do you think West is going to do with the woman from Montana?" Annie asked.

Beside Annie, both Doc and Fleet were looking at Julia intently.

Julia just shrugged. "I honestly don't know. My hope is that West will give the poor woman a little extra drugs, park her in a hotel room, and be long gone before the poor woman wakes up."

"I hope so as well," Lott said. "But I'm not so sure."

"It sounds logical," Julia said, trying to sound more positive than she actually was.

Annie was nodding, but frowning.

"These women only kill inside one carefully arranged method," Julia said, "that patterns what happened to them with their friends in school. We can hope they won't hurt a woman outside of that pattern."

"Let's just hope like hell they don't have the pattern set up somewhere else," Lott said.

That caused silence and nods from everyone.

"So why do you think they would come back here?" Doc asked.

"This is their home," Julia said.

"They have no other homes or property in this city or even close," Fleet said. "Under any name or corporation cover that is linked to them."

"They don't need a home or anything else," Julia said. She pointed around the casino and then up trying to indicate the massive hotel that rose above them. "They just need new looks, some basic fake id, and cash."

Lott nodded, reaching over and taking Julia's hand. "They're here. You're right."

"I know I'm right," Julia said. "But now how do we find them? And even if we can't convict them, we can put them under wraps and stop more deaths."

And with that, the sounds of the casino and the early morning restaurant washed back in over them, filling the silence at the table.

And outside the restaurant, a steady stream of tourists poured into the building.

CHAPTER TWENTY-THREE

August 15th, 2015
7:00 A.M.
Las Vegas

LOTT SCOOTED OVER closer to Julia in the booth as Andor joined them a minute before the waitress came back to take their breakfast order.

"It's a flat madhouse at headquarters right now," Andor said. "FBI, state, and a dozen other police forces from around the area are meeting with the chief. So damn crowded, everyone is shouting to just have the person next to them hear what they are saying."

Lott shuddered. He had only seen headquarters like that once before and he never wanted to be there again when that happened.

"What about the bodies?" Julia asked.

Lott nodded. That was his first thought as well.

"They have men guarding at all sites now, mostly to keep the press away. They are waiting for help from Los Angeles and the FBI before they start taking out the bodies and processing the scenes. They are going to set up a refrigerated warehouse near headquarters for a morgue for the bodies."

Lott didn't even want to imagine what that morgue would look like with so many bodies.

"What about the families?" Annie asked.

"The families are going to be staying at different downtown hotels and I think they have one ballroom in one hotel for only family and another ballroom in another hotel for the press. They won't start being notified until later, though."

Lott was impressed. In just a couple of hours the entire mess was being organized.

"The jerky shops?" Doc asked.

"Shut down, and teams are searching Lynch and West's home and offices and other properties," Andor said.

Doc nodded and Lott was very glad at that moment he had never developed a habit of eating jerky. He just hoped that human jerky could be found because that would tie the two women into the murders solidly and be the evidence they needed.

"So what do we have going on here?" Andor asked, glancing around. "Not a soul at headquarters is going to be thinking of how to capture Lynch and West. Too damn busy trying to wrestle this monster we dumped on them. They are going to leave the capture part up to the FBI and even the FBI is too damn busy with this many bodies."

"Julia thinks Lynch and West will come back here," Lott said. "And I agree."

Andor looked puzzled. "Why would they do that?"

"This is a city of cash," Julia said.

"Impossible to trace and not unusual," Fleet said.

"And thousands and thousands of nice suites," Doc said, nodding.

"So you think they are going to hide right here in plain sight?" Andor asked.

"I do," Julia said. "Change their hair color, get fake IDs, have a lot of cash in bank accounts under various false names, and stay at nice suites. They have had a long time to set it up, so I am sure they are very, very prepared."

Lott could only agree with that as well. The more he thought about Julia's idea, the more he liked it. But something

about it seemed wrong and damned if he could put his finger on it.

"So any ideas how West got back into town?" Andor asked after the waitress brought the first parts of their breakfasts.

Lott had ordered two eggs, a waffle, and some bacon, which smelled wonderful. Not at all his normal breakfast of cereal and coffee, but this morning was far from a normal morning.

"Just as I am sure the panel van is in a storage locker somewhere up north," Lott said, "I'm betting they had other cars that they had bought with cash and registered under a fake name and had stored in various places along West's normal routes."

Andor and Julia both nodded.

"So it would be easy for them to get back here, and no one would expect them to return," Doc said, nodding. "Logical play. And damn near impossible to find and trace."

"And since Lynch and West had a day's notice that the mine had been found," Annie said, "more than enough time."

Lott hated the idea that the two killers were more than likely holed up in a nice room watching the firestorm break over the news. Maybe in this very hotel.

But Lott had no idea at all how to find them. Las Vegas was a huge city and the two women could look so different, without major facial recognition software, they would never be recognized.

Then suddenly Lott realized what he had been thinking.

He turned to Doc and Fleet. "The security systems of these casinos have facial recognition, don't they?"

"They do," Doc said, smiling. "It's not perfect and it can be fooled, but it will see through an easy disguise."

Beside him Annie was almost bouncing.

"We need to get access to the casino's security systems," Fleet said, grabbing his phone.

Lott didn't want to know how Fleet planned to do that. Casino security systems were more protected than any bank by a long, long ways.

"Would Lynch and West be that stupid?" Julia asked. "They would know about that software as well."

"It's worth a shot," Doc said. "A fake nose or a change in eyebrows and cheek bones made to look higher would fool the system. But still worth the shot."

"It is," Lott said. Then before Fleet could start talking, Lott said to Fleet. "Set the search to find women of Lynch's and West's age who can't be recognized due to one factor or another."

Fleet nodded and turned slightly to give instructions to his computer people while Lott dug into his waffle.

Maybe, just maybe, they might get lucky.

He doubted it would be that easy. And so far, they hadn't caught much of a break on this case.

Luck was going to have nothing to do with capturing those two murdering women. It was going to take some skill and planning and a bunch of work, of that he had no doubt.

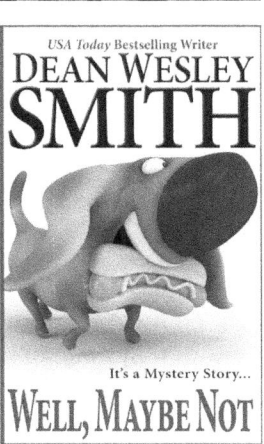

Some Classic Dean Wesley Smith Stories
Available at your favorite booksellers.

PART FOUR
All-In Call

CHAPTER TWENTY-FOUR

August 15th, 2015
9:00 A.M.
Las Vegas

EVEN THOUGH THEY had just had breakfast, Lott and Julia stopped for a bucket of KFC on the way back to Lott's home. The plan was to go down to the poker room and watch the television coverage break. The two of them just couldn't think of anything else to do at the moment.

And for Lott, feeling helpless and useless was something he didn't much like at all.

Doc and Annie and Fleet had all headed off to their Las Vegas corporate office to help coordinate the casino's facial recognition search. Doc and Fleet were pulling in a lot of favors to have the casinos do this for them, but at this moment, every casino in town was all on the same side.

Finding this many kidnapped dead women around the town was bad for business and this needed to be put to rest quickly.

Very quickly. Because it was very, very bad for tourism.

Andor had headed back for headquarters, to, as he said, "stick his nose into places it didn't belong."

Lott had no doubt that if anyone in that madhouse could come up with information, it would be Andor.

Lott poured him and Julia a glass of iced tea and they headed downstairs, leaving the bucket of chicken in the fridge.

The custom-made poker table sat to the left of the stairs with a five-bulb light fixture made of wood over it. When that fixture was on, even the oldest of eyes could see cards clearly and read old police files.

A polished oak bar ran down the left wall with black-and-white pictures of old poker masters on the wall behind it, plus a few stacks of different types of glasses and a row of bottles of premium bourbon, scotch, and liquor, most of which had never been opened.

The bar looked impressive, but most of the Cold Poker Gang didn't drink that much, if at all. Lott figured it was too many years on the force watching what booze did to people sort of cut the enjoyment.

Five file folders of varied colors sat on one end of the bar. Those were the cold cases the gang hadn't figured out a way to close yet. Lott sure hoped this ugly mess wouldn't end up on the end of the bar.

A large leather couch filled the wall beyond the bar and two large recliners on either side of it, with an oak coffee table that matched the bar in front of the couch. A large screen television with complete surround sound filled the right wall facing the couch.

Lott flat loved this room, more than any room in the house. It felt totally comfortable and was all his. He had brought nothing of his wife Carol down here. He was so glad that Annie had pushed him to remodel this basement into this wonderful space.

And not only had the Cold Poker Gang met down here for the last couple of years, but Lott and Julia had spent many a wonderful evening on the couch watching movies.

Lott turned on the television to a local channel and a woman news reporter looking young and slightly panicked was talking, going on about a massive breaking murder story.

Lott glanced at his watch. It surprised him when he realized it was still only a little after nine in the morning. It had already seemed like a long day. No wonder the woman on the screen looked panicked. She wasn't the main news anchor.

He and Julia sat on the couch, sipping iced tea and listening until the woman started to repeat herself. Then Lott muted the television sound.

"Nothing until a press conference at one in the afternoon," Julia said, nodding. "Makes sense. The chief and the other agencies need to get this all under control before they brief the public."

Lott could only nod.

They sat there in silence for a short time, both half-staring at the "Breaking News" banner over the poor young announcer's head. He didn't envy the chief's job of trying to explain what filled the old mines around Las Vegas.

Then Julia turned to Lott. "You think I'm right about the women being here?"

"I do," Lott said.

And he did. But again that nagging feeling came up that they were missing something and damned if he could figure out what.

"So let's back up and see if we can figure out when they started to plan this escape," Julia said. "Maybe then we can get a hint as to the plan."

"I know exactly when," Lott said. "When Andor and I found that mine fifteen years ago. We must have scared them to death."

"So they have had fifteen years to plan this exactly," Julia said, sounding as dejected as Lott felt.

"All this time to plan disguises," Lott said, "get fake names, stash away more money than I want to think about under those fake names."

Nothing at all Julia could say to that, so she said nothing.

They sat in silence, watching the poor reporter cut to different reporters around town, clearly not getting any kind of information.

All Lott could think about was the victims.

So many victims.

If somehow he and Andor could have broken this case fifteen years ago, it would have saved so many lives.

Suddenly, Lott turned to Julia. "Did anyone say anything about the woman from Montana? Missy Andrews? Has she been found yet?"

Julia shook her head. Then she quickly pulled out her phone and called Annie.

Lott could hear his daughter's distinctive voice come over Julia's phone.

"Any recovery yet of the woman from Montana?" Julia asked.

"I'll have Fleet do a search of police records and get back to you," Annie said and hung up.

Julia clicked off her phone and put it on the coffee table in front of her. "You think I'm wrong about the woman being left and not killed?"

Lott shook his head. "Honestly, I don't think you are wrong."

He didn't like at all what he was thinking.

"But…?" Julia asked.

Lott took a deep breath and looked into the eyes of the woman he had come to love.

"Andor and I made the assumption that us finding the mine fifteen years ago might have stopped the killer or killers. We could never catch any lead or even a hint that they continued."

Julia nodded, her face now pale. "You think these two might just continue on?"

Suddenly Lott understood what had been nagging at him.

"What happens if they took turns?"

CHAPTER TWENTY-FIVE

August 15th, 2015
9:45 A.M.
Las Vegas

JULIA JUST LOOKED at Lott, the odd question not making any sense at all.

"Took turns?" she asked.

He nodded, clearly not happy. "We know that West took a leave of absence every month for a week."

Julia nodded.

"What if Lynch did the same thing on a different week?"

Julia felt she might just be sick. In all her years of working as a detective, she had never imagined anything like this even being possible, let alone for this many years in a row.

"If Andor and I spooked Lynch and West fifteen years ago," Lott said, "what happens if they set up their cover identities then and a parallel operation under one of those cover identities? So Lynch could have some fun as well."

"I hope you are wrong," Julia said, grabbing her phone from the coffee table.

"I hope like hell I am as well," Lott said, sitting back to stare at the poor reporter on the screen doing the best she could with no information.

Julia dialed Annie and quickly put the phone on speaker.

Annie picked up the phone and said simply, "The woman from Montana has not yet been found."

Julia glanced at Lott, who was nodding that he had heard.

"You father has come up with a horrid theory," Julia said. "And I need you and Doc and Fleet to disprove it."

"Go ahead," Annie said, clearly hesitant.

"Your father thinks that when he and Andor found the mine fifteen years ago, they spooked Lynch and West into setting up a parallel system under fake names. Fake everything. And Lynch went out every two weeks to get a victim just as West did."

"Oh, shit," Annie said.

"Search the region for missing women with different hair color," Lott said. "Maybe Lynch had a crush on another girl on that bus. Clearly West was into black hair and had a crush on one of the two girls with black hair who died on the bus. Lynch might have been into a blonde or redhead or brunette."

"Got it," Annie said.

"Prove me wrong," Lott said. "Please?"

"We're going to do our best," Annie said and clicked off the phone.

Julia put the phone down between them on the couch.

"You don't think you are wrong, do you?" Julia asked, looking at Lott, a man she had grown to love and admire over the last year. He was one of the smartest people she knew when it came to putting together crime pieces.

"I hope I am wrong," Lott said. "But if I am right, where would they hide even more bodies?"

"Everything comes back to old mines," Julia said.

"Or old school busses," Lott said, holding up a second finger. "What happens if Lynch is putting her victims, if there are any, in old school busses?"

"Oh, no," Julia said, her heart racing. She knew instantly Lott might be right. And all she could do was sit there and be silent and hope like hell he was wrong.

After what seemed like an eternity of silence, the phone rang, jarring her from horrid and sick thoughts of women being baked alive in school busses. She nodded to Lott and reached down and hit the speaker button.

"Got us both here," Julia said.

"A fourth friend that ran with Lynch and West and the black-haired girl when they were in school was named Cynthia Peters," Annie said. "She had blonde hair, kept her hair long, and she also died on the bus."

Julia didn't like at all where this was going.

Beside her on the couch, Lott was just shaking his head.

Annie went on. "Fleet dropped everything and did a preliminary search of the western states through all the missing person databases, same as he did before, and again he and his people found almost three hundred missing women that matched that very general description of long blonde hair and age range that have gone missing in the last fifteen years. There were almost none before that."

"Shit," Lott said softly. "Just shit, shit, shit."

Annie ignored him. "We are pulling up records of when Lynch was in town now from her business," Annie said. "And Fleet is going to start a search of more mines in the area."

"Tell him not to bother," Lott said.

"Why?" Annie asked. Then she said, "Hang on, let me put Fleet on speaker."

"No need for more mine searches because I'm betting we need to look for

a bus graveyard," Lott said when it was clear that Fleet could hear him as well.

"I agree," Julia said. "It would need to be very isolated, yet not a huge distance from Las Vegas. In the desert and the heat, yet well protected."

She didn't like at all what she was thinking, but now that she knew it was possible, and that many women had gone missing, they had to keep working to disprove it.

"I'll get some satellite images coming to you at once," Fleet said. "And we'll work over them here as well."

"Thanks," Julia said as Annie hung up.

"Can this get any worse?" Lott asked, shaking his head.

Julia didn't know what to say.

Then Lott laughed, but without humor. "You know, I remember Andor and me asking ourselves that very same question fifteen years ago."

CHAPTER TWENTY-SIX

August 15th, 2015
11:00 A.M.
Las Vegas

LOTT HAD CALLED Andor right after hanging up from Annie and said simply, "Get over here. This has gotten worse. We're downstairs. And don't touch the chicken in the fridge when you come in. Trust me, you won't have the stomach for it."

Then he hung up.

Andor had arrived just as the satellite images arrived from Fleet. Annie had told

him that they were digging into where old busses went to be recycled or sold. So far no luck, since it was August and a lot of the school districts' personnel were on vacation.

Each satellite image covered about six square miles of desert and there were hundreds of images, at least.

Lott put the images all on a memory stick and then plugged the stick into his television, hooking up his computer keyboard as well so the big screen worked as a computer screen.

Then he and Julia and Andor all pulled chairs from the poker table over to the big screen so they could get moderately close to it.

"So you want to tell me what the hell we're looking for?" Andor asked, sipping on a bottle of water and patting his neck with a wet towel.

"Bus graveyard," Julia said.

"A what?" Andor asked.

"Your partner here believes Lynch went out every month to get a victim just as West did," Julia said.

"Serious?" Andor asked.

"Over three hundred women with long blonde hair missing since we spooked these two monsters fifteen years ago," Lott said.

"So you think they set up their back-up and escape plan then?" Andor asked.

"I'm guessing that's exactly what happened," Lott said, glancing at the white face of his partner.

"So we're looking for a bus graveyard in the desert," Julia said, "well-protected and more than likely hidden from normal view."

"Think the busses will be buried?"

"No," Lott said. He just knew they wouldn't be. Again, these women were recreating in a very sick fashion that bus accident over and over and over. Lynch on the bus side, West on the mine side.

"Before we start into this," Julia said, "Any news from headquarters?"

Andor shook his head. "Nothing but the fact that none of the jerky in any of the Lynch shops was made of human flesh."

That jarred Lott. He had expected them to find some, at least behind the counter in some special reserve.

"So where did all that human flesh go?" Julia asked.

Lott just shook his head. "We're missing something there as well."

"We're missing an entire case," Andor said. "We got bodies, but not one lick of evidence. Nothing, and that's driving the chief and the fine people from the FBI nuts."

"Nothing?" Julia said.

"Nothing," Andor said, clearly angry. "Even if we caught these two women, they couldn't be charged with anything. They own mines. So what? West takes a vacation every month? So what? The murders pattern some tragic deaths in their own pasts. So what? No evidence, not a lick of proof so far."

"Is the chief even going to mention them as persons of interest?" Julia asked.

"And get sued from here to Canada and back?" Andor asked. "Their lawyers are already fighting every search warrant. So not a chance."

Lott agreed completely. He had hoped that the human jerky would be the real link. Maybe fifteen years ago, it might have been. But fifteen years ago, he and Lott put these two monsters on notice that they might get caught and the monsters learned.

"So we find their mistake," Lott said, pointing to the screen.

They all turned to stare at the image of the Nevada desert taken from a satellite shot far overhead. The date on the image said it was taken five days before. Newer than Lott would have expected.

On the big screen, they could see almost each individual sagebrush. A large faded-yellow school bus was going to jump off the image like a bad pimple on clear skin.

Lott quickly got them through forty of the images when they found it. Sixty or more school busses filled a corner of the image, most faded to almost white, many parked within feet of each other in rows. A single dirt road led into the compound that was surrounded by what looked like a very high fence.

Julia grabbed the phone and called Annie as Lott leaned in closer, studying the area around the busses. It appeared to be in a shallow rock valley with walls on three sides. It would be impossible to see from any distance at all.

"We found it," Julia said, putting the phone on speaker again so Lott and Andor could hear.

Julia quickly gave the picture image number.

"Tell Fleet to tread lightly with the computer searches on this property," Lott said. "Expect the two killers to have high level warning systems on any search of this property."

"Good thinking, Dad," Annie said. Then, from the sounds of it, she turned slightly away from the phone. "Did you get that, Fleet?"

"Got it," Fleet said from the background. "They will never know anyone looked, I promise. Give me just one minute, so hold on."

Lott went back to studying the images of the busses, wishing he could fly in low like Google images did and see what was in those busses. He had a hunch he would see it much closer soon enough.

"Wampler Recyling Inc. owns the property," Fleet said.

Lott snapped around and looked at Julia, whose eyes were wide.

"Careful, real careful," Lott said. "But can you get us images of Wampler?"

"Why is that name ringing a bell?" Annie asked.

"Kirk Wampler was the kid who survived the bus tragedy and then was killed by a bus," Julia said.

"These two sickos sure have a sense of irony," Andor said.

"Oh, shit," Annie said.

"We are being very careful," Fleet said. "My people have gone to what we call Def-Con Five, meaning any hint of a search could explode everything."

Lott shook his head. There would be no way in hell they could solve some of these cases without Doc and Fleet and Annie and all the power they wielded with their vast money and expert teams.

"You were right," Fleet said. "My team is telling me that very sophisticated search alarms were set on this site. We triggered none of them."

"Good work," Julia said.

Lott made himself take a deep breath.

"Kirk Wampler is the founder of the company," Fleet said after a moment. "It was started in 2001 and has a dozen business locations around the area specializing in metal repurposing and recycling. I am sending an image of Kirk Wampler to all three of you now."

Julia quickly took her iPad and clicked it on, then got her e-mail, opening the image.

The image was of Lynch, hair very short, large fake eyebrows, wearing a three-piece suit. She disguised perfectly as a man.

"Let me guess," Lott said. "Wampler is married."

"In 2001," Fleet said, "to Cynthia Peters. Picture on the way."

Lott didn't need to see the picture. He had no doubt it would be West.

CHAPTER TWENTY-SEVEN

August 15th, 2015
11:30 A.M.
Las Vegas

JULIA SAT STARING at the image of the bus graveyard on the screen. She didn't want to even try to imagine what the inside of fourteen or so of those busses would be like. She had no intention of going and looking. She needed to sleep again at some point and her imagination was already enough to keep her awake for more nights than she wanted to think about.

She turned to Lott and Andor, who both seemed to be lost in thought. Andor was just staring at his feet and Lott was doing the same thing she had been doing, just staring at the image of the bus graveyard.

"We need some chicken," she said, standing and turning for the stairs, her phone and iPad in her hand. "And then we need to figure out proof to stop these killers before that woman from Montana becomes the first victim sitting against the wall in another mine."

She headed up the stairs taking them two at a time to try to get some blood flowing back to her shocked brain.

She was putting out paper plates and napkins when both Lott and Andor joined her. Lott had her iced tea glass in his hand and refilled hers and his as Andor pulled out the new bucket of chicken and grabbed himself another bottle of water.

The smell of the chicken filled the kitchen almost instantly. No one said a word until they were all seated and had taken a few bites of the still slightly-warm chicken. To Julia, the taste overcame her desire to never eat again, and actually calmed her some. She figured that was because KFC was part of her normal life, not this insane case.

After another bite, she pulled a spiral notebook from the counter behind her and opened it to a clean page. It was a notebook Lott used for groceries and other items he needed to pick up around town.

"So we are going to make a list," she said. "Of all the things we don't yet know."

"I'd suggest you write the word 'everything' and be done with it," Andor said, wiping chicken grease off his fingers. "But I don't suppose that would help much."

Julia ignored him and said, "Montana woman. Missy Andrews. She's still more than likely alive and out there."

"We can hope," Andor said.

She wrote "Montana Woman" as #1 on the list and circled it.

"Where were all these women baked?" Lott asked.

She wrote that down.

"Why take the meat?" Andor asked.

She wrote that down as well.

"Can we trace the school clothes and where they were bought?" Lott asked. "A lot of years of buying clothes."

Julia doubted that would be possible, but she wrote it down anyway. But it caused her to think of something else as Lott and Andor sat staring at their chicken.

"They are using two names now from the bus tragedy," Julia said. "Are they using others?"

"Oh, shit!" Andor said, standing and moving to where they had left the folder with the information and names from the bus tragedy.

Julia grabbed the phone and called Annie, who answered almost at once.

"You have the file on the bus tragedy and the victims?" Julia asked.

Across the table, Andor was flipping through the old file and Lott was staring at her, nodding.

"We got them all," Annie said.

"We're betting Lynch and West are using all the names in one way or another that were associated with that bus tragedy, including the teacher," Julia said. "Can you have Fleet and his people do the super-careful searches on all the names?"

"Damn, great idea," Annie said. "We should have thought of that. Back with you shortly." She hung up.

Julia put the phone down beside the list, trying to decide if she wanted to try to eat another piece of chicken.

Lott was nodding. "Really good idea."

"I have an even sicker idea," Andor said.

Julia wasn't sure she could imagine a sicker idea in this case.

Andor had taken the file folder from the case 15 years ago and was looking at an autopsy photograph of one of the women.

Julia caught a glance at the picture and instantly looked away. Nothing about a baked and carved up human body that was appealing.

Andor looked up from the file at both of them and closed the folder over the autopsy photographs. He seemed to have a haunted look in his eyes. Julia had never seen Andor look that way before.

He then pointed to the folder of the bus tragedy victims.

"I think we need to quietly dig up a few of these graves," he said.

Julia just stared at Andor, as did Lott. For the life of her she couldn't imagine why they would need to do that, or what it would help.

Finally Lott asked bluntly, "And why would we do that?"

"When I asked about why they take the meat," Andor said, "it dinged me. We have always assumed they took it for eating, standing jokes around headquarters and all. But what happens if that assumption has been flat wrong for all these years."

"What else are you thinking they would take it for?" Julia asked, just about as puzzled as she had been in a long time.

"They take the women's butts, top back of their legs, and underwear," Andor said, pointing to the autopsy file.

Lott and Julia both nodded.

Then she understood where Andor was going.

Silence filled the kitchen like a heavy weight. All Julia could do was blink as she imagined a woman's butt, legs, and underwear mounted on some sort of surface. And over a hundred of them stretching off into the distance.

Nightmare didn't begin to describe that image.

The chicken she had eaten now threatened to make a second showing.

Lott shoved his plate away and stood, clearly angry. He paced over to the counter, then came back.

Julia didn't look up at him. She was afraid to. It was everything she could do to clear the image and keep her lunch down.

"You thinking they went back and got trophies from their first kills?" Lott asked Andor.

Andor nodded.

Lott again paced over to the counter and then came back.

"When you bake a human like that," Lott said, "As I discovered with my long bake of a roast, the flesh becomes easier to cut precisely with very sharp knives."

"Exactly," Andor said. "They could then add moisture back into the skin and then coat it with an epoxy or something else like is done with those parts of human bodies in museums."

Lott nodded. "We have seen sicker trophies taken by killers."

Julia had as well, but not on this scale.

"Looks like both women have a thing for women's butts," Andor said, shaking his head.

"Not both women," Julia said, trying her best to not imagine what they might find in those busses. "We haven't seen the busses. We don't know which part Lynch is cutting off to use as a trophy."

Again the silence just slammed into the kitchen like a hammer, pounding at a headache that was threatening Julia. She forced herself to take long, deep breaths and move her shoulders around and the headache faded back a little. She doubted it would leave until this was all over.

Finally, Lott said, "you are right, we need to dig up a few graves."

At that moment the phone rang.

"It's Annie," Julia said, picking up her phone. "Let's hope we don't have to, because now, if we find their trophy room, we can stop these two cold. We will have the evidence."

Now Available
from all your favorite booksellers
in trade paper and electronic editions.

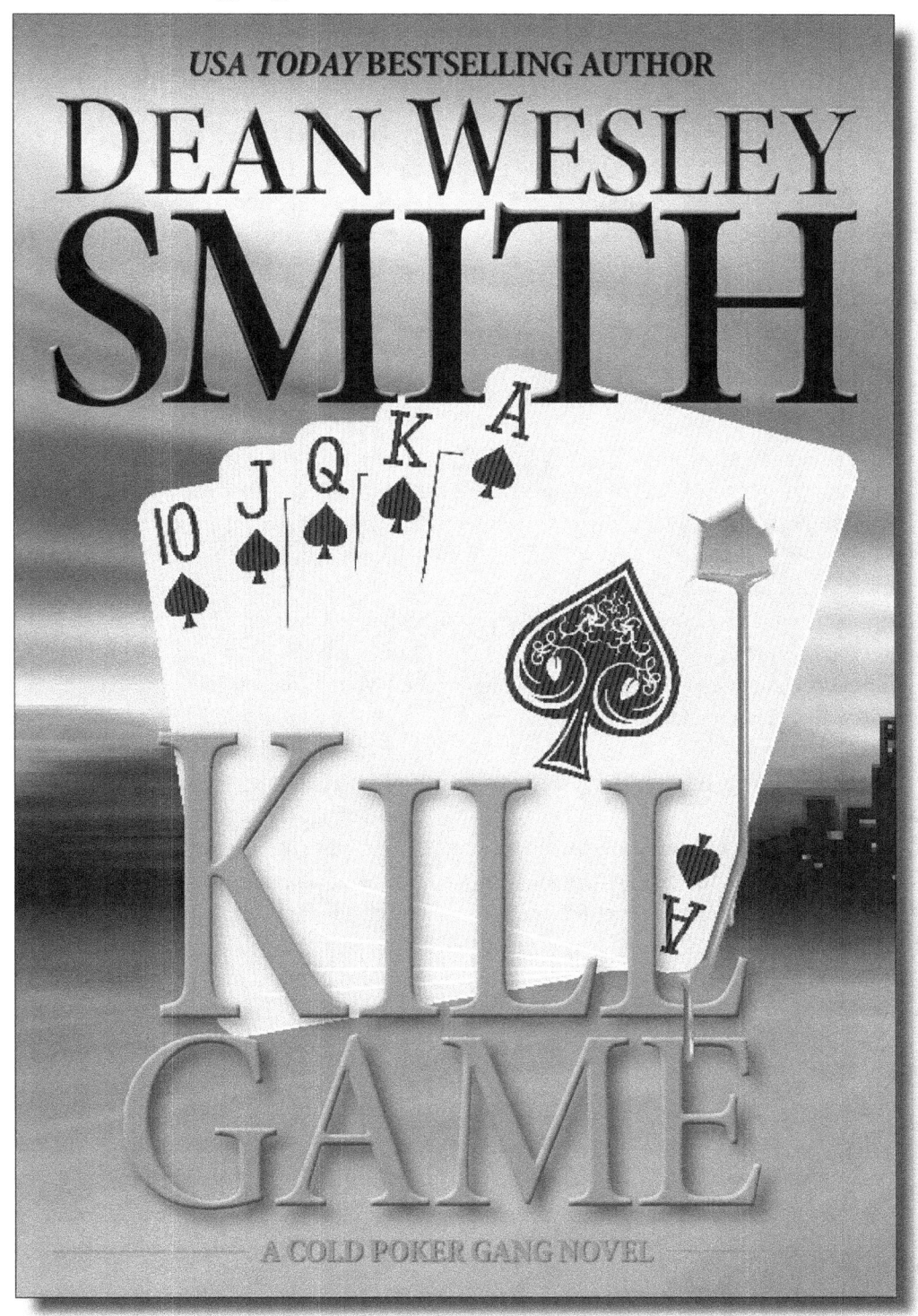

CHAPTER TWENTY-EIGHT

August 15th, 2015
12:30 P.M.
Las Vegas

LOTT LISTENED OVER the speakerphone and was stunned when Annie and Fleet told them that not only were a few of the names from the bus tragedy being used, but that all of them were active. Including the teacher's name.

"At first glance," Fleet said, "the names all have property and accounts and cash in six western states. All of it started a couple of years after Kirk died. We are digging carefully to not set off any alarms and will be back with you with results in an hour."

"Can you also check in those accounts if one of them bought a lot of clear epoxy-like material," Lott had said.

"The stuff used to seal human flesh like in the museum shows of exposed human skin and muscles," Andor said.

"Something you haven't told us yet?" Annie asked.

"Just see if you can find any reference to that," Lott said, not really wanting to explain any more to his daughter at this point. "Or any kind of taxidermy products that could be used to preserve human muscle and skin."

"Oh, shit," Annie said. "You are kidding."

"A theory is all," Julia said.

"I may never eat again," Fleet said.

Annie hung up.

"So we have another thing to add to our list," Julia said. "Where would they display that many trophies?"

Lott watched as she added that to their list of questions. Then she looked up. "What other details are we missing? Let's start with the bus crash because it seems everything else does."

"Did these two have other friends in school at the time of the accident?" Andor asked.

Lott nodded. Good question and he watched as Julia wrote it down.

They sat there for a short time in silence, thinking. Then Lott realized the one large thing they were missing.

"The school itself," Lott said. "Is it still in operation and if not, who owns it now?"

"Great question," Julia said, and wrote that down as well.

"How about we take a drive past it," Andor said. "I got the address and I need to move around some to let this chicken find a place a little lower than my throat."

Lott could only agree to that.

He grabbed all three of them fresh bottles of water as Julia put the tub of chicken back into the fridge and tossed the paper plates into the garbage.

Andor took a dishtowel, soaked it in cold water, and put it over his neck. Then they headed out the back door and into the afternoon August heat.

It was like stepping into a blast furnace, but at the moment, just the change felt good as far as Lott was concerned. It cleared his mind.

He climbed into his Cadillac SUV and got it started, letting the air-conditioning run at full blast.

Andor got into the back seat and Julia climbed into the passenger seat. She had her phone and his grocery notebook. After this, Lott had no doubt he was going to need a new notebook.

Lott worked his way through traffic out the old Boulder Highway. The ten-minute drive was done in silence. They all needed a change of scenery more than anything else at this point.

From the backseat, Andor said, "Turn right off the highway up here. Three blocks down. If these two killers own this place as well, they will have it monitored, so stay back and don't stop."

"Good thinking," Lott said. He had no doubt that if the school was involved, they would have it monitored.

The neighborhood had long ago seen better days. Most of the homes were built in the 1960s and many of them looked like they hadn't had a coat of paint since they were built. Standard trash neighborhood with junked cars in front yards and no hint at all of landscaping besides rows of tires melting in the sun.

"Go right! Quick," Julia shouted.

Without question, Lott swung the big white SUV down the street to the right. He had just caught a glimpse of the old school ahead of them. It was surrounded by two layers of tall fence with many "No Trespassing" signs. From what he could see, it looked like it had once been under construction, but that had long ago stopped.

The school must have been something nice back in the 1950s. Brick, with tall windows and a wide porch out front. It seemed to be two stories tall and had a bell tower of some sort. No wonder someone had wanted to fix it up at one point.

He had no idea what Julia had seen, but there had been something that had alerted her.

"Why right?" Andor asked just a second before Lott did.

"Stop here, on the side of the street," Julia said. "See the home beside the old school."

Lott nodded. From where they were parked in front of a patch of dirt and weeds, he could barely see the home she mentioned. It looked slightly more kept up than many in this area.

"I am sure I saw Kirk Wampler, otherwise known as Lynch, get in that dark

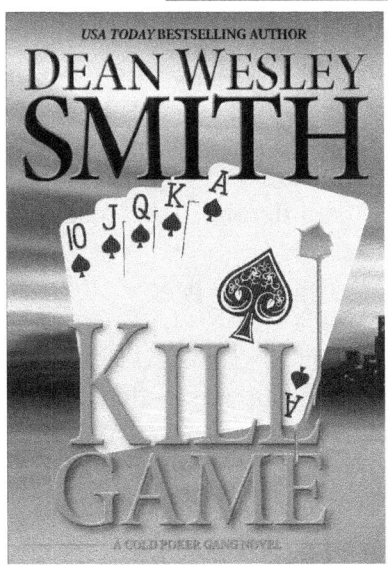

sedan beside the house. And West got in the passenger seat."

"Oh, shit," Andor said.

At that point, the sedan backed out of the driveway slowly, then turned away from them and vanished along the street that ran in front of the old school and parallel to the one they were on.

Julia was instantly on the phone.

Damn Lott hoped she was right. If so, this would be the first piece of luck they had had in this case in fifteen years.

It was about damn time they had some luck.

Lott swung the big SUV around and headed parallel along the street they had seen the sedan go down. He knew that both of these streets dead-ended in a few blocks into a freeway, so the sedan would have to turn toward them to get to the Old Boulder Highway.

After a block, Lott pulled over in front of one of the only houses in the neighborhood that looked kept up. He didn't want them to see him moving.

Just as he did, the sedan went past in front of them, headed for the highway.

Lott eased back into the street.

"Annie, we have an emergency," Julia said, making sure the phone was on speaker. "I think I just saw Lynch and West."

"They are stopped," Lott said, "waiting to turn toward town on the Old Boulder Highway two blocks away from us."

"They are in a dark, late model Chevy sedan," Andor said. "Four-door, can't spot the license plate."

"Can you track them in case we lose them?"

"Fleet?" Annie shouted away from the phone.

"Already on it," Fleet shouted back from what must have been across the office.

Lott just shook his head. Again, no chance they could solve any of this without Doc and Annie and Fleet doing their computer magic.

The sedan turned onto the highway in traffic and headed into town.

Lott got to the intersection and then into traffic quickly, making one car brake suddenly, but at least he was only a dozen cars behind the sedan.

"Can you track us with my phone's location?" Julia asked. "The sedan is only a dozen cars ahead of us in the same lane."

"I got them," Fleet said. "Two people in the car. I'm following them on traffic cams, so you can back off."

Lott let himself take a deep breath and move over a lane.

The sedan made it through a stoplight while they got held up, but Fleet told them not to worry.

After a mile or so of silence, Fleet said, "The car is registered to Kirk Wampler. You hit it on the head. And I know exactly where they are going."

"You're kidding," Julia asked.

"We just got into one of their bank accounts," Fleet said. "Don't ask how. But twice a week they go for a late lunch at the Golden Nugget Buffet. They haven't missed in years."

"So murderers have date nights," Andor said.

"So you can follow them?" Lott asked.

"Without an issue," Fleet said. "Doc and Annie are already out the door headed to the Golden Nugget to alert the security there and let me get plugged into the casino security systems and cameras."

"Don't let them know they are being watched," Lott said.

"No one will get close to them," Fleet said, "and we will make sure any signal trying to reach them from any of their alarms will be shut down completely while they are in there."

"Good," Lott said, "because we're going back to the school."

"School?" Fleet asked.

"The Saint Mary's Girl's School where all this started," Lott said, getting the big white Cadillac turned off the highway and then around and on the highway headed back to the school. "They came from a home beside the old school. I'm betting there is a reason for that."

"We'll keep you on the line," Julia said to Fleet.

They didn't have a lot of time. But they had some.

And Lott had a hunch that the woman from Montana didn't have much time left at all.

PART FIVE
Calling Dead

CHAPTER TWENTY-NINE

August 15th, 2015
1:15 P.M.
Las Vegas

JULIA HAD BEEN stunned for a moment when she saw Lynch dressed as Wampler come out of that home and get into the sedan. Luckily she reacted as fast as she did. Lott's Cadillac was certainly not a car normally seen in this neighborhood, so they would have stuck out and been spotted.

Andor leaned forward between the two front bucket seats as Lott managed to get them headed back toward the school.

"You thinking what I'm thinking?" Andor asked. "Missy Andrews from Montana is being baked as we speak?"

"I am," Lott said.

"Shit," Fleet said over the phone that Julia held up between the three of them.

Julia just shook her head. If that was the case, the woman might already be dead. Or nearly dead.

"I'll get us an emergency search warrant," Andor said. "We play this by the book if we can."

"Agreed," Lott said. "But we go in warrant or not."

Andor nodded and was on the phone a moment later. He simply said his name, then asked for the chief, and less than ten seconds later was connected with the chief. Julia was impressed, considering the firestorm that must be going on at headquarters.

"Chief," Andor said, "We have Lynch and West under surveillance and we think the Montana woman is in immediate danger. We need an emergency warrant. Fast as you can get it."

Julia watched as Lott got parked in front of the old school and Andor gave the address to the chief.

"Fleet," Lott said, "we need to know the instant Lynch and West are blocked from any reception of an alarm."

"A moment," Fleet said.

Julia forced herself to take a deep breath and try to stay calm as each second ticked away in silence.

The old brick school clearly had been special in its day, but now, with two layers of ten-foot tall wire fence around it and construction half done on a bunch of stuff, the school looked just tired. More like an old prison building than anything else. The tall windows had long since been boarded up and the front door was also boarded over.

Julia was surprised that it wasn't bigger. It didn't look much larger than the size of a regular church. But it was two stories tall and the brick bell tower was a bell tower, not a steeple. From what she could tell, the bell was long gone.

"My people just found that Lynch and West," Fleet said on speaker on her phone, "under the Wampler name, own the old school as well, under another shell company that was buried damn deep. And they own three of the homes around the old school."

"Where are they now?" Julia asked. "We're about to go into the school and we don't want to alert them."

"You are clear," Fleet said. "They are just pulling into the valet parking at the Rush Tower side of the Golden Nugget. They are shut down for any incoming messages. Annie and Doc have me linked into all the casino's security cameras and they are standing by in security as well."

"Completely?" Julia asked.

"Completely," Fleet said. "No one in the casino area is going to get a phone call on a cell phone while those two are in there."

Julia glanced at Lott who nodded. "Let's go."

She nodded. They now could go into the school without setting off alarms that would send Lynch and West fleeing.

"We'll let you know what we find in just a few minutes, Chief," Andor said from behind her. "Stay tuned and stall that press conference just a few more minutes."

He clicked off his phone. "Got the warrant."

All three of them climbed out into the baking heat.

Julia kept her connection to Fleet on and held her phone out in front of her as Lott and Andor opened the back of the SUV and dug out a couple large pair of wire and bolt cutters and two large crowbars.

Then they started right at the front gate on the fence.

Two minutes of work in the heat and with the hot wire fence and they had the first gate open enough for the three of them to get inside the area between the two fences. It took less than a minute to get the second fence gate open.

Both Lott and Andor were sweating. But Julia knew that if Missy Andrews was inside, time was of the essence.

"Lynch and West just reached the lobby of the buffet," Fleet said.

"Got a floor plan of this old school?" Lott asked.

"I will pull one up and walk you through it," Fleet said. "Door on the east side might be your best bet to get in."

Julia glanced around as both Fleet and Lott shook their heads. "We're going through the front."

Julia watched, holding the phone out in front of her, wishing there was something she could do as the two of them started ripping boards down. It took them less time to expose the old front door than it had to get through the fence.

"Doors rotted," Lott said, staring up at the casing.

Julia could see that as well.

"Let's hope there's nothing solid behind this," Andor said.

Then with a solid kick, the door smashed inward and came away from the frame, twisting into a wall and sending a cloud of dust swirling through the air.

"Watch for nails," Lott said as they three of them went over the debris and inside.

The place smelled musty and old and unused. A wide main hallway led away in front of them, covered in dust and broken trim and doors, illuminated by the bright light from the broken front door only. On the inside, the place looked much bigger than it did from the outside.

Both Andor and Lott had grabbed flashlights and both started carefully down the hallway.

"Fleet," Julia asked, flipping an old light switch without any success. "Is this place pulling any power?"

"Hold on," Fleet said.

They had taken another five steps down the old high-ceilinged hallway before Fleet came back. "It is. Massive amounts, actually. That started ten minutes ago."

"Oven," Julia said. "Damn it!"

"Basement," Lott said.

"Fleet, is there a basement?" Julia asked.

"There is," Fleet said. "Staircase on the right as you come in from the main door. There is an old gym and locker rooms down there."

Andor cut the lock on the old door with his bolt cutters and they went down the old stairs quickly, plunging into darkness that even the two flashlights didn't seem to push back much.

"Still with us, Fleet?" Julia asked.

"Loud and clear," Fleet said.

At the bottom of the stairs there were two doors, both of which looked like they had been used a great deal. Both had high-level security locks on them. Keypad electronic types.

"That door looks like it goes off underground toward the home next door," Lott said.

Julia agreed. "A logical way to get unseen into the old school."

"Let's hope they didn't set any kind of explosive trap on this door," Lott said.

"Too damn late now if they did," Andor said.

Two Seeders Universe Novels
Available at your favorite booksellers.

Julia agreed as both Lott and Andor started banging at the door, smashing anything that would smash.

"That's some noise," Fleet said.

"Breaking into the old gym area, from the looks of it," Annie shouted over the destruction.

Finally, the door frame started to move where it had rotted out along one side. And then a moment later, it fell inward with a smash, sending dust swirling into the big room.

Cool air swept over them as they stepped forward.

A switch on the wall beside the ruined door worked this time as Julia tried it and lights in the old gym came up full and bright.

At first she didn't understand what she was seeing exactly.

Then the details came clear and she covered her mouth and turned away and for the first time in all her years as a detective, she threw up.

And right beside her, Lott did the same thing.

On the phone in Julia's hand, Fleet said softly, "That doesn't sound good."

CHAPTER THIRTY

August 15th, 2015
1:40 P.M.
Las Vegas

LOTT HAD NEVER, not once, lost his lunch over a crime scene. But what faced them in this room was so much more than a crime scene. This was a sick trophy room.

And just the vastness of the death had overwhelmed him.

He managed to clear his mouth by spitting a few times, then eased Julia up from where she was bent over and together they both turned around again.

The scene in front of them was a nightmare that he had no doubt he would ever forget.

On what looked like very narrow twin beds, with sheets, women's butts, partially covered with underwear, and the backs of their legs were posed, two per bed. It looked like the rest of the woman's body was simply covered up under the sheet, so it looked very much like women were laying there, face down, side-by-side on the narrow beds.

That would have been bad enough, but it didn't stop there.

Between each bed were two child mannequins dressed in the black and white schoolgirl uniforms, standing posed as if watching the two partial bodies on the beds. One watched one bed, another watched another bed.

Only each child mannequin had a real woman's head with long blonde hair.

The bus graveyard was going to be full of headless women's bodies. Lynch took their heads as a trophy.

The scene was repeated like a giant dormitory all the way around the outside of the large gym and also had started another row down the middle.

Sick trophies from over three hundred dead women.

"We need to find that oven," Andor said, his breathing heavy, his voice raspy.

"Damn," Julia said, shaking her head.

Lott also snapped back into focusing on what was important. It was as if his mind had just gone from him for a moment and now it was suddenly back. He forced himself to not look into the faces of all the women whose heads were posed on the child mannequin bodies.

A door stood partially open on the other side of the gym and Andor pointed to it.

Lott, with Julia at his side, followed Andor toward the door as fast as they could go, not looking at anything on or beside any of the beds.

"You still with us?" Julia said into the phone she carried.

"Right with you," Fleet said. "All three of us are here on the phone if you need anything at all."

Lott was glad to hear that, but his strongest hope at the moment was that his daughter would never see anything like this.

Once through the door, Julia again flicked on the light and there, in front of them, was what looked like a massive pizza oven.

And it was radiating heat.

Andor moved to the control panel to the right of the big door and shut everything down quickly. Then with a glance at Lott and Julia, he opened the door.

Heat, as if they had stepped back outside into the hot August sun, flooded the small room.

Inside the oven, stretched out nude, was a black-haired woman lying on what looked to be a very think pad of some sort.

Lott had not seen a picture of Missy Andrews, but he was betting that was her.

He grabbed an oven mitt and tossed a second one to Andor, then the two of them rolled the large tray the woman was on out of the oven. Lott wasn't surprised that it came easily.

Julia quickly touched the woman's hot skin searching for a pulse.

"She's still alive. And her heartbeat is strong."

Lott couldn't believe the relief he felt at that instant.

"Fleet," Julia said into her phone. "Get an ambulance headed here at once."

"On the way," Fleet said.

Andor had his phone to his ear as well. "Chief, I need just you, the head of the FBI, and the State Police person in charge to come here at once. Don't let reporters follow you."

Andor listened for a moment. "Postpone it for an hour and then you can announce you have wrapped this all up."

A pause.

"Not kidding," Andor said.

Another pause as Andor listened. Then he said simply, "We found their trophy room and the Montana woman is alive."

"Make it fast," Andor said. Then hung up.

Lott just shook his head, then pointed to the woman on the big oven tray. "We have to get her upstairs and out of here."

Julia nodded. "We can't have some poor ambulance drivers seeing that room out there."

"Agreed," Andor said. "No one deserves to live with that image."

Lott looked around and spotted the ambulance-like gurney tucked to one side of the oven. More than likely Lynch and West had used it to bring their victims in. It was set at the same height as the oven tray.

Lott grabbed the gurney and pulled it so that it was in front of the oven. With Julia keeping the gurney from moving, Lott and Andor lifted the woman, pad and all, onto the gurney.

Then Julia used a light sheet from a table nearby to cover her up a little.

"Back through the nightmare," Andor said.

Lott nodded.

He knew he was going to be living this nightmare for a very long time.

CHAPTER THIRTY-ONE

August 15th, 2015
1:55 P.M.
Las Vegas

JULIA LED THE way back through the gym, focusing on making sure the gurney they were pushing didn't hit anything. The last thing she wanted to do was stop and look at the heads of murder victims and all the parts of bodies from other women.

At the ruined door, Lott and Andor managed to get the gurney over the wood on the floor and to the bottom of the old staircase. It was markedly warmer out in the foyer area, and Julia didn't much like taking a woman clearly overheated out into the Vegas sun and heat, but they had no choice.

Lott lifted one end of the gurney and then put it back down. "We should be able to get this up the stairs if we are careful."

"I'll pull from the top," Julia said.

Andor nodded and he and Lott got around behind the gurney as Julia got up a few stairs.

"Fleet," she said into her phone, "I'm keeping the connection, but putting the phone in my pocket while we try to get this poor woman up these stairs."

"Understood," Fleet said. "Lynch and West just got their first salad course."

Julia put the phone in her front pocket as Andor and Lott nudged the gurney up against the bottom of the old staircase.

"Count of three," Lott said.

"Three," Andor said.

Andor and Lott lifted while Julia pulled up and lifted. Surprisingly the gurney went up the step easily.

"Three," Andor said again.

Another step.

They repeated that as fast as they dared, with Andor and Lott almost holding one end of the gurney up at chest level.

Finally, they had the poor woman and the hospital gurney in the main hallway. They wheeled it quickly toward the front door just as sirens were sounding outside.

They stopped just inside the front door. Lott and Andor were both sweating and breathing hard, but looked as if they would be all right if they got into some cool air and a bottle of water or two.

Julia again checked to see how the woman was doing. Her heart rate was still strong.

"Still doing fine," Julia said.

Lott, breathing hard, and sweating, looked at Julia and nodded and smiled.

Julia was breathing as hard as he was, and she had no doubt her light blouse was stained through sweat and dirty from all the dust. But at this moment, she didn't care. They had managed to rescue this poor woman from two of the worst serial killers in modern times.

And stopping any more killing.

And that was all that mattered.

She pulled the phone from her pocket as Andor went out through the smashed front door and waved as the ambulance pulled up.

"Fleet," Julia asked, taking the phone from her pocket. "You still there?"

"I am," Fleet said. "Are you three all right?"

"We needed a workout today," Lott said.

"And the woman?"

"Still alive," Julia said.

"Great job," Annie said.

"Oh, thank heavens," Fleet said.

Julia could not have agreed more. They had gotten very lucky to be here in time.

Barely in time.

From just outside the front door, Andor turned back to Lott and Julia. "Chief just pulled up as well."

"We give him a ten minute explanation of the bus graveyard and everything Fleet and his people have found," Lott said. "Fleet, you all right with that?"

"I'll put it in a presentable package as supposition and suggestions," Fleet said, "they can research it themselves then so it can go in as evidence."

"Perfect," Lott said.

"So after we tell them everything, what next?" Julia asked.

"We let the chief and his friends go downstairs and lose their lunches," Lott said. "We have a couple at the Golden Nugget I want to join for a late lunch."

"Oh, I'm going to look forward to watching that," Fleet said.

Julia was as well.

At that moment, two men dressed in medical uniforms came in and immediately started working on Missy Andrews.

"She was exposed to high heat and is drugged," Julia said. "So extreme heat stroke measures are in order."

Julia then gave the ambulance men Missy's name and that the police would be contacting her and her family shortly. That she needed to stay away from any press until the police talked with her when she recovered.

Both men nodded.

The chief and two other men in suits picked their way through the rubble as the two from the ambulance changed the woman over to their gurney and headed out into the heat, covering her with a light sheet held up and off her body.

Julia pushed the gurney they had gotten from downstairs off to one side.

"Great job saving her," the chief said, staring after the two ambulance drivers.

"Please keep us out of it," Andor said.

Lott and Julia nodded, and the other two looked puzzled.

Julia didn't do this for credit and she knew that Andor and Lott wanted none either.

The chief turned to the medium-sized man with the blue tie and no hair. "FBI Regional Director Steve Couch."

The man nodded.

"And this is Chief Carl Landers with the State Police," Chief Beason said, indicating a tall, skinny man with hard, dark eyes.

"This is Detectives Lott, Williams, and Rogers," Chief Beason said, finishing the introduction.

Julia noticed that he didn't add the word "retired" to the introduction, which was good because at the moment she felt a long ways from retired.

"Here's what we got, Chief," Andor said. "This morning we started down the idea that Lynch killed just as West did. We discovered that the girl she had a crush on that died in the bus tragedy was named Cynthia Peters. She had long blonde hair at the time."

"West has long blonde hair," the chief said.

All three nodded.

"So we had Doc and Fleet's people do a search for missing women with long blonde hair," Lott said.

"Fleet," Julia said, holding up the phone so that everyone could see it and hear Fleet clearly, "tell them what you found on that search."

"Chief," Fleet said, "We found in a first-pass search the same pattern as the black-haired women. It seems that over the last fifteen years almost two hundred blonde-haired women have gone missing in the western states."

"Oh, shit," FBI Director Couch said.

Julia was glad that Andor pushed on at that point.

"We figured," Andor said, "that if West was hiding the bodies in mines, Lynch had to be hiding the bodies she took in another way."

Before the chief could ask a question, Lott kept the story going. "We then figured out that all the names of the kids in the original bus tragedy were all being used."

"And we had the idea to look for bus graveyards," Julia said, "since that tragedy happened in a bus and these two seemed to be duplicating so much from that tragedy."

The chief and the other two men just nodded. All three of them were sweating in the heat of the hallway. The chief had pulled off his suit jacket and had it over his shoulder.

"We found a bus graveyard," Andor said, "owned by Wampler Industries, heavily protected outside of the city in a hidden valley."

"We didn't go near it because we knew, just as with the mines, it would be watched," Julia said.

"Wampler?" the chief asked.

"Kirk Wampler was the son of the bus driver in the original tragedy," Lott said.

"He was the only one who survived and then supposedly committed suicide by stepping in front of a school bus."

"Under a shell company," Fleet said, from the phone, "the old school and some of the homes around the school are owned by Wampler and his wife, Cynthia Peters."

The chief nodded. "Let me guess. Cynthia Peters is West, Wampler is Lynch pretending to be a guy."

"Exactly," Andor said. "Next we worked on why there was no human jerky out there. It seems that assumption we all made fifteen years ago was wrong. They didn't take the body parts as food, they took them as a trophy."

"A woman's butt, underwear, and back of her legs?" Director Couch asked.

"Cut off after baking," Lott said, "then brought back and preserved like they do the skin and muscles in those museum shows on human bodies."

"Oh, shit," Couch said again.

"You found that woman in the oven baking, didn't you?" the chief asked.

Andor nodded.

The chief just shook his head. "Thank heavens you three and Doc and Annie and Fleet and his people never seem to rest."

No one said anything to that, but Julia was glad the chief noticed at least, especially the incredible work that Doc and Annie and Fleet were doing.

"So did Lynch and West leave evidence this time?" FBI Director Couch asked.

"I think in this old school," Julia said, "and that home connected by a tunnel next door, you are going to find all the evidence you will ever need on these two."

Both Lott and Andor nodded to that.

"You said you had them wrapped up?" FBI Director Couch asked.

Julia was starting to like the bald guy. He was direct and seemed to keep on focus.

"We do," Andor said. "They don't know it yet and Lott and I want to pay them a short visit first before you take them."

The chief looked puzzled.

"We have been living with this nightmare for fifteen years," Lott said. "Since that first step into that mine. We just ask for a minute. Trust us, we won't hurt the case in any way."

"Besides," Andor said. "All three of you are going to need to be there with some press to record the capture, and we want no part of that. But first, you need to see what those two women did."

Andor pointed to the staircase leading down. "When you have this place secured and are ready for the photo arrests, call me and we'll let you know where we are at. But don't take longer than fifteen minutes."

The chief nodded and the three men started for the stairs.

"Gentlemen," Julia said. "I would suggest you leave your coats and ties on the gurney there."

"That bad?" the chief said, taking off his tie and putting it with his coat.

"Your worst nightmare," Andor said. "But you all need to see it to understand everything about this case and what kind of monsters you are dealing with."

With that, Julia led the way out the shadows of the hallway and through the front door of the old girls school, picking her way through the rubble to finally be in the hot, blazing sun of a Las Vegas afternoon.

It felt wonderful.

CHAPTER THIRTY-TWO

August 15th, 2015
2:20 P.M.
Las Vegas

LOTT GOT THE air-conditioning blowing hard and the Cadillac headed toward town on the Old Boulder Highway. It felt great to just have that much be normal for a moment.

None of them said a word as he drove, being careful.

Finally, after a few minutes, Fleet spoke from the phone Julia still held in her hand.

"Update on the Missy Andrews' condition," Fleet said. "She's going to make a full recovery and she has some relatives who are local who are headed to the hospital now."

"Wonderful," Lott said.

Julia beamed at him and he smiled back. That felt flat out wonderful.

They hadn't been able to save all the other lives, but one was enough for the day. And now they were going to stop any more killing from happening.

"Thanks, Fleet," Lott said. "For everything. We wouldn't have saved her without you."

Nothing from the other side of the phone this time.

"So how are the two monsters?" Andor asked.

"Just finishing their main course," Fleet said. "Doc and Annie are sitting about five tables away. Casino security has the entire place secured down."

"Have them keep an opening for three right beside Lynch and West."

"Will do," Fleet said. "But something you should know."

"Go ahead," Lott said, suddenly being worried again.

"Security scans show they are both carrying concealed weapons. Small pistols."

Lott glanced at Julia, then back at Andor, who just nodded.

"Thanks, Fleet," Lott said. "We'll keep that in mind."

Ten minutes later, Fleet handed a five-dollar tip to the parking valet at the Golden Nugget Rush Tower entrance and the three of them headed inside.

All three of them stopped at a rest room to splash water on their faces and Lott had never felt anything so wonderful as the handfuls of cold water.

Andor took some wet paper towels and just wiped off the back of his neck. Then they went back out and joined Julia, whose face looked flushed as well from the cold water.

"Our trapped mice are starting into their desserts," Fleet said.

"Thanks, Fleet," Julia said. "I'm leaving the connection, but putting the phone in my pocket again."

"I'll be watching," Fleet said. "But just remember, they are trapped and therefore dangerous."

"Copy that," Lott said.

At that moment, Andor's phone rang. He listened for a moment, then said, "They are in the buffet at the Golden Nugget. I would come in with only you three and cameras and a few arresting officers. We'll sit on them until you get here."

Then he put his phone away and smiled at Lott and Julia. "Seems we are about to wrap this up after fifteen years."

"And close a lot of cases and save a lot of lives," Julia said.

Andor nodded to that and turned and headed for the escalator that led up to the buffet.

Julia took Lott's hand and he squeezed her hand in appreciation. He couldn't imagine going through all this with anyone else. They made an amazing team.

As they walked around the planter that divided the buffet from the lobby area, Lott was surprised at how simply normal the two looked.

Lynch made a decent man in looks, and wore a light blue sports coat that clearly screamed money.

West had her long blonde hair pulled back and had on a light blue blouse with pearls around her neck and pearl earrings.

How could two of the worst serial killers in history look so plain and normal?

Doc and Annie sat two tables over to the left of the killers, with an empty table between them and the killers.

Andor led over to the table on the other side of the two killers and sat down.

Julia sat the farthest from the two, while Lott sat across from Andor.

Both of them were close and could move quickly. Lott was almost right beside Lynch.

"Something to drink?" A waitress asked as they were being seated.

"Two glasses of water each," Lott said. "Climbing around inside an old school building is thirsty work."

Both Lynch and West glanced at them, then West did a double-take.

Lott was surprised that she recognized them. He wasn't sure what he thought of that.

"You know," Andor said, "for being dead, Kirk, you are looking pretty nice. A real girly-man if you get my meaning."

"Cynthia here looks much better than she did after being baked on that bus," Lott said. "She has recovered so well."

Both Lynch and West just stared at their half-finished desserts, their hands on the table in front of them. Lynch had been eating apple pie with a slight bit of ice cream. West had been working on a Key lime pie.

Lott didn't much like how they were acting. They had the look of desperation which could mean they would go for their guns at any moment.

Lott glanced at Andor, then at Julia.

Both were clearly seeing the same warning signs.

"You had to assume that someday your killing spree would be over," Andor said, continuing to poke at the two killers. "But I bet you didn't expect two old detectives to be the ones to stop you, now did you?"

"You are right, Detective Williams," West said. "We did expect this to come to an end.

"And you planned for it, right?" Lott said. "All sorts of ways of escape."

"We planned for every contingency," Lynch said, looking at West. "Didn't we, my love."

"We did," West said, nodding.

Lott's alarm bells went off inside his head as he suddenly realized the two of them were planning a mutual suicide, more than likely right here in the casino. And that was their key words to do it.

He jumped at Lynch at the same time as Andor jumped at West.

Lynch's hand was on a gun, and Lott wrestled with her until suddenly Doc and Annie were there as well.

Lott got the gun away and put it on the table where he had been sitting.

Then he made sure Lynch was sitting back in front of her dessert.

Andor and Julia had gotten the gun from West and had done the same thing.

Casino security had materialized all around the buffet, but when Doc waved them away, none of them came in.

"Just stay seated," Lott said to the two killers. "You have some fine folks to meet in a few minutes. Trust me, you do not want to miss this by doing something silly like killing yourselves."

Around them, the buffet was buzzing with noise as both women adjusted where they sat, both looking shocked that their suicide plan had failed so quickly.

Doc and Annie took the two guns and tucked them away and then moved back toward the cashier, but didn't go back to their table.

Lott and Andor sat back down, as did Julia.

Lott glanced at the two killers. "You know why we didn't let you two just save the state a ton of money and kill yourselves?"

Neither woman moved.

"Because there are upwards of three hundred families out there that need closure on the family members you killed," Andor said.

"And we want your two faces to be known as the ugliest killers in modern times," Lott said.

"There will be no escape for either of you," Andor said.

Both women said nothing, simply stared at their hands in front of them.

"Calvary," Julia said, softly.

Lott glanced around and saw the chief and the director of the FBI coming up the escalator.

Lott and Andor and Julia all stood.

"We needed this little time as well for some closure for us," Lott said.

Andor pointed to the half-eaten desserts. "Might want to finish those. Might be the last dessert either of you see in a very long time."

Then, as Lott turned away, he decided to ask just one question.

"That bus tragedy was horrible," Lott said, stopping over the two women. "But not sure why both of you decided to continue to live it over and over."

West looked up at Lott and just shook her head. "You don't understand yet, do you, detective?"

"It wasn't horrible," Lynch said, looking at Lott with cold, dark eyes. "It was gloriously wonderful."

"Better than we had planned," West said.

"A lot better than we had ever hoped," Lynch said.

"Glorious," West said, softly. "Just glorious."

With that the two women reached forward and took each other's hands.

CHAPTER THIRTY-THREE
Three Weeks Later…

September 3rd, 2015
5:30 P.M.
Las Vegas

LOTT UNLOADED the snacks and drink supplies for the poker game later while Julia got the bucket of KFC on the kitchen table and then put out a few large piles of napkins and three paper plates.

In theory, Andor was bringing a new cold case for the gang tonight and Lott had made him promise to not make it personal to him or Julia. They hadn't taken

on a new case since finally getting rid of Lynch and West.

Both Lynch and West had spent the last three weeks on suicide watch as the national news descended on Las Vegas. A media storm didn't even begin to describe what hit.

The chief had done as he had promised and kept the three of them, plus Doc and Annie and Fleet, out of it all. When asked how the police had come up with all this and solved this very cold case, he had just said simply, "Great detective work."

All the bodies had been removed from the mines and the bus graveyard and all but a few of the victims had been claimed by families.

The national news for a week was full of funerals all over the west as closure finally came for so many.

And the chief had also played up the rescue of Missy Andrews from Montana and her last minute save from an oven. Luckily, Missy made a full recovery and remembered nothing from the moment in the parking lot with a flat tire to when she woke up in the Las Vegas hospital.

Gory details about the two killers had come out, and slowly more and more charges were being placed against them, both in state courts and in federal courts, since kidnapping and murder over state lines were federal crimes.

It seemed like every district attorney with a victim wanted a part of the two killers. It was going to take a lot of time to sort out who got to them first. More than likely the Feds would win, Lott was sure.

Doc and Annie and Fleet had headed back to Idaho after a few days and Doc and Annie had gone in rafting on the River of No Return in central Idaho, where Doc was a guide. They were due out in three more days.

Lott had only had major nightmares a few times during the last few weeks, and Julia had been there for him on both.

She had had her share of bad dreams as well, and he had been there to help her through those. A perfect team to fight nightmares.

But for Lott, it seemed that closing this case, locking up the two killers, cleared out so many of the nightmares that had haunted him for years.

And now, after three weeks, that was feeling very light and freeing and he was ready to get back to work on another case.

Just as Julia got the plates out and Lott had taken the lid off the tub of KFC to release the fantastic smell of hot chicken into the kitchen, the back door opened and in walked Andor, followed by Chief Beason.

Lott was surprised, but not that surprised. He had come to really like and admire the chief and how he handled all this massive turmoil.

"Wow, does this place smell great," Beason said, smiling.

"Great seeing you, Chief," Julia said as she grabbed him a paper plate and a pile of napkins and pointed to a spot at the table where Annie usually sat.

"Great seeing you as well, Chief," Lott said. "Andor tells me things are finally starting to calm down some."

"Some," Beason said, slipping around to the spot Julia had pointed to at the table. "I just wanted to come by and thank all three of you personally. And the Cold Poker Gang in general."

Lott smiled. "Thanks," he said.

Julia nodded, as did Andor in agreement.

"But thanks go to you," Lott said, "for giving us the permission to do the job we love and make a difference."

Chief Beason laughed. "I get three of the best detectives I have ever had the pleasure to meet working for me for free and making me and the rest of the clowns

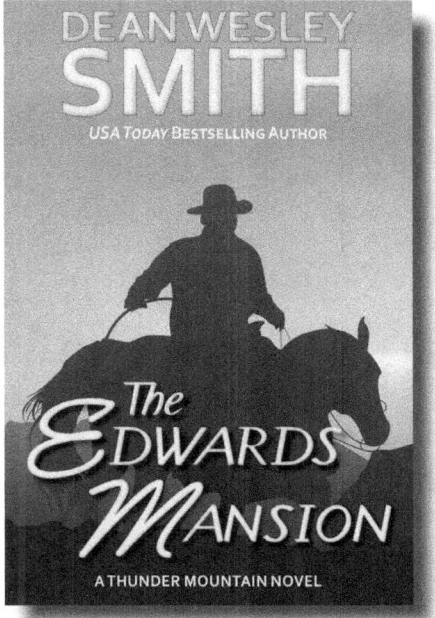

Two Thunder Mountain Novels
Available at your favorite booksellers.

down at headquarters look smart. What's not to love on my side?"

"Perfect," Lott said.

"We got a new case," Andor said, pointing to a file he had put on the counter.

"One close to my heart," Chief Beason said, smiling. "So hope you all can pull your magic on that one."

"Oh, great," Lott said, shaking his head, but smiling.

"By the way," Beason said, "I do have one bone to pick with you three from this last case. You could have saved me going into that basement."

Andor laughed and shook his head. "You and Couch and Landers needed to see that to really understand the depth of sickness of those two women."

"And the scale of the tragedy that needed to be dealt with," Julia said.

"Yeah, I know," Beason said. "Just glad no cameras were around to catch the three top law enforcement officers in the area all throwing up together. Felt like a bad night back in college. First time I ever lost my lunch over any crime scene."

"You weren't alone with that one," Lott said.

"So what is your secret?" Beason asked. "Besides being smart and having your daughter and Doc and Fleet helping, how does the Cold Poker Gang solve so many unsolved cases?"

"You honestly want to know?" Andor asked, staring with his look of intensity at the chief.

Lott smiled at Julia.

"I do," the chief said, looking slightly puzzled that his light question was being taken so seriously.

"KFC before every meeting," Andor said, pulling the bucket toward himself and grabbing a wing.

"He's not kidding," Julia said, yanking the bucket to her and grabbing a wing as well.

"He's not," Lott said, grabbing a leg and biting into the juicy, warm meat.

The chief smiled, shook his head, and then pulled the bucket toward himself and grabbed a thigh, biting into it and letting the grease get on his face.

"See what I mean?" Andor asked.

The Las Vegas Chief of Police nodded and smiled. "I do. I feel smarter already."

"Best crime-fighting food ever," Lott said, holding up a half-eaten chicken leg in salute.

They all saluted with their own half-eaten chicken part, and with that the laughter filled the room and the Cold Poker Gang was ready for a new case.

~

Coming Next Issue in Smith's Monthly
A return to the Ghost of a Chance Series
in a brand new novel.
HEAVEN PAINTED AS A FREE MEAL

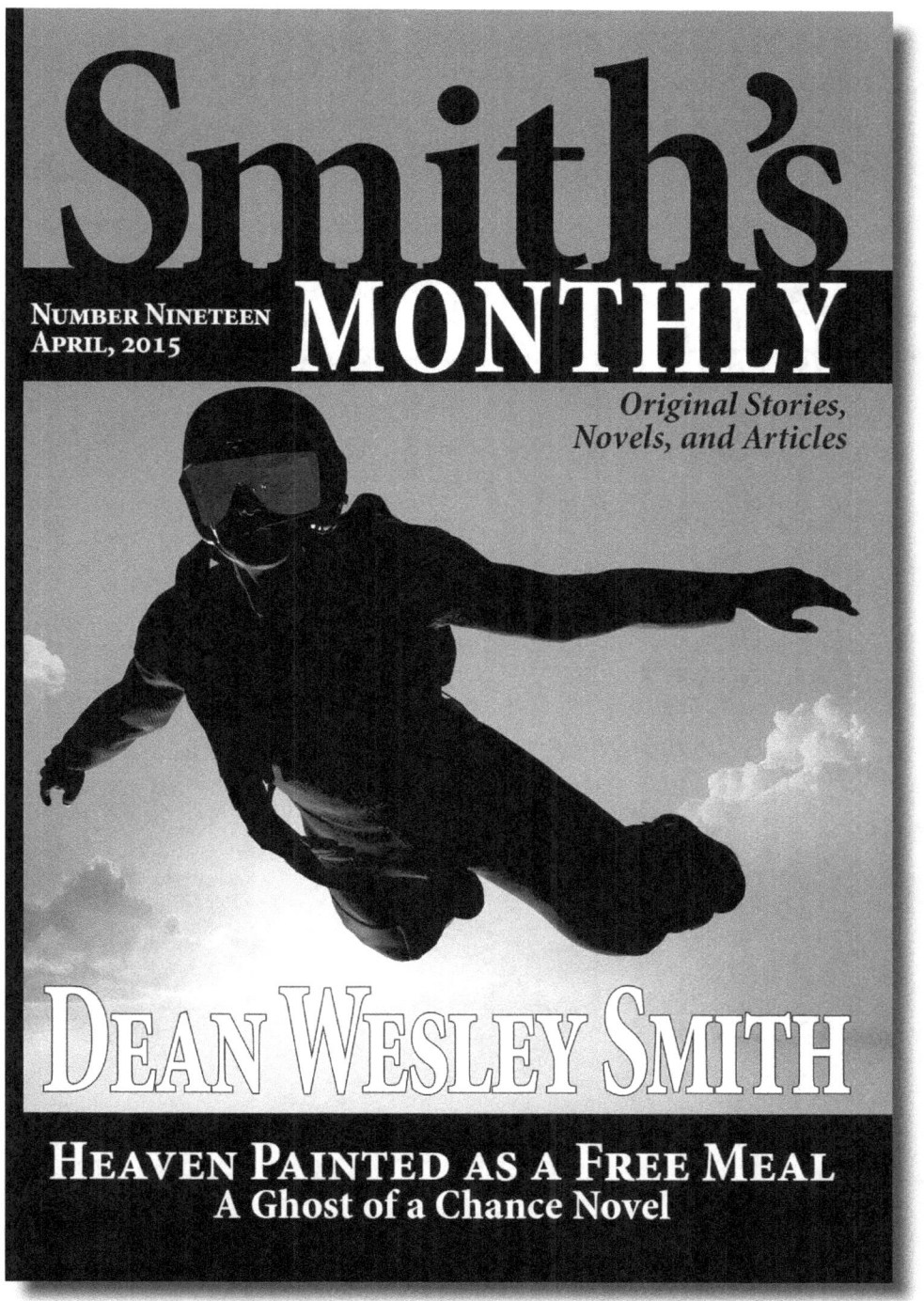

#1... October 2013

#2... November 2013

#3... December 2013

#4... January 2014

#5... February 2014

#6... March 2014

#7... April 2014

#8... May 2014

#9... June 2014

#10... July 2014

#11... August 2014

#12...September 2014

#13...October 2014

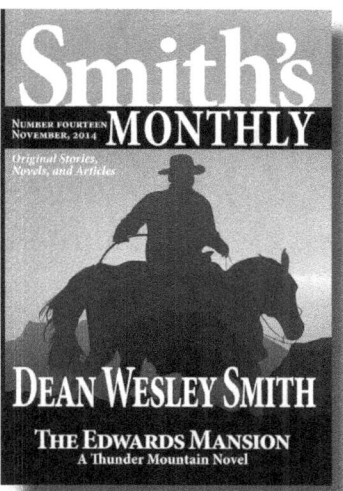

#14...November 2014

#15...December 2014

#16...January 2015

#17...February 2015

#18...March 2015

Thank You!!

Walter White Cat and I would like to thank
the following wonderful people who support my blog
and my work through Patreon.
Your support is very important to me.
Thanks!

Rob Cornell

Erick Lindman

Christopher Ridge

Miguel Angel Alonso Pulido

Nancy Hendrickson

Ryan M. Williams

Jacob Proffitt

Ryan Whiteside

Marian Goldeen

John Connelly

Gary Speer

Megan Bryce

Michelle Tatam

Scott Gordon

Kathryn Rooney

Sherman Cox

Livia Quinn

Amri Ackers

Robin Brande

J.R. Murdock

Kathleen McClure

Michael Kelberer

Gunnar Gunderson

F.I. Goldhaber

Mary Jo Rabe